Praise for the *New York Ti*

GWENDY'S BUTTON BOX

"A different sort of coming-of-age story about a mysterious stranger and his odd little gift. . . . Cowritten with Richard Chizmar, King's zippy work returns to the small-town Maine locale of *The Dead Zone*, *Cujo*, and other early novels . . . Extremely well-paced . . . a fun read that never loses momentum. . . . *Gwendy's Button Box* feels like it belongs in this locale that's always been a pit stop for scary Americana and the normal turned deadly . . . Nicely captures that same winning dichotomy between the innocent and the sinister."
—*USA Today*

"Man, I love this story! The whole thing just races and feels so right-sized and scarily and sadly relevant. Loved the characters . . . and the sense of one little girl's connection to the whole world through this weird device. It all just sang."
—J. J. Abrams

GWENDY'S MAGIC FEATHER

"Chizmar carries the tale forward into Gwendy's future with sympathy and grace. The result is at once an independent creation and a particularly intimate form of collaboration. . . . Chizmar's voice and sensibility dovetail neatly with [Stephen] King's own distinctive style, and the book ultimately reads like a newly discovered chapter in King's constantly evolving fictional universe."

—The Washington Post

"[An] appealing chiller. . . . Short, punchy chapters keep the pages turning. . . . The charming protagonist and thrill of temptation will enthrall fans and new readers alike."

—Publishers Weekly

GWENDY'S FINAL TASK

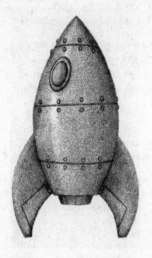

STEPHEN KING AND RICHARD CHIZMAR

G

GALLERY BOOKS

NEW YORK LONDON TORONTO SYDNEY NEW DELHI

G

Gallery Books
An Imprint of Simon & Schuster, Inc.
1230 Avenue of the Americas
New York, NY 10020

First Gallery Books trade paperback edition May 2022

GALLERY BOOKS and colophon are registered trademarks of Simon & Schuster, Inc.

For information about special discounts for bulk purchases, please contact Simon & Schuster Special Sales at 1-866-506-1949 or business@simonandschuster.com.

The Simon & Schuster Speakers Bureau can bring authors to your live event. For more information or to book an event, contact the Simon & Schuster Speakers Bureau at 1-866-248-3049 or visit our website at www.simonspeakers.com.

Manufactured in the United States of America

10 9 8 7 6 5 4 3 2

Library of Congress Cataloging-in-Publication Data is available.

ISBN 978-1-9821-9155-9
ISBN 978-1-9821-9156-6 (ebook)

For Marsha DeFilippo,
a friend to a couple of writers.

1

It's a beautiful April day in Playalinda, Florida, not far from Cape Canaveral. This is the Year of Our Lord 2026, and only a few of the people in the crowd standing on the east side of Max Hoeck Back Creek are wearing masks. Most of those are old people, who got into the habit and find it hard to break. The coronavirus is still around, like a party guest who won't go home, and while many fear it may mutate again and render the vaccines useless, for now it's been fought to a draw.

Some members of the crowd—again, it's mostly the oldies, the ones whose eyesight isn't as good as it once was—are using binoculars, but most are not. The craft standing on the Playalinda launch pad is the biggest manned rocket ever to lift off from Mother Earth; with a fully loaded mass of 4.57 million pounds, it has every right to be called Eagle-19 Heavy. A fog of vapor obscures the last 50 of its 400-foot height, but even those with fading vision can read the three letters running down the spacecraft's side:

T

E

T

And those with even fair hearing can pick up the applause when it begins. One man—old enough to remember hearing Neil Armstrong's crackling voice telling the world that the Eagle had landed—turns to his wife with tears in his eyes and goosebumps on his tanned, scrawny arms. The old man is Douglas "Dusty" Brigham. His wife is Sheila Brigham. They retired to the town of Destin ten years ago, but they are originally from Castle Rock, Maine. Sheila, in fact, was once the dispatcher in the sheriff's office.

From the Tet Corporation's launch facility a mile and a half away, the applause continues. To Dusty and Sheila it sounds thin, but it must be much louder across the creek, because herons arise from their morning's resting place in a lacy white cloud.

"They're on their way," Dusty tells his wife of fifty-two years.

"God bless our girl," Sheila says, and crosses herself. "God bless our Gwendy."

2

EIGHT MEN AND TWO women walk in a line along the right side of the Tet control center. They are protected by a plexiglass wall, because they've been in quarantine for the last twelve days. The techs rise from behind their computers and applaud. That much is tradition, but today there's also cheering. There will be more applause and cheers from the fifteen hundred Tet employees (the patches on their shirts, jackets, and coveralls identify them as the Tet Rocket Jockeys) outside. Any manned space mission is an event, but this one is extra special.

Second from the end of the line is a woman with her long hair, now gray, tied back in a ponytail that's mostly hidden beneath the high collar of her pressure suit. Her face is unwrinkled and still beautiful, although there are fine lines around her eyes and at the corners of her mouth. Her name is Gwendy Peterson, she's sixty-four, and in less than an hour she will be the first sitting U.S. senator to ride a rocket to the new MF-1 space station. (There are cynics among Gwendy's political peers who like to say MF stands for a certain incestuous sex act, but it actually stands for Many Flags.)

The crew are carrying their helmets for the time being, so nine of them have a free hand to wave, acknowledging the cheers. Gwendy—technically a crew member—can't wave unless she wants to wave the small white case in her other hand. And she doesn't want to do that.

Instead of waving she calls, "We love you and thank you! This is one more step to the stars!"

The cheers and applause redouble. Someone yells, "*Gwendy for President!*" A few others take up the call, but not that many. She's popular, but not *that* popular, especially not in Florida, which went red (again) in the last general election.

The crew leaves the building and climbs into the three-car tram that will take them to Eagle Heavy. Gwendy has to crane her neck all the way to the reinforced collar of her suit to see the top of the rocket. *Am I really going up in that?* she asks herself, and not for the first time.

In the seat next to her, the team's tall, sandy-haired biologist leans toward her. He speaks in a low murmur. "There's still time to back out. No one would think the worse of you."

Gwendy laughs. It comes out nervy and too shrill. "If you believe that, you must also believe in Santa Claus and the Tooth Fairy."

"Fair enough," he says, "but never mind what people would think. If you have any idea, any at all, that you're going to freak out and start yelling '*Wait, stop, I've changed my mind*' when the engines light up, then call it off now. Because once those engines go, there's no turning around and no one needs a panicked politician onboard. Or a panicky billionaire for that matter." He looks to the car ahead of them, where a man is bending the ear of the Ops Commander. In his white pressure suit, the man bears a resemblance to the Pillsbury Doughboy.

The three-car tram starts to roll. Men and women in coveralls applaud them on their way. Gwendy puts the white case down and holds it firmly between her feet. Now she can wave.

"I'll be fine." She's not entirely sure of that but tells herself she has to be. *Has* to. Because of the white case. Stamped in raised red letters on both sides are the words **CLASSIFIED MATERIAL**. "How about you?"

The bio-guy smiles, and Gwendy realizes that she can't remember his name. He's been her training partner for the last four weeks, only minutes ago they back-checked each other's suits before leaving the holding area, but she can't remember his name. This is NG, as her late mother would have said: not good.

"I'll be fine. This'll be my third trip, and when the rocket starts to climb and I feel the g-force pressing down? Speaking just for myself, it's the best orgasm a boy ever had."

"Thank you for sharing," Gwendy says. "I'll be sure to put it in my first dispatch to the down-below." It's what they call Earth, the down-below, she remembers that, but what's Bio Boy's damn name?

In the pocket of her jumper she's got a notebook with all sorts of info in it—not to mention a very special bookmark. The names of all the crew members are in there, but no way can she get at the notebook now, and even if she could, it might—almost certainly *would*—raise suspicions. Gwendy falls back on the technique Dr. Ambrose gave her. It doesn't always work, but this time it does. The man next to her is tall, square-jawed, blue-eyed, and has a tumble of sandy hair. The women think he's hot. What's hot? Fire's hot. If you touch it, you might get a—

Bern. That's his name. Bern Stapleton. Professor Bern Stapleton who also happens to be Major Bern Stapleton, Retired.

"Please don't," Bern says. She's pretty sure he's talking about his orgasm metaphor. There's nothing wrong with her short-term memory, at least not so far.

Well . . . not *too* wrong.

"I was joking," Gwendy says, and pats his gloved hand with her own. "And stop worrying, Bern. I'll be fine."

She tells herself again that she must be. She doesn't want to let down her constituents—and today that's all of America and most of the world—but that's minor compared to the locked white box between her boots. She can't let *it* down. Because there's a box inside the box, made not of high-impact steel but of mahogany. It's a foot wide, a bit more than that in length, and about seven inches deep. There are buttons on top and levers so small you have to pull them with your pinky finger on either side.

They have just one paying passenger on this flight to the MF, and it's not Gwendy. She has an actual job. Not much of one, mostly just recording data on her iPad and sending it back to Tet Control, but it's not entirely a cover for her real business in the up-above. She's a climate monitor, her call designation is Weather Girl, and some of the crew jokingly refer to her as Tempest Storm, the name of a long-ago ecdysiast.

What is that? she asks herself. *I should know.*

Because she doesn't, she resorts to Dr. Ambrose's technique again. The word she's looking for is like paint, isn't it? No, not paint. Before you paint you have to get rid of the *old* paint. You have to . . .

"Strip," she murmurs.

"What?" Bern asks. He has been distracted by a bunch of applauding men standing beside one of the emergency trucks. Which please God won't have to roll on this fine spring day.

"Nothing," she says, thinking, *An ecdysiast is a stripper.*

It's always a relief when the missing words come. She knows that all too soon they won't. She doesn't like that, is in fact terrified of it, but that's the future. Right now she just has to get through today. Once she's up there (where the air's not just rare but nonexistent), they can't just send her home if they discover what's wrong with her, can they? But they could screw up her mission if they found out. And there's something else, something that would be even worse. Gwendy doesn't want to even think about it but can't help herself.

What if she forgets the real reason she's up there? The real reason is the box inside the box. It sounds melodramatic, but Gwendy Peterson knows it's true: the fate of the world depends on what's inside that box.

3

THE SERVICE-AND-DELIVERY STRUCTURE BESIDE Eagle Heavy is a crisscross latticework of steel beams housing a huge open elevator. Gwendy and her fellow travelers mount the nine stairs and get inside. The elevator has a capacity of three dozen and there's plenty of room to spread out, but Gareth Winston stands next to her, his considerable belly pooching out the front of his white pressure suit.

Winston is her least favorite person on this trip to the up-above, although she has every confidence he doesn't know it. Over a quarter-century in politics has taught Gwendy the fine art of hiding her feelings and putting on a you're-so-darn-fascinating face. When she was first elected to the House of Representatives, a political veteran named Patricia "Patsy" Follett took Gwendy under her wing and gave her some valuable advice. That particular day it was about an old buzzard from Mississippi named Milton Jackson (long since gone to that great caucus room in the sky), but Gwendy's found it useful ever since: "Save your biggest smiles for the shitheads, and don't take your eyes off theirs. The women will think you love their earrings. The men will think you're smitten with them. None of them will know that you're actually watching their every move."

"Ready for the biggest joyride of your life, Senator?" Winston asks as the elevator begins its slow 400-foot trundle up the side of the rocket.

"Ready-ready-Teddy," Gwendy says, giving him the wide smile she reserves for shitheads. "How about you?"

"Totally excited!" Winston proclaims. He spreads his arms and Gwendy has to take a step back to keep from being bopped in the chest. Gareth Winston is prone to expansive gestures; he probably feels that being worth a hundred and twenty billion dollars (not as much as Jeff Bezos, but close) gives him the right to be expansive. "Totally thrilled, totally up for it, totally *stoked!*"

He is, needless to say, the paying passenger, and in the case of space flight that means paying through the nose. His ticket was $2.2 million, but Gwendy knows there was another price, as well. Mega-billions translates into political clout, and as it gears up for a manned Mars mission, TetCorp needs all the political allies it can get. She just hopes Winston survives the trip and gets a chance to use his influence. He's overweight and his blood pressure at last check was borderline. Others in the Eagle crew may not know that, but Gwendy does. She has a dossier on him. Does *he* know she knows? It wouldn't surprise Gwendy in the least.

"To call this the trip of a lifetime would be an understatement," he says. He's speaking loudly enough for the others to turn around and look. Operation Commander Kathy Lundgren gives Gwendy a wink, and a small smile touches the corners of her mouth. Gwendy doesn't have to be a mind reader to know what that means: *Better you than me, sister.*

As the slow-moving elevator passes the lower **T** in **TET**, Winston gets down to business. Not for the first time, either. "You're not here just to send back rah-rah dispatches to your adoring fans, or to look down at the big blue marble and see how the fires in the Amazon are affecting wind currents in

Asia." He looks meaningfully down at the white box with its CLASSIFIED stamp.

"Don't sell me short, Gareth. I took meteorology classes in college and boned up all last winter," Gwendy says, ignoring both the comment and the implied question. Not that he's afraid to ask outright; he already has, several times, both during their four weeks of preflight training and their twelve days of quarantine. "It turns out that Bob Dylan was wrong."

Winston's broad brow creases. "Not sure I'm following you, Senator."

"You actually *do* need a weatherman to know which way the wind blows. The fires in the Amazon and those in Australia are making fundamental changes in Earth's weather patterns. Some of those changes are bad, but some may actually be working in the environment's favor, strange as that seems. They could put a damper on global warming."

"Never believed in all that stuff myself. Overblown at best, nonexistent at worst."

Now they are passing the **E.** *Get me away from this guy,* Gwendy thinks . . . then realizes that if she didn't want to be in close quarters with a guy like Gareth Winston, she should have avoided this trip altogether.

Only she couldn't.

She looks up at him, maintaining what she thinks of as the Patsy Follett Smile. "Antarctica is melting like a Popsicle in the sun and you don't think global warming is real?"

But Winston won't be led away from what interests him. He may be an overweight blowhard, but he didn't make all those mega-billions by being stupid. Or distractable. "I would give a great deal to know what's in your little white box, Senator, and I have a great deal to give, as I'm sure you know."

"Ooo, that sounds suspiciously like a bribe."

"Not at all, just a figure of speech. And by the way, since we're going to be space-mates very shortly, can I call you Gwendy?"

She maintains the brilliant smile, although it's starting to hurt her face. "By all means. As for the contents of this . . ." She lifts the box. "Telling you would get us both in very big trouble, the kind that lands you in a federal facility, and it's really not worth it. You'd be disappointed, and I'd hate to let down the fourth richest man in the world."

"Third richest," he says, and gives her a smile that equals Gwendy's in brilliance. He waggles a gloved finger at her. "I won't give up, you know. I can be very persistent. And no one is going to put me in prison, dear." *Oh my*, Gwendy thinks. *We've progressed from Senator to Gwendy to dear in the course of one elevator ride. Of course, it's a very slow elevator.* "The economy would collapse."

To this she makes no reply, but she's thinking that if the box inside the box—the button box—fell into the wrong hands, *everything* would collapse.

The sun might even gain a new asteroid belt between Mars and Venus.

4

AT THE TOP OF the gantry there's a large white room where the space travelers stand, arms raised and doing slow pirouettes, as a disinfecting spray that smells suspiciously like bleach wafts over them. It's their last cleansing.

Not long ago there was another room in here, a small one, with a sign on the door reading WELCOME TO THE LAST TOILET ON EARTH, but Eagle Heavy is a luxury liner equipped with its own bathroom. Which, like the three cabins, is actually little more than a capsule. One of the private cabins is Gareth Winston's. Gwendy reckons he deserves it; he paid enough for it. The second is Gwendy's. Under other circumstances she might have protested this special treatment, U.S. senator or not, but considering her main reason for being on this trip, she agreed. Mission Control Director Eileen Braddock suggested that the six members of the crew without flight responsibilities (Ops Commander Kathy Lundgren and Second Ops Sam Drinkwater) draw straws for the remaining cabin, but the crew voted unanimously to give it to Adesh Patel, the entomologist. His live specimens have already been loaded. Adesh will sleep in a cramped bunk surrounded by bugs and spiders. Including (*Oh, ag*, Gwendy thinks) a tarantula named Olivia and a scorpion named Boris.

The lavatory belongs to all, and no one is any happier about that than their mission commander. "No more diapers,"

Kathy Lundgren told Gwendy during quarantine. "*That*, my dear Senator, is what I call one giant leap for mankind. Not to mention womankind."

"*Ingress*," the loudspeakers on Mission Control boom. "*T-minus two hours and fifteen minutes. Green across the board.*"

Kathy Lundgren and Second Ops Sam Drinkwater face the other members of the crew. Kathy, her auburn hair sparkling with tiny jewels of disinfectant mist, addresses all eight, but it seems to Gwendy that she pays special attention to the senator and the billionaire.

"Before we begin our final prep, I'll summarize our mission's timeline. You all know it, but I am required by TetCorp to do this once more prior to entry. We will achieve Earth orbit in eight minutes and twenty seconds. We will circle the earth for two days, making either thirty-two or thirty-three complete circumnavigations, the orbits varying slightly to create a Christmas bow shape. Sam and I will be charting space junk for disposal on a later mission. Senator Peterson—Gwendy— will begin her weather monitoring activities. Adesh will no doubt be playing with his bugs."

General laughter at this. David Graves, the mission's statistician and IT specialist, says, "And if any of them get free, out the hatch they go, Adesh. Along with you." This provokes more laughter. To Gwendy they sound pretty loosey-goosey. She hopes she sounds that way herself.

"On Day Three, we'll dock with Many Flags, which just now is pretty much deserted except for a Chinese enclave—"

"Spooky," Winston says, and makes an *ooo-OOOO* sound.

Kathy gives him a flat look and continues. "The Chinese keep to themselves in Spoke 9. We're in Spokes 1, 2, and 3. Spokes 4 to 8 are currently not occupied. If you see the Chinese at all, it will be while they're running the outer ring.

They do a lot of that. You'll have plenty of room to spread. We're going to be up there for an additional nineteen days, and room to spread is an incredible luxury. Especially after forty-eight hours in Eagle Heavy.

"Now here comes the important part, so listen to me carefully. Bern Stapleton is a veteran of two previous trips. Dave Graves has made one. Sam, my second in command, has made five, and I've made seven. The rest of you are newbies, and I'll tell you what I tell all newbies: This is your final chance to turn around. If you have even *the slightest doubt* about your ability to pull your weight from ingress to final egress, you must say so now."

Nobody speaks up.

Kathy nods. "Outstanding. Let's get this show on the road."

One by one they cross the access arm and are helped into the spacecraft by a quartet of white-suited (and disinfected) service personnel. Lundgren, Drinkwater, and Graves—who'll be overseeing the flight from a bank of touch screens—go first.

Below them, on the second level, Dr. Dale Glen, physicist Reggie Black, and biologist Bern Stapleton seat themselves in a row.

On the third and widest level, where eventually more paying passengers will sit (or so TetCorp hopes) are Jafari Bankole, the astronomer who'll have little to do until they're in the MF station, entomologist Adesh Patel, passenger Gareth Winston, and last but not least, the junior senator from Maine, Gwendy Peterson.

5

GWENDY SEATS HERSELF BETWEEN Bankole and Patel. Her flight chair looks like a slightly futuristic La-Z-Boy recliner. Above each of them are three blank screens, and for a panicky moment Gwendy can't remember what they're there for. She's supposed to do something to light them up, but what?

She looks to her right in time to see Jafari Bankole plugging a lead into a port in the chest of his suit, and things come into focus. *Keep it together, Gwendy.*

She plugs in and the screens above her first light up, then boot up. One shows a video feed of the rocket on its launch pad. One shows her vital signs (blood pressure a little high, heart rate normal). The third shows a rolling column of information and numbers as Becky, Eagle Heavy's computer, runs an on-going series of self-checks. These mean nothing to Gwendy, but presumably they mean something to Kathy Lundgren. Also to Sam and Dave Graves, of course, but it's Kathy—plus Eileen Braddock, the Mission Control director—who will be watching the readouts with the greatest attention, because either one of them can scrub the mission if they see something they don't like. That decision, Gwendy knows, would cost upward of seventeen million dollars.

Right now all the numbers are green. Above the marching columns is a countdown clock, also in the green.

"Hatch closed," Becky tells them in her soft, almost human

voice. "Conditions remain nominal. T-minus one hour, forty-eight minutes."

"Downrange check," Kathy says from two levels above Gwendy.

"Weather downrange . . . ," Becky commences.

"Belay that, Becky." Kathy can't turn her head much because of her suit, but she waves an arm. "You give it to me, Gwendy."

For a terrible moment Gwendy has no idea what to do or how to respond. Her mind is a mighty blank. Then she sees Adesh Patel pointing below her seat and things click into place again. She understands that stress is making her condition worse and tells herself again that she has to calm down. *Must.* She's a lot less terrified about sitting on megatons of highly combustible rocket fuel than she is of the relentless neurological decay going on in the gray sponge between her ears.

She grabs the iPad out of its clips beneath her seat, PETERSON stamped on the cover. She thumbprints it and swipes to the current weather app. The cabin's superb WiFi overrides the diagnostic screen above her. What takes its place is a weather map similar to one on a TV newscast.

"It's grand downrange," she tells Kathy. "High pressure all the way, clear skies, no wind." And, she knows, it would take hurricane-force winds to knock Eagle Heavy off course once it was really rolling. Most weather concerns have to do with lift-off and reentry.

"How about the up-above?" Sam Drinkwater calls back to her. There's a smile in his voice.

"Thunderstorms seventy miles up, with a slight chance of meteor showers," Gwendy returns, and everyone laughs. She turns off her tablet, and the diagnostic screen resumes.

Jafari Bankole says, "If you would like the porthole seat, Senator, there is still time for us to switch."

There are two portholes on the third level—again, with an eye to future tourism. Gareth Winston, of course, has one of them. Gwendy shakes her head. "As the crew astronomer, I think you should have an observation post. And how many times have I told you to call me Gwendy?"

Bankole smiles. "Many. It just does not come naturally to me."

"Understood. Appreciated, even. But as long as we're crammed together in the world's most expensive sardine can, will you give it your best shot?"

"All right. You are Gwendy, at least until we dock with the Many Flags station."

They wait. The minutes drain away (*the way my mind is draining away*, Gwendy can't help thinking). At T-minus 40, Becky tells them the service structure is retracting on its gigantic rails. At T-minus 35, Becky announces, "Fuel loading has commenced. All systems remain nominal."

Once upon a time—actually just ten or twelve years ago, but things move fast in the twenty-first century—the fuel was loaded before the human cargo, but SpaceX changed that, and a lot of other things. There are no more flight controls, just the ubiquitous touch screens, and Becky is really running the show (Gwendy just hopes the Beckster isn't a female version of HAL 9000). Lundgren and Drinkwater are basically just there for what Kathy calls "the dreaded holy-shit moment." Dave Graves is actually more important; if Becky has a nervous breakdown, he can fix it. Probably. Hopefully.

"Helmets," Sam Drinkwater says, putting on his. "Let me hear your roger."

One by one they respond. For a moment Gwendy can't

remember where the catches are, but then it comes to her and she locks down.

"T-minus 27," Becky informs. "Systems nominal."

Gwendy glances at Winston, and is meanly pleased to see that some of his rich-guy bonhomie has evaporated. He's looking out his porthole at blue sky and a corner of the Mission Control building. There's a red patch on the fleshy cheek Gwendy can see, but otherwise he looks pale. Maybe thinking this wasn't such a good idea, after all.

As if catching her thought, he turns to her and gives her a thumbs-up. Gwendy returns the gesture.

"Got your special box all secure?" Winston asks.

Gwendy has it beneath one knee, where it won't fly away unless she does. And she's secured with a five-point harness, like a jet fighter pilot.

"Good to go." And then, although she's no longer sure what it means—if it means anything: "Five-by-five."

Winston grunts and turns back to the window.

On her left, Adesh has closed his eyes. His lips are moving slightly, almost certainly in prayer. Gwendy would like to do the same, but it's been a long time since she had any real confidence in God. But there is *something*. That she's sure of, because she cannot believe that any power on Earth made the strange device currently hidden inside a steel container that can only be opened with a seven-digit code. Why it has ended up in her hands again is a question to which she supposes she knows the answer, or at least part of it. Why she's saddled with it while suffering the first stages of early-onset Alzheimer's is less understandable. It's also hideously unfair, not to mention absurd, but since when did questions of fairness ever enter into human events? When Job cried out to God, the Almighty's response was mighty cold: *Were you there when I made the world?*

Never mind, Gwendy thinks. *Third time is the charm, last time pays for all. I'll do what I have to do, and I'll hold on to my mind long enough to do it. I promised Farris, and I keep my promises.*

At least she always has.

If not for the innocent people with me, she thinks, *for the most part good people, brave people, dedicated people (maybe with the exception of Gareth Winston), I'd almost wish we'd blow up on the launching pad or 50 miles downrange. That would take care of everythi—*

Except it wouldn't; that's something else that's slipped her increasingly unreliable mind. According to Richard Farris, the author of all her misery, it wouldn't take care of everything any more than weighting the goddamned button box down with rocks and dropping it into the Marianas Trench would take care of everything.

It had to be space. Not just the final frontier but the ultimate wasteland.

Give me strength, Gwendy prays to the God whose existence she highly doubts. As if in response, Becky—the god of Eagle Heavy—tells them they are now at T-minus 10 minutes, and all systems remain green.

Sam Drinkwater says, "Visors down and locked. Let me hear your roger."

They snap down their visors, firing off their responses. At first everything looks dark to Gwendy, and she remembers her polarizing visor also came down. She shoves it up with the heel of her gloved hand.

"Initiate oxygen flow, let me hear your roger."

The valve is somewhere on her helmet, but she can't remember where. God, if only she could get to her notebook! She looks at Adesh in time to see him twist a knob on his helmet's left side, just above the pressure suit's high collar.

Gwendy copies him and hears the soft shush of air into her helmet.

Remember to turn it off once we achieve orbit, she tells herself. *Cabin air after that.*

Adesh is giving her a questioning look. Gwendy makes a clumsy **O** with her thumb and forefinger. He gives her a smile, but Gwendy is afraid he saw her hesitation. Again she thinks of her mother's NG: not good.

6

TIME IN TRAINING HAS been slow. Time in quarantine has been slow. The walk-out, the elevator ride, the insertion, all slow. But as those last earthbound minutes begin, time speeds up.

In her helmet—too loud, and Gwendy can't remember how to turn it down—she hears Eileen Braddock in Mission Control say, "T-minus five minutes, terminal countdown begins."

Kathy Lundgren: "Roger that, Mission Control, terminal countdown."

Use your iPad, Gwendy thinks. *It controls everything in your suit.*

She touches the suit icon, finds the volume control, and uses her finger to decrease the blare. *See how much you remember?* she thinks. *He'd be proud.*

Who would be proud?

My handsome hubby. She has to fish for his name, which is appalling.

Ryan, of course. Ryan Brown is her handsome hubby.

Sam Drinkwater: "Eagle is in auto idle. All fuel is on."

On her iPad and on the screen above her, T-minus 3:00 gives way to 2:59 and 2:58 and 2:57.

A gloved hand grips hers, making Gwendy startle. She looks around and sees Jafari. His eyes ask her if it's okay or if she'd like him to let go. She nods, smiles, and tightens her grip. His lips form the words *All will be well.* Winston has his bought-and-paid-for porthole, but it's going to waste, at least

21

for now. He's staring straight ahead, his lips pressed so tightly together that they're almost not there, and Gwendy knows what he's thinking: *Why did this seem like a good idea? I must have been crazy.*

Kathy: "Arm for launch?"

Sam: "Roger that, armed for launch. Eleven minutes from stars in the daytime, folks."

Seemingly only seconds later, Eileen from Mission Control: "Crew okay? Let me hear you roger."

One by one they reply. Gareth Winston is last, his *roger* a dry croak.

Kathy Lundgren, sounding as cool as the other side of the pillow: "Flight termination armed. T-minus one minute. Are we go for launch?"

Sam Drinkwater and Eileen Braddock answer together: "Go for launch."

With the hand not holding Jafari's, Gwendy feels for the steel box. It's there, it's safe. Only the box inside it is *not* safe. The box inside is the most dangerous thing on Earth. Which is why it must *leave* Earth.

Eileen Braddock: "First Ops Commander Lundgren, you have the bird."

"Roger that, I have the bird."

On the screen above Gwendy, the final ten seconds begin to count off.

She thinks: *What is my name?*

Gwendy. My father wanted a Gwendolyn and my mother wanted a Wendy, like in *Peter Pan*. They compromised. Hence, I am Gwendy Peterson.

Gwendy thinks: *Where am I?*

Playalinda, Florida, the Tet Corporation's launch complex. At least for a few more seconds.

Why am I here?

Before she can answer that question, a vast rumble begins 450 feet below where she sits reclined in her ergonomic chair. Eagle's cabin begins to vibrate—gently, at first, then more strongly. Gwendy has a fragmentary memory of being five or six and sitting on top of their washing machine as it goes into its final spin cycle.

"We are firing green," Sam Drinkwater says.

A second or two later Kathy says, "Lift-off!"

The roar is louder, the vibration more intense. Gwendy wonders if that's normal or if something has gone wrong. On the center screen above her she now sees Mission Control and the rest of the complex through a red-orange bloom of fire. How far below is it? Fifty feet? A hundred? A shudder runs through the craft. Jafari's grip tightens.

This isn't right. This can't be right.

Gwendy closes her eyes, asking herself again why she's here.

The short answer is because a man—if he *is* a man—told her that she had to be. At this moment, waiting for her life and all the others' to end in a vast explosion of cryogenic liquid oxygen and rocket-grade kerosene, she can't remember the man's name. A crack has opened in the bottom of her brain and everything she has ever known has started to leak into the darkness below it. All she can remember is that he wore a hat. Small and round.

Black.

7

THIS IS THE THIRD time the button box has come into Gwendy Peterson's life. The first time it was in a canvas bag with a drawstring top. The second time she found it in the bottom drawer of a filing cabinet in her Washington, D.C., office. During her freshman term as Maine's second district representative, that was. The third time was in 2019, while she was running for the Senate, a campaign that Democratic committee insiders felt had as much chance of succeeding as the Charge of the Light Brigade. Each time it was brought by a man who always dressed in jeans, a white shirt, a black suit-coat, and a small bowler hat. His name was Richard Farris. On the first occasion, the button box was in her possession all through her adolescence. On the second, her custodianship was much shorter, but she believed it saved her mother's life (Alicia Peterson died in 2015, years after cancer should have killed her).

The third time was . . . different. *Farris* was different.

Gwendy retired from the House of Representatives in 2012, although she could have gone on getting elected well into her eighties, perhaps even into her nineties, if she had so chosen. "You're like Strom Thurmond," Pete Riley, head of the Maine Democratic Committee once told her. "You could have gone on getting reelected even after you were dead."

"Please, no comparisons to that guy," Gwendy had said.

"Okay, how about John Lewis? Whoever you use for a

comparison—hell, Margaret Chase Smith from right up the road in Skowhegan spent thirty-three years in D.C.—the point is the same: you're the fabled automatic. And we need you."

But what Gwendy needed to do was write books. Fiction was her first love. She had published only five novels, and time was marching on. Retirement from public service opened up that side of her life and made her happy in a way life under the Capitol dome never had. She published *Bramble Rose* in 2013 and then, in 2015, a serial killer novel called *Desolation Street*. That one, featuring a charming maniac who harvested the teeth of his victims, was set in D.C. but based on certain events in her hometown.

She was considering another book, one full of romance and family secrets, when Donald Trump was elected president. Many in Maine's second district rejoiced, feeling the Washington swamp would be drained, the budget would be balanced, and the flood of "bad hombre" illegal immigrants from South America would finally be dammed up. For life-long Democrats—the kind of people who avoided Fox News as if it might give them rabies—it was the beginning of a four-year nightmare. Gwendy's own father, perhaps the most apolitical member of the Democratic party in the entire state of Maine, looked at Gwendy with sober eyes the day after the election and said, "This is going to change everything, Gwennie. And probably not in a good way."

She was deep into the novel, this one set in Maine at the time of the Bradley Gang massacre in Derry, when Pete Riley came to see her again. The poor man looked as if he'd lost twenty pounds between election night in 2016 and that early winter day a little over two years later. He kept it simple and he kept it brief. He wanted Gwendy to run against Paul Magowan for the Senate in 2020, which he called "the year of perfect eyesight." He said only Gwendy would have a chance of beating the Republican businessman, who expected his campaign to be little more than a formality on the way to a foregone conclusion.

"If nothing else, you could slow his roll and give some hope to all the good folks suffering TD."

"Which is what?"

"Trump Depression. Come on, Gwendy, open your mind to this. Give it fair consideration."

Fair consideration was one of her trademark phrases, used at least once at every town hall gathering during her political career. If Pete expected it to turn the key in her lock, he was disappointed. "You're joking. You have to be. Aside from the fact that I'm writing a new book—"

"And I'm sure it will be as good or better than the others," Pete said, flashing his most winning Clark Gable smile.

"Don't bother blowing smoke up my skirt," Gwendy (who that day was wearing a pair of old Levis) said. "Better men than you have tried and failed. What I was going to say is that aside from the new book, where there's a lot of hot sex that I'm enjoying vicariously, that idiot Magowan won by fifteen points in '14. And after spending two years with his lips firmly attached to Donald Trump's ass, he's got an eighty percent approval rating."

"Bullshit," Pete said. "Republican propaganda. You know it is."

"I know nothing of the kind, but let's say it is. I was quite popular during my run in the House, I'll give you that, but memories are short. Magowan is the man of the hour, and I'm the woman of yesterday. There's a tide in politics, and right now it's running strong conservative. You know that as well as I do. I probably wouldn't lose by fifteen points, but I'd lose."

Pete Riley went to the window of Gwendy's small study and looked out with his hands stuffed deep in his pockets. "Okay," he said, not looking at her. "Barring a miracle, you'd lose. I think we've settled that point. So lose. Make a pretty concession speech about how the voters have spoken but the fight continues and blah blah blah. Then you can go back to writing about Derry, Maine, in the 1930s. But this isn't the '30s, it's 2018, and you know what?"

He turned back to her like a good defense attorney addressing the jury.

"Yeats's blood-dimmed tide is also running. People are turning away from women's rights, from science, from the very notion of equality. They're turning away from *truth*. Politics aside, somebody needs to stand up and make them look at all the stuff it's easier and more comfortable not to believe in. You always did that, *always*. I'm asking you to do it again."

"To be your noble Joan of Arc and let the good people of Maine burn me at the stake?"

"Nobody is going to burn you alive," Pete said . . . not knowing that eight years later Gwendy would be atop a flaming torch called Eagle Heavy and more than half expecting to be transformed into superheated atoms at any moment. "You're going to lose an election. But in the meantime, you could make that fat prick Magowan sweat bullets. Get him on the debate stage and make people see that he's sticking up for ideas that aren't just bad, they're unworkable and downright dangerous. *Then* you can go back to writing your books."

Gwendy had been ready to be angry with Pete, but she saw he was at least partly right. She was being melodramatic.

Which, she supposed, went with writing fiction full of secrets and hot sex. "Take one for the team, in other words. Would that be accurate?"

He gave her the big Clark Gable grin. "Hole in one."

"Let me think about it," she'd said.

Probably a mistake.

8

BUT NOT AS BIG *as this one*, Gwendy thinks as the roar of the engines increases to a bellow. Jafari Bankole's grip has become paralyzing, even through the thickness of their two gloves. She goes to CREW on her iPad with her free hand, highlights Jafari's name with the pad-sensitive tip of her index finger (it's easier to remember stuff when you're not trying, she has discovered), and speaks to him comm to comm, so it's private. "Let up a little, Jaff, okay? You're hurting."

"Sorry, sorry," he says, and relaxes his grip. "This is . . . such a very long way from Kenya."

"And from western Maine," Gwendy says.

The cabin's shudder-shake begins to lessen, and her recliner starts to turn slightly on its gimbals. Or is it? Maybe what's really happening is that the altitude of the cabin is changing. Tilting.

Gwendy punches for Ops Comm so she can listen to Kathy, Sam, and Mission Control.

"Three hundred fifty miles downrange and the sound barrier is just a happy memory," Eileen says. She sounds calm, and why not? Eileen is safe on the ground.

"Roger that," Kathy says. She also sounds calm, which is good.

"Looking fine, Eagle Heavy. Nominal burn, all three engines."

"Roger." Sam Drinkwater this time.

The cabin's tilt is gradually becoming more pronounced, and the ride has become smooth. For the time being, at least.

"You are go for throttle up, Eagle Heavy."

Kathy and Sam together: "Roger."

Gwendy can't hear any real difference in the engine roar, but an invisible hand settles on her chest. Ahead of her, Dale Glen, the mission's doctor, appears to be making notes on his iPad, and never mind the pad-sensitive fingertip; he has stripped his glove off. *He could be in his Missoula consulting room,* Gwendy thinks.

She goes to FLIGHT INFO on her pad. They are less than two minutes into the flight but already 22 miles high and traveling at 2,600 miles an hour. For a woman who considers driving at 80 on the Maine state turnpike living dangerously, she finds the number hard to comprehend, but there's no doubt about the increasing pressure on her body. Gravity doesn't want to let go.

There's a thud, followed by a bright flash in the porthole to her left, and for a moment she thinks it's all over. Jafari's hand clamps down again.

"Solid booster rocket has separated," Sam says, to which Dave Graves responds, "Hallelujah. Swivel those jets, BoPeep."

"Call me that again and I'll tear your face off," Kathy says. "Let me hear your roger."

"Roger that," Dave says, grinning.

The tilt of the cabin increases. Outside, the blue sky has darkened to violet.

"Three main engines all firing beautifully," Kathy says, and Gwendy sees Bern Stapleton lift his hands with the thumbs up. A moment later he's in her helmet, comm to comm. "Enjoying the ride, Senator?"

And because for the moment it's just the two of them, she says, "Best orgasm a girl ever had."

He laughs. It's loud. Gwendy winces. She needs to turn down the sound, but how does she do that? She knew a little while ago, she even did it, but now she can't remember.

It's on your iPad. Everything is.

Before she can turn down the volume, Bern has clicked off and Ops Comm returns. Below and now far behind, Eileen Braddock is telling them they've passed the point of negative return.

Kathy: "Roger that, negative return."

No going back now, Gwendy thinks, and her fear is replaced by a feeling of what-the-hell exultation that she never would have expected. *Space or bust.*

She motions for Jafari to raise his visor and she raises her own. Not protocol, but it's only for a few seconds, and she has something she wants to say. Needs to say.

"Jaff! We're going to see the stars!"

The astronomer smiles. "God's grace, Gwendy. God's grace."

9

AFTER PETE RILEY'S VISIT, Gwendy began to read up on Paul Magowan, the Republican junior senator from Maine. The more she read, the more disgusted she became. The younger Gwendy Peterson would have been outright horrified, and even at fifty-eight, with several trips around the political block in her resume, she felt at least some horror.

Magowan was an avowed fiscal conservative, declaring he wouldn't allow tax-and-spend progressives to mortgage the futures of his constituents' grandchildren, but he had no problem with clear-cutting Maine's forests and removing the commercial fishing bans in protected areas. His attitude seemed to be that the grandchildren he was always blathering about could deal with those things when the time came. He promised that with the help of President Trump and other "friends of the American economy," he was also going to get Maine's textile mills running again "from Kittery to Fort Kent."

He waved aside such issues as acid rain and polluted rivers—which had given up such wonders as two-headed salmon in the mid-twentieth century, when the mills had been booming 24/7. If he was asked how the product of those mills could compete with cheap Chinese imports, Magowan told voters, "We're going to ban all Chinese imports except for moo-shu pork and General Tso's chicken."

People actually laughed and applauded this codswallop.

While she was watching that particular video on YouTube, Gwendy found herself remembering what Pete Riley had said on his exploratory trip in December of '18: *People are turning away from women's rights, from science, from the very notion of equality. They're turning away from truth. Somebody needs to stand up and make them look at all the stuff it's easier and more comfortable not to believe in.*

She decided she was going to be that somebody, but when Pete called her in March of 2019, she told him she still hadn't decided.

"Well, you better hurry up," Pete told her. "It gets late early in politics, as you well know. And if you're going to take a shot at this, I want to be your campaign manager. If you'll let me, that is."

"With that smile of yours, how could I say no?" Gwendy asked.

"Then I need to start positioning you."

"Ask me again in April."

Pete made a low moaning sound, as if she'd stepped on his foot. "That long?"

"I need to deliberate. And talk to my husband, of course." Although she was pretty sure she knew what Ryan's reaction would be.

What she needed to do was to finish her book, *City of Night* (a title already used by John Rechy, but too good not to use again), and clear the decks. Then she was going to go after Senator Paul Magowan with everything she had. As someone with absolutely no chance of winning, she felt good about that.

When she told Ryan, he reacted pretty much as she had expected. "I'm going to go out and buy a bottle of wine. The good stuff. We need to celebrate. *Ladies and gentlemen, Gwendy Peterson is BACK!*"

10

OUTSIDE THE PORTHOLE NEAREST to Gwendy, the sky is now dark. More than dark. "Blacker than a raccoon's asshole," Ryan might have said. The cabin rotates further, her chair compensates, and all at once her three monitor screens are directly ahead of her instead of over her head. The roaring of the engines stops, and all at once Gwendy is floating against her five-point restraining harness. It reminds her of how it feels when a roller-coaster car takes its first dive, only the feeling doesn't stop.

"Crew, helmets can come off," Sam says. "Unzip your suits if you want to but keep them on for now."

Gwendy unlocks her helmet, takes it off . . . and watches it float, first in front of her and then lazily upward. She looks around and sees three other helmets floating. Gareth Winston snatches his down. "What the hell do I do with it?" He sounds shaky.

Gwendy remembers this, and Winston should; God knows they had enough dress rehearsals.

Reggie Black says, "Under your seat. Your compartment, remember?"

"Right," Winston says, but doesn't add a thank-you; that doesn't seem to be in his vocabulary.

Gwendy stows her helmet, opening the hatch by feel and waiting until she hears the small click as the helmet's magnetized circle finds the corresponding circle on the side of her personal stowage area, which is surprisingly large. There's also room for her pressure suit when the time comes, but for the time being the only thing she wants to put in there is the steel box with its dangerous cargo. She takes it from beneath her knee, places it in the compartment, and discovers she has to hold it down so it won't float back up like a helium balloon.

Steel floats, she marvels. *Holy God, I'm in a place where steel floats.*

"Senator Peterson," Kathy calls. "Gwendy. Come up here. I want to show you something. Do you remember how to move around?"

She doesn't. It's gone. It shouldn't be, but it is.

Reggie Black, the mission physicist, bails her out. "One or two slow strokes," he says. "Easy, so you—"

Now she remembers. "So I don't bump my head on the DESTRUCT button." A joke they learned in training.

"Exactly so," Adesh says, beaming. "Must not bump that one, no!"

Winston says nothing. Gwendy can see he's miffed not to have been invited up top first; he is, after all, the paying passenger. The guy may be worth an obscene amount of money, but with his lower lip stuck out the way it is now, he looks like a petulant child.

Gwendy unbuckles and laughs when she rises slowly from her seat. She pulls her knees up to her chest as she was taught during training and goes into a lazy forward roll. She extends her legs. She could be lying on her stomach in bed, except of course there *is* no bed. And she doesn't have to stroke. Jafari closes his hand around her ankle and gives her a gentle push. Laughing, delighted, she floats toward the top of the cabin (only it's now the front of the cabin), over the heads

of Reggie, Bern, and Dr. Glen. *It's like being in a dream*, she thinks.

She grabs the back of David Graves's seat and pulls herself in between Kathy and her second in command, whose name has slipped her mind. It's something about water, but she can't remember what.

There are no portholes in the control area, but there's a narrow slit window four feet long and six inches wide. "You can see this better on your center screen," Kathy says quietly, "and of course on your tablet, but I thought you might like your first look this way. Since you're part of the reason these missions are still flying."

I had my own reason, Gwendy thinks. *Space exploration, advancing human knowledge, sure. But now there's something else.*

For one horrifying moment she can't remember what that something else is, even though it's the biggest thing in her life. Then that concern is driven from her mind by what she's seeing below her . . . and yes, it's definitely below.

The home world hangs in the void, blue-green and wearing many scarves of white cloud. She has seen pictures, of course, but the reality, the firsthand *reality*, is staggering. Here, in all the black nothing of empty space, is a world teeming with improbable life, beautiful life, lovely life.

"That's the Pacific Ocean," the second in command says quietly, and now that she's not trying, she can remember his name: Sam Drinkwater.

"How can America be gone so fast, Sam?"

"Speed will do that. Hawaii just passing below us. Japan coming up."

She can see a whirlpool down there, white twisting away in the middle of the blue, and remembers the monsoon she saw while checking the weather dump on her computer early that morning when she couldn't sleep. But this is no computer screen; this is a God's eye view.

"Pure beauty is what it is," she responds to Sam, and begins to cry. Her tears rise and hang above her, perfect floating diamonds.

11

Of course the opposition was laying for her.

They could do that, because Gwendy was the only viable candidate for the Democratic nomination. She announced her intentions in August of 2019, with her husband by her side. She spoke from the Castle Rock bandstand on the town common, where she'd announced her candidacy for the House of Representatives each time she ran. There were reporters and camera crews from all the Maine television stations in attendance, plus bloggers and even a national guy, who probably just happened to be in the area: Miguel Almaguer, from NBC News. There was also an excellent turnout of locals, who cheered their fannies off. Gwendy even spotted some home-made signs. Her favorite, waved by her old friend Brigette Desjardin, read HEY, MAINE! SENDY GWENDY!

The coverage of her speech was good (local NPR stations ran the whole ten minutes that night). Paul Magowan's comment on the late news was typically condescending: "Welcome to the race, little lady—at least you'll have your books to fall back on when it's over."

The Magowan campaign would hold most of its advertising for another full year, because Mainers don't really get interested in the local races until three or four months before the election, but they fired an opening salvo on August 27, the day after Gwendy's announcement. Full-page newspaper advertisements and sixty-second TV spots began with the statement that "Maine's Favorite Writer Is Running for the United States Senate!"

Printed below it in the newspaper ads and narrated on TV for the reading challenged was a selection from *Bramble Rose*, published in 2013 by Viking. Gwendy was sourly amused by the portentous tones of the narrator in the TV ad.

"Andrew embraced her from behind with one hand planted firmly on her bare midriff. With his other he stroked her **bleep** *until she began to breathe hard.*

" 'I want you to **bleep** *me now,' she said, 'and don't stop until I* **bleep**.*

He carried her to the bedroom and threw her down on the four-poster. Panting, she turned on her side and grasped his **bleep**, *breathing, 'Now, Andy. I can't wait any longer.' "*

Below this in the print ads, and across an especially unflattering picture of Gwendy in the TV ads (mouth open, eyes squeezed half shut, looking mentally disabled), was a question: *ISN'T THERE ALREADY ENOUGH PORNOGRAPHY IN WASHINGTON?*

Gwendy was amused by the sheer scurrilousness of this attack. Her husband was not. "You ought to sue them for defamation of character!" Ryan said, throwing down the Portland *Current* in disgust.

"Oh, they'd love me to get down in the dirt with them," Gwendy said. She picked up the newspaper and read the excerpt. "Do you know what this proves?"

"That Magowan will stoop to anything?" Ryan was still fuming. "That he's low enough to put on a tall hat and crawl under a rattlesnake?"

"That's good, but not what I was thinking of. It proves that context is everything. *Bramble Rose* is a better book than this suggests. Maybe not a lot, but still."

When asked about the so-called pornography in the weeks that followed, Gwendy responded with a smile. "Based on Senator Magowan's voting record, I'm not sure he could tell you the difference between porn and politics. And since we're on the subject of porn, you might want to ask him about his pal Donald Trump's romance with Stormy Daniels. See what he's got to say about that."

What Magowan had to say about Stormy Daniels, it turned out, was not much, and eventually the whole issue blew away, as teapot tempests have a way of doing. Both campaigns dozed as the autumn of 2019 burned away Indian summer and brought on the first cold snap. Magowan might bring back the carefully culled passage from her book when the election run started in earnest, but based on her sharply worded retort, he might not.

Gwendy and Ryan helped serve Thanksgiving dinner that year to a hundred homeless people at the Oxford Street shelter in Portland. They got back to Castle Rock late and Ryan went right to bed. Gwendy put on her pajamas, almost got in beside him, then realized she was too wired to sleep. She decided to go downstairs and have a juice glass of wine—just two or three swallows to calm the post-event jitters she still felt even after years in the public eye.

Richard Farris was sitting in the kitchen, waiting for her.

Same clothes, same round black hat, but otherwise how he'd changed. He was old.

And *sick*.

12

WHEN GWENDY TURNS AROUND to stroke her way back from officer country to the crew's launch area, she almost bumps heads with Gareth Winston, who is floating just behind her. "Make way for the big fella, Senator."

Gwendy turns on her side, grabs a handhold, and pulls herself back to her seat while Winston crams between Graves and Drinkwater. He peers out through the slit for a few moments, then says, "Huh. View's better from the porthole."

"Enjoy it, then," Kathy says. "Suggest you let those who don't have a porthole come up and have a peek."

Dave Graves is checking a run of computer figures and murmuring with Sam, but he takes a moment to give Gwendy a look, eyebrows waggling. Gwendy isn't sure he's communicating *Three weeks with this guy should be fun*, but she's pretty sure that's what it is. Gwendy has met plenty of rich people in Washington. They are attracted to power like bugs to a buglight, and most of them are pretty much okay; they want to be liked. She thinks Gareth is an exception to the general rule.

She grabs her seatback, does a neat little twist (in zero-g, her sixty-four-year-old body feels forty again), and settles in. She buckles her harness and unzips her suit to the waist. She takes her notebook from the elasticized pocket of her red Eagle jumpsuit, not because she needs it at this moment but just to verify it's there. The book is crammed with names, categories, and information.

Some of it she doesn't need yet, but she's read enough about what's wrong with her to know she will as the mental rot in her brain advances. *1223 Carbine Street*. Her address. *Pippa*, the name of her father's ageing dachshund. *Homeland Cemetery*, where her mother is buried. A list of her medications, presumably now stored in her tiny cabin along with the scant wardrobe she was allowed to bring. No telephone numbers, her iPhone won't work up here (although Eileen Braddock assured her such service was only a year or two away), but a complete list of her phone's functions, plus a list of her duties as Eagle's weather officer. That may be a make-work job, but she intends to do it well.

The most important thing in her memory book (that's how she thinks of it) is halfway through, written in red ink and boxed: *1512253*. It's the code that opens the otherwise unopenable steel case. The idea of forgetting that number, and thus finding herself unable to get to the button box inside, fills Gwendy with horror.

Adesh has pulled himself over to look out of Winston's porthole, and Jafari Bankole is looking over his shoulder. There's currently no Earth to look at from that one, but Dr. Glen has pulled himself down to look out the other side. "Amazing. *Amazing*. It's not like looking at photos, or even film footage, is it?"

Gwendy agrees and opens her notebook to the crew page, because she has forgotten the doc's first name. Also, Reggie Black—what's his job? She knew only minutes ago, but it's slipped away.

A feather floats up from her book. Winston, now swimming his way back, reaches for it.

"Don't touch that," Gwendy says sharply.

He pays no attention, simply plucks it out of the air, looks at it curiously, then hands it to her. "What is it?"

"A feather," Gwendy says, and keeps herself from adding, *Are you blind?* She has to live with this man, after all, and his support of the space program is vital. If they find signs of life in the solar system—or beyond—that might not be the case, but for now it is. "I use it as a bookmark."

"Lucky charm, perhaps?"

The shrewdness of this startles her and makes her a little uneasy. "How did you guess?"

He smiles. "You have the same feather tattooed on your ankle. Saw it in the gym while you were on the treadmill."

"Let's just say I like it."

Winston nods, seeming to lose interest. "Gentlemen? May I have my seat back? And my porthole?" He puts a slight but unmistakable emphasis on *my*.

Adesh and Jafari move out of his way, a couple of swimming trout making way for an overfed seal.

"It's marvelous," Adesh murmurs to Gwendy. She nods.

Once she's got some clear space to maneuver, Gwendy releases her harness again and takes off her pressure suit. She does an involuntary forward roll in the process and thinks that weightlessness isn't all it's cracked up to be. Once the suit is stowed under her seat, folded on top of the steel case, she descends to the next and last level down, which will be the passenger common room on later orbital flights . . . and perhaps on flights to the moon. Such an amenity is brand new, and it won't be there on craft that go directly to the MF station. This is its maiden run.

The area is shaped like a great big Contac capsule and surprisingly roomy. There are two large viewscreens set into the floor, one showing empty black space and the other featuring the vast shoulder of Mother Earth with its gauze of atmosphere (faintly dirty, Gwendy can't help but notice). Two of the cabins are on the port side, the other and the head on the starboard. The shiny white doors can't help but remind her of morgue lockers on some of the TV crime shows she enjoys. A sign on the toilet says ALWAYS REVIEW PROCEDURE BEFORE OPERATING.

Gwendy doesn't need the john yet, so she gives a lazy kick of her feet and floats to the cabin with SEN. PETERSON on the door. The latch is like the one on a refrigerator. She pulls it and uses the grip over the door to yank herself inside. The cabin—actually more of a nook—is also in the shape of a cold capsule but much smaller. Claustrophobic, really. This time she's reminded of the crew quarters in World War II submarine films. There's a bunk with a harness to keep the sleeper from floating up to the curved ceiling a foot or so above, a miniscule fridge big enough for three or four bottles of juice or soda (maybe a sandwich, if you really crammed), and—of all things—a Keurig coffee maker. *Coffee in your cabin*, she thinks. *The height of space travel luxury.*

On top of the tiny fridge, held in place by a magnet, is a steel-framed photograph of Gwendy and Ryan and her parents, the four of them on the beach at Reid State Park, laughing with their arms around each other.

Gwendy will soon start her weather duties, but for now she needs to mentally refocus and review the crew information. She lies down on her bunk and buckles herself in. Servos are humming somewhere, but otherwise her little cold capsule is eerily silent. They may be circling the planet at thousands of miles an hour, but there's no sense of movement. She opens her red notebook and finds the crew pages. Names and thumbnail bios. Reggie Black is the physicist, of course he is. And Dr. Glen's first name is Dale. Easy-peasy, clear as a freshly washed window . . . but it could be gone again in an hour, maybe just fifteen minutes.

I'm crazy to be here, she thinks. *Crazy to be covering up what's wrong with me. But he gave me no choice. It has to be you, Gwendy, he said. I have no one else. So I agreed. In fact, I was sort of excited by the prospect. Only . . .*

"Only then, I was all right," Gwendy whispers. "At least I thought I was. Oh God, please get me through this."

Here in the up-above, after what she has seen below her—Earth so fragile and beautiful in the black—it's easier to think He or She might really be there.

13

"WHAT—" GWENDY BEGAN, MEANING to finish with either *are you doing here* or *is wrong with you*, she didn't know which, and Farris didn't give her time.

He put a finger to his lips and whispered: "Hush." He lifted his eyes toward the ceiling. "Don't wake your husband. Outside."

He struggled to his feet, swayed, and for a moment she was sure he was going to fall. Then he caught his balance, breathing hard. Inside his cracked lips—and were those fever blisters on them?—she saw yellowish teeth. Plus gaps where some were missing.

"Under the table. Take it. Hurry. Not much time."

Under the table was a canvas bag. She hadn't seen that bag since she was twelve, forty-five years ago, but she recognized it immediately. She bent down and picked it up by the draw-string top. Farris walked unsteadily to the kitchen door. There was a cane leaning beside it. She would have expected such a fabulous being—someone straight out of a fairy tale—to have a fabulous walking stick, maybe topped with a silver wolf's head, but it was just an ordinary cane with a curved handle and a scuffed rubber bicycle grip over the base. He leaned on it, fumbled for the doorknob, and almost fell again. Black suit coat, black jeans, white shirt: those garments, which had once fitted him with casual perfection, now bagged on him like cast-off duds on a cornfield scarecrow.

She took his arm (so thin under the coat!) to steady him and opened the door herself. That door and all the others were locked when she and Ryan left, and the burglar alarm was set, but now the knob turned easily and the alarm panel on the wall was dark, not even the message WAITING in its window.

They went out on the screened back porch, where the wicker furniture hadn't yet been taken in for the cold season. Richard Farris tried to lower himself into one of the chairs, but his legs wouldn't cooperate and instead he just dropped, letting out a pained little grunt when his butt hit the cushion. He gasped a couple of times, stifled a cough with his sleeve (which was caked with the residue of many previous coughs), then looked at her. His eyes were the same, at least. So was his little smile.

"We need to palaver, you and me."

It wasn't what he'd said the first time she met him; close, but no cigar. Back then he'd said they *ought* to palaver. *Needing to*, she thought, *takes it to a whole new level.*

Gwendy shut the door, sat down in the porch swing with the canvas bag between her feet, and asked what she would have asked in the kitchen, had he not reminded her that she had a husband upstairs.

"What's wrong with you? And why are you here?"

He managed a smile. "Same Gwendy, right to the point. What's wrong with me hardly matters. I'm here because there's been what that little green fellow Yoda would call 'a disturbance in the Force.' I'm afraid I must ask you—"

He began to cough before he could finish. It racked his thin body and she thought again how like a scarecrow he was, now one blown about on its pole by a strong autumn wind.

She started to get up. "I'll get you a glass of wa—"

"No. You won't." He brought the spasm under control. Coughing that hard should have raised a flush in his cheeks, but his face remained dead pale. His eyes were set in dark circles of sick.

Farris fumbled in his suit coat and brought out a bottle of pills. He started to cough again before he could get the cap off and the bottle dropped from his unsteady fingers. It came to rest against the drawstring bag. Gwendy picked it up. It was a brown pharmacy bottle, but there was no information on the label, just a series of runes that made her strangely dizzy. She closed her eyes, opened them again, and saw the word DINUTIA, which meant nothing to her. The next time she blinked, the dizzying runes were back.

"How many?"

He was coughing too hard to reply but held up two fingers. She pushed the cap off and brought out two small pills that looked like the Ranexa her father took for his angina. She put them in Farris's outstretched hand (there were no lines on it; the palm was perfectly smooth), and when he popped them in his mouth, she was alarmed to see tiny beads of blood on his lips. He swallowed, took a breath, then another, deeper one. Some color bloomed in his cheeks, and when it did she could see a little of the man she'd first met on Castle View, near the top of the Suicide Stairs, all those years ago.

His coughing eased, then stopped. He held out his hand for the bottle. Gwendy looked inside before putting the cap on. There were only half a dozen pills left. Maybe eight. He returned the bottle to his inner coat pocket, sat back, and looked out at the darkened backyard. "That's better."

"Is it heart medicine?"

"No."

"A cancer drug?" Her mother had taken both Oncovin

and Abraxane, although neither of them looked like the little white pills Farris had taken.

"If you really must know, Gwendy—you were always curious—there are many things wrong with me and they're all crowding in at once. The years I was forgiven—there have been many—are rushing back like hungry diners into a restaurant." He offered his charming little smile. "I'm their buffet."

"How old *are* you?"

Farris shook his head. "We have more important things to talk about, and my time is short. There's trouble, and the thing inside that canvas bag is responsible. Do you remember the last time we spoke?"

Gwendy does, vividly. She was at Portland South Airpark, sitting on a bench while Ryan went to park the car. Her luggage, including the button box in her carry-on bag, was piled around her. Richard Farris sat down and said they should palaver a spell before they were interrupted. And so they did. When the palaver was done, the button box was gone from her bag. Presto change-o, now you see it, now you don't. And the same was true of Farris himself. She had turned her head for a moment, and when she looked back, he was gone. She'd thought then she would never see him again.

"I remember."

"Twenty years ago that was." He kept his voice low, but the rasp was gone, his fingers were no longer trembling, and his color was good. *All just for the time being*, Gwendy thought—she had nursed her mother through her last illness, and her father was now in slow but steady decline. Pills could only do so much, and for so long. "You were a lowly House of Representatives backbencher then, one among hundreds. Now you're gunning for a seat of genuine power."

Gwendy gave a quiet laugh. She was sure Richard Farris

knew a great deal, but if he thought she was going to beat Paul Magowan and ascend to the United States Senate, he understood jack shit about Maine politics.

Farris smiled as if he knew exactly what she was thinking (an uncomfortable idea, which didn't make it wrong). Then the smile faded. "The first time you had the box, your proprietorship lasted six years. Remarkable. It's passed through seven sets of hands just since that day at the airport."

"The second time I had it was barely the blink of an eye," Gwendy said. "Long enough to save my mother's life—I still believe that—but not much longer."

"That was an emergency. This is another." Farris toed the canvas bag between her slippered feet with an expression of distaste. "This thing. This goddamned thing. How I hate it. How I *loathe* it."

Gwendy had no idea how to reply to that, but she knew how she felt: scared. Her mother's old saying came to mind: this is NG.

"Every year it gains power. Every year its ability to do good grows weaker and its ability to do evil grows stronger. Do you remember the black button, Gwendy?"

"Of course I do." Speaking through numb lips. "I used to call it the Cancer Button."

He nodded. "A good name for it. That's the one with the power to end everything. Not just life on Earth but Earth itself. And each year the proprietors of the box feel a stronger compulsion to push it."

"Don't say that." She sounded watery, on the verge of tears. "Oh please, Mr. Farris, don't say that."

"Do you think I want to?" he asked. "Do you think I even want to be here, tasking you with this—excuse the language—this fucking thing for a third time? But I have to,

Gwendy. There is simply no one else I trust to do what needs to be done, and no one else who may—I say *may*—be able to do it."

"What is it you want me to do?" She would find out that much, at least, and then decide. If she could, that was; if he left the button box with her, she'd be stuck with it.

No, she thought, *I won't. I'll weight the bag with rocks and throw it into Castle Lake.*

"Seven proprietors since the year 2000. Each held it a shorter time. Five committed suicide. One took his whole family with him. Wife and three kiddos. Shotgun. He kept telling the police negotiator, 'The box made me do it, it was the button box.' Of course they had no idea what he was talking about because by then it was gone. I had it back."

"Dear God," Gwendy whispered.

"One is in a mental asylum in Baltimore. He threw the button box into a crematorium furnace. Which did no good, of course. I committed him myself. The seventh, the last, only a month ago . . . I killed her. I didn't want to, I was responsible for what she became, but I had no choice." He paused. "Do you remember the colors, Gwendy? Not the red and the black, I know you remember those."

Of course she remembered. The red button did whatever you wanted, for good or ill. The black one meant mass destruction. She remembered the other six just as well.

"They stand for the continents of the earth," she said. "Light green, Asia. Dark green, Africa. Orange, Europe. Yellow, Australia. Blue is for North America, and violet is for South America."

"Yes. Good. You were a quick study even as a child. Later you may not be, but if you fight it . . . fight it hard, for all you're worth . . ."

"I'm not following you." Gwendy thought that the effect of the pills he'd taken was beginning to wear off.

"Never mind. The last proprietor was a woman named Patricia Vachon, from Vancouver. She was a schoolteacher working with mentally disabled children, and like you in many ways, Gwendy. Level-headed, strong-willed, dedicated, and with a moral fiber that went bone-deep. Rightness as opposed to righteousness, if you see what I mean."

Gwendy did.

"If existence is a chess game, with black pieces and white ones, Patricia Vachon stood firmly on the side of the white. I thought she might even be the White Queen, as you once were. Patricia had lovely dark skin, but she was of the white. The *light*. Do you understand?"

"Yes."

Gwendy wasn't very good at the kind of chess played on a board—Ryan always beat her on the occasions when she let him talk her into a game—but she had been very good at real-life chess during her years in the House of Representatives. There, she was always thinking three moves ahead. Sometimes four.

"I thought she was perfect," Farris continued. "That she'd be able to take care of the box for years, perhaps even until we were able to decide how to dispose of it once and for all."

"We? Who is *we*?"

Farris paid no attention. "I was wrong. Not about her, but about the box. I underestimated its growing power. I shouldn't have, not after what happened to the others who came after you, Gwendy, but the Vachon woman seemed so *right*. Yet in the end the box destroyed her, too. Even before I put a bullet in her head, she was destroyed. I'm responsible."

Tears began to trickle down Farris's seamed cheeks.

Gwendy observed them with incredulity. He was no longer the man she knew. He was . . .

Broken, she thought. *He's broken. Probably dying.*

"She was going to push the black button. She was struggling mightily—*heroically*—against the impulse, but she actually had her thumb on it when I shot her. And pushing down. Luckily, one might say providentially, the buttons are hard to push. Very hard. As I'm sure you remember."

Gwendy certainly did. The first time she tried to push one—it was the red button, as a kind of experiment—she thought they were dummies and the whole thing was a joke. It wasn't, unless you considered the hundreds dead in the South American country of Guyana as a joke. How much of the Jonestown massacre was actually her fault she still didn't know, and wasn't sure she wanted to.

"How did you get there in time to stop her?"

"I monitor the box. Every time it's used, I know. And usually I know when the proprietor is even thinking of using it. Not always, but there's another way I can keep track."

"When the levers are pulled?"

Richard Farris smiled and nodded.

There were two levers, one on each side of the box. One dispensed Morgan silver dollars, uncirculated and always date-stamped 1891. The other dispensed tiny but delicious chocolate animals. They were hard to resist, and Gwendy realized that made them the perfect way to monitor how often the proprietor was using the box. Handling it. Picking up its . . . what? Cooties? Germs? Its capacity to do evil?

Yes, that.

"Proprietors who pull the levers too frequently to get the chocolates or the dollars raise red flags. I knew that was happening with the Vachon woman, and I was disappointed, but

I thought I had more time to find another proprietor. I was wrong. When I reached her, she had already pushed one of the other buttons. Probably just to take the pressure off for a little while, poor woman."

Gwendy felt cold all over. The hair on the back of her neck stirred. "Which one?"

"Light green."

"When?" Her first thought was of the Fukushima disaster, when a tsunami caused a Japanese nuclear reactor to melt down. But Fukushima was at least seven years ago; maybe more.

"Near the end of this October. I don't blame her. She held on as long as she could. Even while her thumb was on that light green button, trying to overcome a compulsion too strong to resist, she was thinking, *Please, no explosion. Please, no earthquake. Please, no volcano or tidal wave.*"

"You heard this in your head. Telepathically."

"When someone touches one of the buttons, even the lightest caress, I go online, so to speak. But I was far away, on other business. I got there as quickly as I could, and I was in time to stop her before she could push the one you call the Cancer Button, but I was too late to stop her from pushing the Asia button."

He ran a hand through his thinning hair, knocking his little round hat askew, making him look like someone in an old-time musical about to start tap-dancing.

"This was just four weeks ago."

Gwendy spun her mind back, trying to think of a disaster that had occurred in one of the Asian countries during that timespan. She was sure there'd been plenty of tragedy and death, but she couldn't think of a mega-disaster strong enough to displace Donald Trump from the lead story on the evening news.

"Maybe I should know, but I don't," she said. "An oil refinery explosion? Maybe a nerve gas attack?" Knowing either would be too small. Things like the red button handled the small stuff.

Jonestown, for instance.

"It could have been much, much worse," Farris said. "She held back as well as she could, and against mighty forces from the black side of the board. But it's bad enough. Only two people have died so far, one of them the owner of what in Wuhan Province is called a wet market. That's a place where—"

"Where meat is sold, I know that." She leaned forward. "Are you talking about a sickness, Mr. Farris? Something like MERS or SARS?"

"I'm talking a *plague.* Only two dead now, but many more are sick. Some are carrying the disease and don't even know it. The Chinese government isn't sure yet, but they suspect. When they do know, they'll try to cover it up. As a result it's going to spread. It's going to be very, very bad."

"What can I do?"

"That's what I'm going to tell you. And I'll help, if I can."

"But you're—"

She doesn't want to finish, but he does it for her. "Dying? Oh yes, I suppose I am. But do you know what that means?"

Gwendy shook her head, for a moment thinking of her mother, and a night when they looked up at the stars.

Farris smiled. "Neither do I, dear girl. Neither do I."

14

WHEN GWENDY PETERSON WAS a young girl, she and her best friend Olive Kepnes played a game called "mermaids" at the Castle Rock Community Pool. They waded side-by-side into the shallow end until the water, chilly even in August, reached the middle of their chests. Then they took turns sitting on the bottom while the other girl remained standing and recited a series of secret, made-up words. Once her breath gave out and she resurfaced, the underwater girl—the mermaid—would try to guess what had been said. There were no winners or losers in this game. It was simply for fun.

When Gwendy opens her eyes to the bright overhead lights, the memory notebook pinned against her chest by one tightly clenched fist, Olive Kepnes and this long-ago game is the first thought that pops into her head. The voice coming from the other side of the shiny white door, no more than a half-dozen feet away, sounds distant and garbled, like she's hearing it from underwater.

She lifts her head and looks around, her eyes settling on the black and silver Keurig coffee maker. She blinks at it in confusion. She knows she's on a rocket ship traveling through space—she remembers that much—but what in the blue blazes is a coffee machine doing there?

She tries to sit up and experiences a flash of ice-cold panic when she discovers the restraints holding her in place, and then an immediate flood of relief when she realizes she must have dozed off in her bunk. She unbuckles the harness and floats upward from the narrow mattress. *Just like Tinkerbell*, she thinks in a moment of pure amazement.

There's a hollow knock at the door and the muffled voice comes again. Gwendy doesn't recognize it—in fact, is unable to determine if it's male or female—but it sounds like someone is saying, *"My dog is lost in the hay."* Even in the swirling gray mist of her half-awake stupor, she's pretty sure that's not right.

Whoever it is outside the door thumps again, a loud triple-knock this time, and then there's that same voice. *"I went fishing in the bay,"* it murmurs, with even more urgency this time around.

Gwendy slips the notebook into her pocket, then gives a single lazy kick and glides across the capsule-shaped cabin. As she reaches out to unlatch the door, it occurs to her that there's no peephole centered at eye level like there is on her front door back home in Castle Rock. This bothers her for some reason and she hesitates, suddenly afraid. *Is this what it feels like to lose your mind?*

Holding her breath, she pulls open the heavy white door. Adesh Patel and Gareth Winston are floating above the common room floor, the pair of large viewscreens lapping at the bottom of their boots like dark hungry mouths. Mother Earth, still surrounded by that gauzy haze Gwendy noticed earlier, winks at her from hundreds of miles away and keeps right on spinning.

Adesh, brown eyes wide with concern, swims closer and asks, "Gwendy, are you okay?"

It had been the entomologist's voice she'd heard calling out from the other side of the cabin door. Winston, bobbing up and down a few feet behind him, looking like a plump marshmallow in his unzipped pressure suit and grinning that I'm-better-than-you-and-you-know-it grin of his adds, "Sounds like you were having a whopper of a nightmare, Senator."

Gwendy speaks a little too cheerfully to come across as entirely convincing. "I'm fine, boys. Just dozed off and took a little catnap. Space travel does that to a girl."

15

"A PLAGUE . . . FROM CHINA?" Gwendy stared at the skeleton of a man sitting across from her on the screened-in back porch. "How bad? Will it come here to the States?"

"Everywhere," Farris answered. "There will be body bags stacked like cordwood outside of hospital loading docks. Funeral homes will bring in fleets of refrigerated trucks once the morgues begin to fill up."

"What about a vaccine? Won't we be able to—"

"Enough," he hissed, flashing a glimpse of decaying teeth. "I told you, I don't have much time."

Gwendy leaned back in the wicker porch swing, cinching her robe tight across her chest. *I don't have much time.* She thought once again: *He's dying.*

"And I don't have a choice, do I?"

"You, Gwendy Peterson, of all people should know that you always have a choice." He let out a deep, wavering breath.

And that's when Gwendy figured it out—what had been nagging at the back of her brain ever since they'd first come outside onto the porch. The temperature in Castle Rock had dropped to single digits on Thanksgiving evening; she and Ryan had heard a weather report on the radio as they were pulling into the driveway no more than an hour ago. She was shivering, and every time she opened her mouth a fleeting misty cloud appeared in front of her face—*fairy breath* they used to call it when they were kids—yet when Farris spoke, there was nothing, not even a trace.

"I wouldn't call it much of a choice," she said, glancing at the canvas bag resting between her feet. "I'm stuck with the damn thing no matter what I say."

"But what you choose to *do* with it is entirely up to you." He coughed into his hand, and when he pulled it away, she once again noticed a fine spray of blood across his knuckles.

"You said the box was going bad, that it killed the last seven people you entrusted it with. What makes you think I'll be any different?"

"You've always been different." He held up a slender finger in front of her face. "You've always been *special*."

"Bullshit," she said mildly. "It's a suicide mission and you know it."

Farris's cracked lips curled into a gruesome imitation of a smile, and then just as abruptly the smile disappeared. He cocked his head, staring off to the side, listening to something only he could hear.

"Who's coming?" Gwendy asked. "Where are they from? What do they want?"

"They want the button box." When he turned around again, it was the Richard Farris she'd first met on a bench in Castle View Park staring back at her—if only in his eyes, which were now strong and clear and focused with intensity. "And they're very angry. Listen to me carefully." He leaned forward, bringing with him a whiff of rotting carrion, and before Gwendy could shrink away, he reached over and took her hand in his. She shuddered, staring down at their intertwined fingers, thinking: *He doesn't feel human. He's not human.*

In a surprisingly sturdy voice, Richard Farris explained what needed to be done. From the first word to the last, it took him maybe ninety seconds. When he was finished, he released her hand and slumped back into the patio chair, the remaining color draining rapidly from his face.

Gwendy sat there motionless, staring out at the dark expanse of backyard. After awhile she looked at him and said, "What you're asking is impossible."

"I sincerely hope not. It's the only place they can't come for it. You have to try, Gwendy, before it's too late. You're the only one I trust."

"But how in the—"

Sitting upright, he raised a hand to stop her from speaking. He turned his head and peered next door into the deep pool of shadows beneath a weeping willow tree.

Gwendy got to her feet and slowly walked closer to the wire screen, following his gaze. She saw and heard nothing in the frozen darkness. A few seconds later, the wood-framed screen door to the back porch banged closed behind her. She turned and looked without much surprise. The wicker chair was empty. Richard Farris had left the building. Like Elvis.

16

"I ONLY GOT THERE right at the end," Adesh says, keeping his voice low, "but it sounded like you were whimpering. I thought perhaps you had injured yourself."

Both he and Gwendy are once again strapped into their flight chairs on the third deck of Eagle Heavy. The steel box marked **CLASSIFIED MATERIAL** is tucked safely beneath her seat. Gwendy cradles her iPad in her ungloved hands, the screen silent and dark.

"Winston said you sounded frightened and were calling out . . . something about a 'black box.' He claims he couldn't understand the rest of it."

Gwendy doesn't remember falling asleep and dreaming, but the very idea that Gareth Winston could be telling the truth makes her feel light-headed and causes her stomach to perform an uneasy cartwheel. She carries too many deep, dark secrets inside to start talking in her sleep now.

She steals a glance at Jafari Bankole, who's busy studying one of the overhead monitors, and at the opposite end of the craft, Gareth Winston, now buckled in tight and snoring loudly in his flight seat next to the porthole. *His* porthole. *Is he really asleep?* For the second time since boarding, the same crystal clear thought surfaces inside Gwendy's muddled head: *That man is smarter than he appears.*

"What was he doing down there in the first place?"

"He said he was going to use the toilet, and maybe he

did," Adesh tells her, leaning close enough for Gwendy to smell cinnamon on his breath. He drops his voice to a whisper. "But when I went down a short time later to check on my specimens, I found him standing there with his hand in the proverbial cookie jar."

Gwendy waits for him to continue, dreading what's coming next.

"He was fiddling with the latch on your cabin door."

NG, Gwendy thinks. *Not good at all.*

A smile comes onto Adesh's round face, and not a friendly one. "When he finally turned around and saw me, his eyes bugged out—pardon the pun—and he practically jumped out of his pressure suit. That's the nice thing about being weightless. No one can hear you coming."

"Well, I'm grateful you came along when you did. I . . . I . . ."

And just like that her brain short-circuits and shuts down. All the information that was stored there just a moment earlier suddenly vanishes as if an invisible eraser has been swept across the inside of her head. *Where has it gone?* She doesn't know that. All she *does* know is that her name is Gwendy Peterson and she's a passenger on a spaceship and she's trying to save the world. But save it from what? She has no memory at all of that, nor what she was just talking about or whom the person is she was just talking to. The abrupt and overwhelming sense of loss—of abandonment—frightens her so badly that sudden tears bloom in the corners of her eyes.

"Senator Peterson? Gwendy? Are you okay?" Adesh asks. His eyes narrowed in concern, he appears on the verge of calling out for help.

"I'm . . ." she begins to answer, and then, just like that, everything is back where it's supposed to be. She's talking to Adesh Patel, the Bug Man, about Gareth Winston, the nosy and noisy lout sleeping just over yonder. Winston's a billionaire with a capital "B," and Gwendy isn't sure he can be trusted. Judging from the look on Adesh Patel's face, the Bug Man's not entirely convinced Gwendy can be trusted, either.

"I'm fine," she finally says. "I was in the middle of a thought and something my late mother used to say came along and hijacked my brain. I'm not sure why, but it's happening more and more often these days."

Adesh's brown eyes immediately soften. "Oh, Gwendy, I'm so sorry you lost her."

It's a nasty trick on Gwendy's part and she knows it—but she has no regrets. "Don't be. Please. It was a lovely thought and I'm glad I had it." She thumbprints her iPad and the blank screen flashes to life. "I just wish I had better control over when those sorts of memories resurface. It can be a bit . . . embarrassing."

"Please, don't be embarrassed. I'm sure you miss her terribly."

Gwendy sighs. "And you would be right about that." She musters a halfhearted smile. "To tell the truth, I'm more embarrassed that it's my first day in the up-above and I'm already off schedule." She studies the readout on her iPad. "I'm not due for a sleep break for another six hours."

Adesh wrinkles his brow and *pish-toshes* her. "You took a twenty-minute nap. So what?" He looks around furtively and gives his stomach a couple of gentle pats. "I'll let you in on a little secret. It's still an hour or so until my first designated meal, and I've already snuck two protein bars."

"You did no such thing!"

"I most assuredly did."

She takes a peek at the level above them. "You better not let the boss hear you say that."

"What happens on third level stays on third level," he says, shrugging his shoulders against the restraining belts.

Gwendy puts a hand to her mouth and stifles a giggle. Throughout the four weeks of intense training and twelve days of close-quarters quarantine, she's gotten to know several of her fellow crew members rather intimately. While Kathy Lundgren and Bern Stapleton are like old and trusted friends by now, she feels like she's barely scratched the surface with many of the others, including the Indian gentleman they call the Bug Man. She knows that Adesh Patel is quiet and polite and brilliant. He's traveled the world and speaks several languages. He's happily married to a beautiful woman named Daksha, which means "The Earth" in their traditional culture, and they have fourteen-year-old twin sons. She's seen a number of photographs, and the family is always smiling. She also knows that neither of the boys wants to follow in their parents' footsteps and become doctors. Instead, they're determined to become professional baseball players with lucrative shoe contracts and seven-digit social media followings—a fact the humble entomologist admits often keeps him awake at night.

After today Gwendy believes she's learned something else, something very important, about Adesh Patel. He has a kind heart to go along with his kind chestnut eyes, and she likes him a great deal. She believes she can trust him on this journey—and she needs all the allies she can get. Even those—perhaps even especially those—with a pet scorpion and a creepy tarantula.

Across the deck, Gareth Winston begins snorting in his sleep, a cacophony of wet, gurgling, slobbering sounds, not unlike what you might hear from a pair of horny prize hogs going at it in the midst of rutting season.

Gwendy and Adesh gape in astonishment at the blubbering

billionaire, then glance at each other and crack up. Jafari looks up from his iPad. "What? What did I miss?" The mystified expression on the astronomer's face makes them laugh even harder. "What? Tell me."

There's a sudden buzzing sound and Kathy Lundgren's amused face appears on the middle screen of the three over-head monitors. "Hate to be a buzzkill, folks, but some of us are trying to get a little work done up here." She gives them a friendly wink. "A bit quieter, please."

"My apologies," Gwendy says, her cheeks flushing. "I started the whole thing."

"No worries, Senator. I'm glad you're enjoying the trip."

Kathy's face disappears from the screen and is immediately replaced by a series of data charts and multicolored graphs.

"What's all the ruckus about?"

The three crew members turn and stare across the deck. Gareth Winston is rubbing sleep from his eyes with one chubby, balled-up fist. His usually neat short brown hair is sticking up in sweaty spikes. Before any of them can manage an answer, he whips his head around and peers excitedly out the nearby porthole. *His* porthole. "Hey! Are we there yet?"

17

THE MORNING AFTER RICHARD Farris's surprise Thanksgiving visit dawned clear and cold in the town of Castle Rock, Maine. Overnight, a storm sweeping across the upper half of the state took an unexpected dip to the south and slowed its roll just long enough to clip Castle County on its way out to sea, dropping six inches of wet snow on the frozen streets and lawns. Gwendy could hear the plows working even before she opened her eyes.

Slipping out of bed shortly before seven, after a brief stint of troubled sleep, Gwendy got dressed in the dark and left her husband dreaming peacefully beneath the covers. Before she stepped into the hallway, she took a single backward glance at the only man she'd ever truly loved. *No more secrets after today,* she silently promised, easing the door closed behind her.

Trying hard to remain calm, Gwendy checked the alarm system (the panel display was back to reading READY TO ARM; no big surprise there) and turned on the coffeemaker in the kitchen before heading out to the garage.

Using the old wooden stepladder her father had passed down to her the previous summer, Gwendy slowly ascended the rungs until she was able to reach the highest row of metal shelving that ran along the length of the garage's cluttered back wall. She scooted aside an old Tupperware container labeled FISHING TACKLE & BOBBERS, and—breathing heavy with the effort; at fifty-seven, she wasn't nearly as spry as she once was—carefully took down a cardboard box marked SEWING SUPPLIES. Once she was safely down, she placed the box on the cold concrete floor at her feet, dropped to a knee, and opened the flaps. Gooseflesh immediately broke out across her forearms.

The button box, snug in its canvas bag, was waiting for her inside.

She felt the short hairs on the back of her neck begin to tingle, and heard that familiar faint whisper of *something* in the far corner of her brain. She quickly closed up the box, got to her feet, and backed away.

This goddamned thing. How I hate it. How I loathe it.

She shivered, listening to the echo of Farris's voice in the dim silence of the garage, remembering his pale sickly face, scarecrow limbs, rotting and missing teeth.

And then his final words came to her, practically pleading by then: *It's the only place they can't come for it. You have to try, Gwendy, before it's too late. You're the only one I trust.*

"Why me?" she asked, barely recognizing the sound of her own voice.

She waited for an answer, but none came. Certainly not God, asking her if she was there when He made the world.

Summoning her courage, she climbed the ladder again and returned the cardboard box to its hiding place on the top shelf. Locking the garage door—she couldn't remember the last time she'd done that—she went back inside to the kitchen and poured herself a mug of hot coffee. She sipped it staring out the window above the sink at the snow-covered back-yard, once again promising herself that she was going to tell Ryan everything. She was too old and too frightened to go it alone this time around—*third time's a charm*, she thought—but it was more than that. She owed her husband the truth after

all these years, and it would feel good to finally tell it. Damn good.

But that conversation would have to wait until later tonight.

She had a busy day to get through first.

Every year, bright and early on Black Friday morning, her old friend Brigette Desjardin would swing by the house and pick her up. They'd grab a quick breakfast at the Castle Rock Diner before heading off on a ninety-minute road trip to Portland. Once there, they'd lace up their Reeboks and spend the day braving the overflow crowds at not one, not two, but all three of the city's massive shopping malls. They usually returned home late in the evening, the trunk and back seat of Brigette's bright red BMW crammed full with shopping bags and gift boxes, bragging about the great deals they'd gotten and complaining about swollen feet from all the walking and chapped lips from all the talking. And all the greeting: that, too, because a surprising number of people still recognized Gwendy from her stint in the House. For some of those folks, Gwendy Peterson was practically an old family friend; she'd been part of their lives for that long. Political demi-celebrity aside, Christmas shopping with Brigette was a holiday tradition Gwendy always enjoyed and looked forward to. And she liked people, for the most part.

This year would obviously be a different story. All of a sudden, thanks to the man in the little black hat, she had more important matters to worry about than shoe sales and triple value coupons.

She considered bailing out altogether—in fact, she picked up the telephone and went so far as to punch in half of Brigette's number, only to hang up. A last-minute cancellation would give rise to more questions than she was prepared to answer.

No, she told herself, she'd just have to "suck it up, buttercup," as her father liked to say.

Ryan had his own Black Friday activities to participate in. First up, a Chinese buffet for lunch with the guys on the bowling team, followed by a three-game, best-average-score-takes-all competition at the Rumford Rock 'N Bowl (the annual winner was awarded a two-foot-high, gold-plated trophy resembling a kicking donkey's backside; Ryan had taken it home three years running). After bowling, they would head over to Billy Franklin's bachelor pad, where they'd feast on catered Mexican food and watch college football on the big-screen television. Ryan usually rolled home around eight or nine at night suffering from a serious case of dragon breath and immediately rushed upstairs in search of the big plastic container of Tums. He'd spend half the night moaning and groaning in the bathroom and wake up the next morning swearing that he wasn't going back next year. They could keep their damn trophy. The two of them would have a good laugh about it over breakfast—just toast and a big glass of ice water for Ryan—knowing full well that he didn't mean a word of it.

So, yes, she decided, she'd suck it up, buttercup, and they'd both get through their respective busy days. Then they'd come home, change into their PJs, grab a bottle of good red wine and a couple of glasses, and rendezvous in the bedroom. And after all these years, she'd tell him everything.

Only it didn't turn out that way.

Gwendy held up her end of the deal just fine. At first, as was to be expected, she was distracted and quiet. She barely touched her omelet, home fries, and toast at breakfast. Once they got in the car, she found herself staring out the window at the passing countryside, daydreaming about the button box and Richard Farris's pale, waxy skin. And those perfectly smooth, unlined hands of his; she couldn't stop thinking about those. She did her best to keep up with the conversation—nodding when she sensed it was appropriate and tossing in the occasional comment or two—but Brigette wasn't fooled. Halfway to Portland, she turned down the car radio and asked Gwendy if something was wrong. Gwendy shook her head and apologized, claiming she had a lingering headache from the previous night and hadn't gotten much sleep (at least that much was true). She made a show of popping three Advil tablets and singing along with Barry Manilow's "I Write the Songs" when it came on the radio—and that seemed to do the trick for Brigette.

By the time they parked the car and waded into the frenzy, Gwendy actually found herself smiling and laughing. Brigette, with that childlike enthusiasm and goofy sense of humor of hers, had a way of turning back the clock and making the rest of the world melt away. Gwendy often told her husband that spending an afternoon with Brigette Desjardin was a little like stepping into a time machine and traveling back to the late 1970s. Her simple enjoyment of life was contagious.

Both women scored major coups at the first boutique they entered—a half-price carryall purse for Gwendy; a pair of knee-high leather boots for Brigette—and that set the tone for the rest of the day. They spent the next eight hours giggling and gossiping like a couple of happy teenagers.

Often—actually more often than she would have expected—Gwendy was approached by men and women who said they were going to vote for her. One of them, an older woman with perfectly coifed pink hair, touched her on the elbow and whispered, "Just don't tell my husband."

After grabbing soup and salads for dinner at a burstingat-the-seams Cracker Barrel just off I-95, Gwendy finally made it home at 7:45 p.m. She immediately shucked her clothes, leaving them in a messy pile on the bathroom floor, and slipped into a warm bubble bath. An hour later, dressed in her favorite silk pajamas, which Ryan had smuggled home from an assignment in Vietnam, she dozed off on the family room sofa with a true crime paperback laying open in her lap.

Some time later she was awakened by a ringing door-bell. *Big dummy forgot his keys*, she thought, getting up from the sofa. She glanced at the antique grandfather clock on her way to the foyer and was surprised to see that it was after midnight. Still, she wasn't worried until she looked into the peephole and saw Norris Ridgewick standing on the porch. Norris, who once upon a time held the title of Castle County Sheriff for almost two decades, had retired a year earlier and now spent most of his days fishing at Dark Score Lake.

She yanked open the door and immediately knew from the look in her old friend's eyes that Ryan was not coming home tonight. Or ever. Before Ridgewick could manage a single word, Gwendy let loose a sob that tore at her chest and stum-bled back to the sofa with tears streaming down her cheeks.

Norris plodded into the house, head down, and closed the door behind him. Sitting down on the arm of the sofa, he placed a hand on Gwendy's shoulder. As he explained what had happened—a hit-and-run, her husband of so many years taken in mere instants—Gwendy scooted to the far side of the couch and curled into a fetal position, hugging her legs tight to her chest.

"He wouldn't have suffered," Norris said, and then added the very thing she had been thinking: "I know that's no consolation."

"Where?" Thinking it must have been in the Rock 'N

Bowl's parking lot, probably some guy in a pickup truck pulling out too fast after too many beers, maybe reaching down to tune the radio.

"Derry."

"*Where?*" Thinking she must have misheard. Derry was over a hundred miles north of the Rock 'N Bowl and Billy Franklin's Rumford apartment.

Norris, perhaps thinking she wanted the actual location, consulted his notebook. "He was crossing Witcham Street. Near the bottom of what they call Up-Mile Hill."

"Witcham Street in Derry? Are you sure?"

"Sorry to say, dear, but I am."

"What was he doing there?" Still not able to believe this news. It was like a stone lodged in her throat. No, lower: on her heart.

Norris Ridgewick gave her an odd look. "You don't know?"

Gwendy shook her head.

In the days following her husband's funeral, Gwendy found herself searching for an answer to that question with a dogged persistence that bordered on obsession. She discovered from talking to several members of Ryan's bowling team that he had called them early on Black Friday and canceled on the annual tournament, as well as Billy Franklin's after party. He gave no reason, just claimed that something important had come up.

None of it made any sense to Gwendy. It surely wasn't work-related—Ryan was supposed to be taking it easy until after the New Year, a fact she confirmed in a phone call with his editor—much less an assignment that would've required him to make the two-hour drive to Derry on the day after Thanksgiving.

What she knew about Derry wasn't good. It was a dark and dreary town with a violent history. There were an unsettling number of child murders and disappearances lurking in its past, as well as detailed documentation of strange sightings and weird goings-on. Toss in a series of deadly floods and the fact that Derry was home to one of the most blatantly anti-LGBT communities in the state, and you had yourself a place that most non-locals avoided like poison sumac.

A woman Gwendy had become close with during a long-ago fund-raising campaign claimed that back when she was a teenager living in Derry, she'd once been chased down a dark street by a giggling man dressed as a circus clown. The man had had razors for teeth and huge round silver eyes . . . or so she said. She was only able to get away from him by running into the Derry Police Station screaming her terrified head off. While the officer in charge fetched a glass of water and tried his best to calm her, two other policemen went outside to search for the man. They returned fifteen minutes later—faces flushed, eyes wide, breathing heavy—claiming that they hadn't seen a thing. The streets were deserted. But they had sounded scared, the woman told Gwendy. And they had looked it, too. She was certain they weren't telling the truth. The officer in charge drove the girl home later that night in his squad car and watched her from the driveway until she was safely inside.

And there was this: when Gwendy was growing up, her father claimed on more than one occasion—usually after reading something troubling in the newspaper or drinking too many cans of Black Label beer—that Derry was haunted. When he was in his early twenties, years before he married Gwendy's mom, he'd lived for six months in a cramped studio apartment overlooking the canal that split the town in two.

He'd spent his days peddling cheap insurance policies door to door. He'd despised his time in Derry and fled the town as soon as the opportunity presented itself. Although usually practical to his bones, Alan Peterson told his daughter he believed that some places were built on bad ground, thereby ensuring they would forever remain cursed. He insisted that Derry was one of those places.

Many longtime residents of Maine wore their well-earned reputation for coming across as surly and mistrusting to outsiders—if not downright hostile at times—as a sort of badge of honor. Gwendy knew this and accepted it, even going so far in years past as to poke fun at the stereotype in several of her novels, as well as a handful of political speeches. *"I told that flatlandah to git his ass on back down the rud to N'Yawk"* was always good for a warm-up laugh before getting down to business.

But even she was shocked—and angered—by the treatment she received upon her subsequent visit to Derry. In the company of the investigating detective, Ward Mitchell, she spent half an hour at the intersection of Witcham and Carter Streets, where Ryan had died. Mitchell at least was polite—she was, after all, a high-profile politician who'd just lost her husband—but he answered her questions without a hint of warmth. Witnesses? *None.* Ryan's cell phone? *No sign.* She thanked him, bid him a happy New Year, and sent him on his way.

She parked her rental in a nearby garage and set off on foot. Stopping at a handful of shops and restaurants, as well as a rundown bar named the Falcon—many of these establishments bearing red-white-and-blue PAUL MAGOWAN FOR SENATE signs in their front windows—she introduced herself to the employees and explained what had happened to her husband just a few weeks earlier. Then she pulled out a photograph of Ryan from her purse and showed it to them, politely asking if anyone had happened to see or speak with him.

In response, she received any number of ill-mannered grunts and dismissive head shakes. And no one whispered that they were going to vote for her.

Giving up on the local townspeople, Gwendy's final stop of the afternoon was a return visit to the Derry Police Station, where Detective Mitchell greeted her coolly. "I forgot something—what about surveillance video?"

He shook his head. "No cameras anywhere downtown. Oh, maybe in a few stores, but that's all of it. This isn't a nanny state, you know, like California."

"If it had happened in California," Gwendy said tartly, "you might have a license plate, Detective. Has that occurred to you?"

"Very sorry for your loss, Ms. Peterson," he said, pulling a pile of paperwork toward him. His cheap sport coat pulled open and she saw his gun in a shoulder rig. Something else, too. A Magowan campaign button on the breast pocket of his shirt.

"You've been a great help, Detective."

He ignored the sarcasm. "Always glad to assist."

After describing her unsettling visit to Norris Ridgewick at lunch two days later, Gwendy found herself giving serious consideration to Norris's suggestion that she hire a private detective to look further into the matter. He even gave her a business card of someone he knew and trusted. She meant to call and set up an appointment, but before she knew it Christmas was there, and New Year's Eve, and she had her elderly father to take care of.

Not to mention a Senate campaign to run. Shortly after Ryan's death, Pete Riley had called to ask her (dread in his voice) if she wanted to declare herself out of the race. "I'd understand if you did. I'd hate it, but I'd understand."

There were a great many issues that she cared about—Magowan's pledge to resume clear-cutting the forests up north was a major one—but it was the button box she was thinking about when she replied. "I'm running."

"Thank God. Just don't say I'm in it to win it. That didn't work so well for Hilary."

She gave a dutiful laugh, although it wasn't funny. What neither of them said was that the election was less than a year away and early polls had Gwendy Peterson lagging by almost twelve points.

The gray days of winter arrived. The first nor'easter of 2020 blasted Castle Rock during the third week of January, dumping nearly two feet of snow and toppling trees and telephone poles. Most of the town lost power for three days, and a sophomore girl from Castle Rock High lost her right eye in a sledding accident. January turned into February, February into March. The sun rose each morning, and so did Gwendy Peterson. She was too old and out of shape to start jogging again, but she began walking a daily three-and-a-half-mile route, usually in the frigid hours just after dawn when the streets were silent and still. She stopped dyeing her hair and let the gray grow out. She also started writing a new book about a haunted town. A thousand words here, five hundred words there, even scribbling a short chapter on a Dunkin' Donuts napkin during one of her campaign stops. Anything to blunt the keen edge of her grief.

And all of that time, hidden away in a cardboard box marked SEWING SUPPLIES, the button box waited. Sometimes, when the house was as quiet as a church, Gwendy could hear it talking out there in the garage, that faint whisper of *something* echoing deep in the corners of her brain. When that happened, she usually told it to shut the hell up and turned up the volume on the television or the radio. Usually.

Did the idea of pressing the red button and blasting the town of Derry (and all those awful people) off the face of the planet ever enter Gwendy's consciousness? As a matter of fact it did, and on more than one occasion. How about the shiny black button? Did she ever think about pressing the old Cancer Button and ending the whole shebang? Was she ever so tempted in her grief? The sorry truth: she was.

But Gwendy also remembered what Richard Farris had told her that nightmarish evening on the screened-in back porch—the box's last seven proprietors all dead, many of their families in the ground right alongside them—and it occurred to her that perhaps what the button box wanted most of all was a voluntary act of madness and mass destruction from its most faithful guardian. Talk about a win—the win of *all* wins—for the bad guys. And exactly who *were* the bad guys?

Around that time, the plague that Farris had warned her about—the media was calling it the coronavirus or COVID-19, depending on which channel you watched; Gwendy couldn't help but think of it as the Button Box Virus because she knew it had been responsible—finally made landfall in the United States. Only a handful of people had died so far, but many others had fallen sick and were being admitted to hospitals. Schools and colleges all across the country were sending students home to learn online. Concerts and sporting events were being canceled. Half the country was wearing masks and practicing safe social distancing; the other half—led by a frozen-like-a-deer-in-the-headlights President

Trump—believed it was all a big hoax designed to steal their constitutional rights. So far, there was no sign of the stacked-up body bags that Farris had told her about, but Gwendy had no doubt they were coming. And soon.

Some late nights, when she was feeling particularly small and alone, curled up like an orphaned child on her side of the spacious king-size bed or lying awake in a hotel room after a campaign stop, unable to find sleep despite a warm bath and several glasses of wine, Gwendy was certain that the button box was responsible for taking Ryan away from her. *A life for a life*, she thought. *It saved my mother and took my lover.* The goddamn box had always been like that—it preferred to keep things square.

In March of 2020, she got a phone call on her personal cell, a number known to only a handful of people. Perhaps a dozen in total. UNKNOWN CALLER showed in the window. Because spammers were now required to display an actual callback number (legislation she had enthusiastically voted for), Gwendy took the call.

"Hello?"

Breathing on the other end.

"Say something, or I'm hanging up."

"It was a Cadillac that hit your husband." The voice was male, and although he wasn't using one of those voice-distorting gadgets, he was clearly trying to disguise his voice. "Old. Fifty, maybe sixty years, but in beautiful shape. Purple. Or could have been red. Fuzzy dice hanging from the rearview."

"Who is this? How did you get this number?"

Click.

Gone.

Gwendy closed her eyes and ran a review of all the people who had her private cell number (in those days she was still capable of such a mental task). She came up empty. It was only later that she realized she had also given her number to Ward Mitchell of the Derry PD. She doubted it had been him, with his chilly eyes and Magowan campaign button, but it would have been entered into the department's computer system, and she had an intuition that it had been a cop who called her . . . but she never found out who.

Or why.

18

BERN STAPLETON HANDS THE iPad back to Jafari Bankole. The astronomer looks at the screen and shakes his head in disbelief. "I swear I tried that. Twice."

"Probably you did," Stapleton says. "These gadgets are fancy as hell, but they're not perfect." He glances over at Senator Peterson, who's strapped in her flight chair, busy tapping away at her own mini computer. "Let me know if you need anything else, Jaff."

"Thank you," Bankole says, already engrossed in the seemingly endless rows of shifting numbers.

This is Stapleton's third trip to the up–above, which is why he's currently making his rounds on level three of Eagle Heavy. All four crew members on the lower deck are first-timers, what the veterans call Greenies. Stapleton knows from experience that four weeks of training, no matter how rigidly organized, just isn't enough time.

"How're tricks, Senator?"

Gwendy looks up from her iPad screen. "Just finished performing my assigned duties as weather girl, and now I'm checking my emails. Pretty typical afternoon. What are you up to?" Despite her sassy tone, she's genuinely curious. She'd noticed Stapleton speaking quietly with Adesh Patel a few minutes earlier, their heads mere inches apart, and it worried her. Were they discussing her little episode from earlier?

Sneaking glances at her when she wasn't looking? She doesn't think that's the case, but even the possibility makes her uneasy.

"Thought I'd make sure the rookies were pulling their weight," Bern says. "Speaking of that . . ." He looks around. "Where's Winston?"

Gwendy hooks a thumb toward level four. "Either in the bathroom again or hiding in his cabin. I think he's already grown bored with the view from his precious porthole."

"How about you?" Stapleton asks. "You bored yet?"

Gwendy's entire face brightens—and the years fall away. Stapleton stares in amazement, thinking, *This is what Gwendy Peterson looked like as a little girl.* "You're kidding, right?" She holds up her iPad for him to see. "The interior temperature of our current destination, specifically Spoke One of the Many Flags Space Station, is a comfortable seventy-three degrees Fahrenheit. I was curious, so I checked." She taps the screen— once, twice, three times. "TetCorp plans to take a ship very much like the one we're presently flying in to Mars in the next couple of years. Do you know what the current temperature on the surface of Mars is at this exact moment?"

Stapleton actually does know, but he doesn't dream of saying so. Not with Senator Gwendy Peterson looking at him with the cheery (and wonder-filled) eyes of a twelve-year-old. Instead, he shakes his head.

"It's the middle of the night on Mars, and almost two hundred degrees below zero." She lowers the iPad to her lap. "Makes Maine feel like a beach in the Bahamas."

He laughs and gives a gentle kick of his legs to remain in place. "So what was all the commotion about earlier? I heard Kathy had to shut the party down."

"That was my fault. Winston was over there snoring like

a banshee, and it got me to laughing." She shrugs her shoulders. "Once I started, I couldn't stop."

"Sometimes first impressions are correct ones," he says, glancing at the billionaire's empty flight seat.

Gwendy nods, recalling Winston's booming voice and obnoxious behavior during their four weeks of close-quarters training. "I keep reminding myself to give the man the benefit of the doubt, but it's not been easy."

"Maybe this will help." He lowers his voice. "Kathy told me that Winston is responsible for more than half of St. Jude's annual funding, but the press doesn't print a word about it, because he doesn't want them to know. Shocking, huh?"

"Well, if in fact that's true," she says, wondering why the information was missing from her dossier, "then God bless Gareth Winston, and he certainly deserves the benefit of my doubt. May heavenly choirs sing his name."

"Hopefully, you'll still feel that way after spending nineteen days with him on MF-1." He grins. "If you're really lucky, you and Winston might even get partnered up to take a spacewalk together."

Gwendy flashes her training partner a scorching look— but doesn't say anything. She's thinking about Richard Farris's plan for the button box at that moment, and praying she can pull it off.

"I better head back. Reggie and Dale get upset if I leave them alone for too long." He begins to drift slowly upward, then stops himself by grabbing hold of one of the ship's support beams. "Almost forgot to ask. You ready for your video chat?"

In just over two hours, Gwendy has a video conference scheduled with top high school and middle school students from all fifty states, as well as select members of the media. She's not looking forward to it. In fact, she's dreading it. All she can think is: *What if I have one of my Brain Freezes on live television? What then?* That's one question she knows the answer to—it would be an unmitigated disaster and most likely signal the end of her journey.

"As ready as I'm going to be, I guess," she says, craning her neck to look up at him. "I just wish it could wait until we got settled in at the space station. Like Adesh and Jafari are doing with their students."

"No can do. You're a sitting U.S. senator and the VIP on this expedition. The world demands a bigger piece of you."

That's what I'm afraid of, Gwendy thinks.

Gareth Winston emerges from the lower level, a sour look on his face, and passes within a couple feet of Gwendy's flight chair. He doesn't make eye contact with her or any of the other crew members and doesn't say a word. His lower lip is sticking out. Once he's strapped into his seat, he turns his head and stares silently out the porthole.

Wonder what that's all about, Gwendy thinks. And then it comes to her. Winston must've overheard Stapleton calling her a VIP, and now he's in major pout mode. *What a baby!* She's about to lower her voice and say as much to Stapleton when the comm mic attached to the front of his jumpsuit gives out a loud squawk and Kathy Lundgren's voice inquires: "Bern, are you in the middle of something?"

"Just about to head back to level two. What do you need?"

"Can you accompany Senator Peterson to the flight deck? Immediately."

"Roger that. On our way." He clicks off and looks at Gwendy. "Wonder what that's all about."

Gwendy swallows, her throat suddenly sandpaper dry. "You're not the only one."

It takes them less than a minute to make their way up to

the flight deck, but it's long enough for Gwendy to convince herself that the worst is about to happen: Mission Control has somehow discovered her deteriorating condition and they're canceling the scheduled landing at MF-1. There will be no spacewalk. No disposal of the button box. It's over. She's failed.

When they arrive at level one, Operation Commander Kathy Lundgren and two male crew members—Gwendy can't recall their names for the life of her and is too unsettled to try Dr. Ambrose's technique—are buckled into their flight seats surrounded by a U-shaped bank of touch-screen monitors. Directly in front of them is the long, narrow viewing window Kathy had invited Gwendy to look out of a little more than twenty-four hours earlier. Beyond the window lies one of the world's great oceans. Kathy swivels in her chair to face them, her expression unreadable.

"I'm afraid I have some bad news, Gwendy."

Here it comes . . .

"There's been a mishap back in Castle Rock."

"It's not my father, is it?" she asks, all her breath leaving her at once. *Please, he's all I have left.*

Kathy's eyes widen in alarm. "No, no, as far as I know, your father is fine. I'm sorry. I didn't mean to frighten you."

Oh, it's a little too late for that.

"There was a fire at your house, Gwendy. Your neighbor spotted the smoke and called 911. The fire department was able to catch it early. The majority of the damage was limited to your garage and back porch. There was some additional water damage to the kitchen and family room."

"A fire. At my house." Gwendy feels like she's dreaming again. "Does anyone know how it started?"

"You'll be receiving a number of emails—one from someone at your insurance company, another from a retired policeman named Norris Ridgewick—explaining everything they know." Kathy looks at her with sincere regret. "I'm very sorry, Senator."

Gwendy waves a hand in front of her face. "I'm just glad no one was hurt. The rest are just . . . things. They can be replaced."

"Under the circumstances, we didn't know whether we should tell you right away or wait until we docked at MF-1, or even if we should wait until you were back on the ground. But we were concerned that someone in the media might alert you, so we decided you needed to hear it from us first."

"I appreciate that."

"Gwendy . . . would you like me to reschedule the video conference for another time? I'm sure everyone will understand."

She pauses before answering, purposely giving the impression that she's thinking about it. "I'll be okay," she finally says. "The last thing I want to do is disappoint all those children."

Despite being called "one of public education's fiercest advocates" by a reporter from the *Washington Post* two years earlier, Gwendy's true motivation for going ahead with the video chat has little to do with not wanting to disappoint honor roll students from all fifty states. As desperately as she would like to avoid appearing on live television, she believes that canceling at the last minute would be a very bad idea. It would send the wrong message—one of weakness—to whomever it was searching for the button box. And that's the last thing she wants to do.

It's not a coincidence, she thinks on her way back down to level three. *The fire started in the garage and it spread from there. After all these years, they're getting closer.*

19

As SPRING APPROACHED, GWENDY threw herself into the 2020 Senate campaign with what Wolf Blitzer from CNN described as "fevered abandon." Even with the coronavirus raging across the country—with more than 175,000 and counting confirmed deaths by mid-August—she spent the majority of her days and nights connecting face-to-face with the people of Maine. Masked, she visited hospitals and schools, daycare centers and nursing homes, churches and factories. While the incumbent (and defiantly unmasked) Paul Magowan focused the majority of his attention on big business and corporate incentives and continued to hammer strict borders and the Second Amendment, Gwendy went straight to the people and their day-to-day struggles and concerns. Tip O'Neill once said, "All politics is local," and she believed that. Any place of commerce or education that would have her—as long as masks and social distancing were in place—she went. She even spent a blisteringly hot August afternoon walking door to door in Derry. At one house, a man in a wifebeater tee told her to "get outta my face, you fucking harpy." It made the news, with the obscenity bleeped . . . for all the good that might do.

When she came down with a 102-degree fever and a nasty bout of diarrhea a few days later, most members of her campaign committee were convinced that she'd finally caught the virus and this would mean the end of her run. But, as often was the case, they underestimated her. A negative test and two days of bed rest later, Gwendy was back out on the road and speaking to the men and women stationed at Bath Iron Works. She told a couple of "old Maineah" jokes, which got big laughs. Her favorite was the one about moose-shit pie. In the current version, she changed the name of the lumber crew's cook to Magowan.

Gwendy's father—who'd moved to the first floor of the Castle Rock Meadows Nursing Home earlier in the summer— worried about his daughter, and told her so on more than one occasion. He faithfully watched her appearances on the morning and evening news programs and spoke to her almost every night on the telephone, but he couldn't convince her to slow down. Brigette Desjardin—now taking care of Pippa, Alan Peterson's elderly dachshund—pleaded with her best friend to make time to see a grief counselor, insisting that she was self-medicating with her hectic work schedule, but Gwendy wouldn't hear of it. She had places to go and people to see and undecided voters to win over. Even Pete Riley, the driving force behind Gwendy's Senate run, grew concerned after a while and tried to talk her into easing up. She refused.

"You got me into this. No backing out now."

"But—"

"But nothing. If you don't want me to block your number—which would be bad, with you being my campaign manager and all—let me do my thing."

That was the end of that.

What her family and friends and work colleagues didn't understand was that the engine driving her wasn't grief over Ryan's tragic death. Yes, she was still sad and lonely and maybe even clinically depressed, but if there was one thing Gwendy had learned during her lifetime, it was that you had to move on; honor the dead by serving the living, as her mentor Patsy Follett used to say. Nor was it an inflated sense of political importance. It was the button box, of course, still hidden away on the top shelf in her garage. One day soon she would have to step up and save the world. It was ridiculous, it was absurd, it was surreal . . . and it seemed to be true.

On the last Friday of August, new poll numbers came out showing Gwendy only seven points behind Paul Magowan. This was cause for mighty celebration, according to an ecstatic Pete Riley and the rest of the Maine Democratic Committee. Many members of the media attributed the surge to a wave of sympathy for the recently widowed challenger. Gwendy knew that was some of it but not all of it. She was reaching out to people and a surprising number were reaching back.

By late September, the gap had narrowed to five and Gwendy realized that people weren't just listening—they were starting to believe. As Pete Riley had predicted more than a year before during that first exploratory meeting, the tightening poll numbers soon snagged Paul Magowan's attention and his campaign began to play dirty. Step one was an updated series of television spots highlighting the proliferation of profane language and explicit sex scenes in several of Gwendy's novels. "I guess they're not big on originality," Gwendy snarked to the press after one campaign appearance. "I thought they already ran with the 'Peterson Is a Pervert' angle last August?"

She wasn't nearly as flippant two weeks later when a follow-up commercial aired on prime-time television depicting Gwendy's late husband as a raging anarchist, offering as proof a photograph of Ryan standing next to a burning American flag on a riot-ravaged urban street, as well as his arrest two years earlier at a Chicago protest. What the ad failed to mention was that Ryan had been in Chicago on a work assignment for *Time* magazine, had stopped to take photographs of the burning flag and rioters, and despite having proper press credentials displayed in plain view, had been taken into custody. In the Magowan-campaign photo, the credential hanging around Ryan's neck had been artfully blurred out. Nor did the Magowan ads say anything about any charges being almost immediately dropped.

From there it only got worse. The third wave of TV and radio ads shined a glaring spotlight on Paul Magowan's large and successful family—five children, three boys and two girls, plus sixteen grandchildren, all of whom still called the state of Maine their home—and questioned the fact that Gwendy had never had any children of her own.

"If Gwendy Peterson is such a true believer of the good things in this state and country—as she so often claims—then why hasn't she bothered to bring new life into it? Too busy writing smut and jet-setting around the world?"

As recently as a decade before, such a despicable ad would have torpedoed any chance of Paul Magowan holding on to his Senate seat. But this was a brave new world, populated by a brand-new breed of seemingly shameless GOP candidates.

When Gwendy's father saw the commercial for the first time during Game 3 of the American League Division Series, he became so enraged he climbed out a first-floor window at the nursing home and tried to call a taxi to pick him up. When one of the counselors escorted him back inside a short time later and asked where he had planned to go, Mr. Peterson responded, "To Magowan's campaign headquarters to whup his fat ass."

Gwendy reacted much more diplomatically, at least in public, largely because, at the age of fifty-eight, she'd already had years to come to terms with the reality of the situation.

She'd always adored children and wanted kids of her own one day, even before she'd met Ryan and fallen in love. For years after they were married, they tried with no success. It was the fault of neither. They visited the right doctors and took the right tests, and the results always came back the same: Gwendy Peterson and Ryan Brown were two immensely healthy human beings and, according to the rules of medical science, were perfectly capable of producing healthy children. But for some reason, despite all the trying—and they tried a *lot* during those early years—it never happened.

There was a time, not long after the final artificial insemination attempt proved unsuccessful, that Gwendy, alone in the silence of her bedroom, broke down and allowed the tidal wave of grief and anger to crash over her. She'd kicked and screamed and thrown things. Later, after the crying stopped and she'd cleaned up the mess, she called her mother to share the sad news. Mrs. Peterson told her what she always told her: "God works in mysterious ways, Gwendy. I don't understand why this is happening any more than you do, but we have to put our faith in the Lord's hands." And then she added, "I'm so sorry, honey. If anyone in this world deserves to be parents, it's you and Ryan."

Gwendy thanked her mom and hung up the telephone. She walked to the bedroom window overlooking the front yard and street below, and watched as a young curly-haired boy pedaled a bright yellow bicycle past their house. She watched until he disappeared around the corner.

"I understand why this is happening," she said to the empty house around her. "I think I always have and just didn't want to admit it. It's because of the button box. I was only a stupid kid, but I took and I took and I took. And now it's the box's turn."

In October 2020, with mail-in voting underway and physical voting sites opening their doors in just under three weeks, Gwendy Peterson and Paul Magowan met at the Bangor Civic Center for a long-anticipated televised debate. For ninety minutes, the incumbent senator was rude, arrogant, and condescending, the same behavior that had gotten him elected just four years earlier. His challenger was humble, well-spoken, and polite. Except for one fleeting moment in her closing remarks, when she turned to face her opponent and said, "And as for my late husband, you, sir, may try your very best to disparage his good name and reputation, but you know and I know and every person sitting in this auditorium and watching from home on television knows that you, Senator Magowan, are not enough of a man to shine Ryan Brown's shoes or wash the sweat out of his dirty jockstrap."

The majority of the audience in attendance roared their approval and rewarded Gwendy with a standing ovation as she walked off the debate stage. When the new poll numbers came out early the next morning, Magowan's lead had shrunk to a paltry three points.

But even with such impressive results, Gwendy knew it would take a miracle to overcome a three-percent deficit in as many weeks. There were no more debates on the docket and, after the public drubbing he'd taken, little chance that Magowan would agree to add one. Word on the street was that he planned to lay low for the rest of the campaign and lick his wounds until election night, when he would resurface and take the stage to accept a surprisingly narrow victory. Gwendy had events planned for every day leading up to the election—sometimes two or three in the same twelve-hour block—but even taken as a whole, she knew it wasn't enough to move the needle three percentage points. They were simply running out of time.

Gwendy believed there was only one surefire way to guarantee a miracle, and it was sitting on a shelf inside her garage at home in Castle Rock. Over the course of the next two weeks—usually while tossing and turning in one hotel bed or another; after a while, they all looked and smelled the same—there were at least half a dozen instances when she convinced herself that pulling out the button box was the right thing to do. Presto! Push the red button and make Paul Magowan disappear like a rabbit in a magician's hat! But each time, her conscience and Richard Farris's words of warning stopped her: *You must resist. Don't touch the button box or even take it out of the canvas bag unless absolutely necessary. Every time you do, it will get more of a hold on you.*

And then, on the Thursday night before Election Day, Gwendy got her miracle.

Like most of his longtime GOP counterparts, Paul Magowan's bread-and-butter constituency was made up of Pro-Life, Pro-Religion, Pro-Build-the-Wall loud and proud NRA members. As a proclaimed Christian and father of five, he spoke often and passionately of his abhorrence of the ungodly and downright evil practice of abortion. He called the doctors that performed such procedures "soulless butchers" and "devils in blood-smeared white coats."

On that Thursday evening, word leaked to the national press that a front-page article in the next morning's edition of the *Portland Press Herald* would be outlining in great detail and providing written documentation that proved Paul Magowan had not only had a year-long dalliance with a young woman from his local church but that he'd also paid—using illegal campaign funds, no less—for her to abort their unborn child.

Magowan's campaign immediately scheduled a late-night news conference to try to get ahead of the story. But it was too late. The ball had already dropped—right on top of Magowan's arrogant and hypocritical bald head—and started rolling down-hill. Fast.

When the final votes were tallied a few days later, *New York Times* bestselling author Gwendy Peterson became senator-elect of the great state of Maine. She won by a mar-gin of four points, which meant that thousands of full-time residents had still punched their ticket for Paul Magowan.

Life in America, Gwendy thought when she contemplated all those Magowan votes. *Life in pandemic America*.

20

GWENDY SWIPES TO THE CONTROL screen on her iPad, taps VIDEO LINK, and a blank picture-in-picture display opens in the upper right-hand corner. She hits the REVERSE IMAGE icon and the top of her head appears in the small window. Adjusting the angle, she gives one final tap, and her smiling face fills the entire screen.

"Got it," she says with no small measure of pride.

Gwendy's long gray hair is pulled back into a neat pony-tail and there are circles of bright color in her cheeks. Her blue eyes are clear and alert. She looks much younger than her sixty-four years and feels it, too.

"There you are." Kathy Lundgren floats down into view. "Ready for your close-up, Ms. Peterson?"

Gwendy extends her hand. "Of course I am, darling," she says in a haughty tone. Kathy laughs and feigns kissing the senator's hand.

Kathy was worried about Gwendy earlier—when she first told her the news about the fire, the senator had appeared lost, almost in a daze—but now that she's down here face-to-face, she finds that she can't stop staring at her. "My goodness, a couple hours of rest did wonders for you. You look and sound terrific."

"That and a strategic touch or two of makeup." Only Gwendy didn't bring much on this trip. Why would she? She's about as low-maintenance as they come.

"Well, whatever it is, send some my way, why don't you." Adesh Patel glides past Kathy on his way to his flight chair. She gives him a friendly nod and looks back at Gwendy. "A little less than five minutes til go."

Gwendy adjusts the straps on her flight seat and wiggles her hips until she's comfortable. She glances up at the overhead monitors and then down at her iPad. Licking her lips, she tastes a hint of chocolate on the back of her tongue. She instantly feels the *thump-thump-thump* of her heart beginning to race beneath her jumpsuit.

The tiny piece of chocolate had been in the shape of an ostrich. When she'd pulled open the drawstring of the canvas bag and slid out the button box, she'd been amazed at how heavy it felt in her hands despite their weightless environment. Much heavier than she remembered, and somehow significantly heavier than when she was carrying it around inside the reinforced steel case. She knew that made little sense—no sense at all, in fact—but didn't spend much time thinking about it. All things were possible when it came to the button box.

Her decision had already been made by the time she'd punched in the seven-digit code and opened the small white case marked **CLASSIFIED MATERIAL**, so there was little hesitation once the moment came. She lifted the box onto her lap, reached down, and pulled the lever on the left side, the one closest to the red button. And then she'd thought: *If you're monitoring this, Farris, you can kiss my bony white ass.*

The narrow wooden shelf slid soundlessly open from the center of the box. She picked up the chocolate ostrich and popped it into her mouth, barely taking the time to appreciate its fine detail. Closing her eyes, she allowed it to melt on her tongue, savoring the familiar burst of exotic flavor. Once the chocolate was gone, she immediately thought about pulling the lever a second time but fought back the temptation. She knew she was already pressing her luck.

After leaving the control room earlier and assuring a concerned Bern Stapleton that she was okay and just needed to rest, Gwendy retired to her cabin. When she stretched out atop the cramped bunk and buckled herself in, she hadn't even been thinking about the button box and its magic treats. All she wanted was to close her eyes and make the world go away for a short time. She was physically and mentally exhausted—and she was scared. Despite what Kathy Lundgren and Bern Stapleton believed, it wasn't the fire in Castle Rock that had Gwendy so distraught, although that certainly didn't help matters. It was a combination of *everything*. The video conference worried her greatly. One untimely misstep and she knew she was finished. Her heart ached fiercely. Despite the friendships she'd made, she hadn't realized how alone she'd feel on this trip. It had been almost seven years now, but not having Ryan waiting for her back at home left Gwendy feeling forlorn and adrift. And then there were the Brain Freezes. Ever since quarantine—and especially ever since they'd boarded Eagle-19 Heavy—they were coming with an increasing frequency that terrified her. Initially, she'd believed it was stress worsening her symptoms. But in her heart, she knew that wasn't the case. The button box had somehow discovered her plan and was trying to stop her before they reached MF-1.

Reaching down and touching the notebook tucked safely inside the pocket of her jumpsuit, she thought: *How long until the only things I remember are the words inside this notebook? And what about when I no longer remember how to read . . . ?*

Just the thought of that happening made Gwendy want to pull her hair out, or scream, or do both. Lying there, head spinning, staring up at the curved ceiling of her cabin, she'd eventually dozed. And dreamed . . .

Gareth Winston sits cross-legged on the floor beneath his port-hole. No other crew members are in sight and the ship is eerily silent. Winston is naked except for a saggy pair of soiled tighty-whities. His man-boobs and bright pink nipples are ringed by unruly snatches of curly dark hair. The button box rests atop his pale chubby legs and at first glance it appears to be smeared in blood. But then Gwendy sees that Winston's sausage-like fingers are dripping with globs of melting chocolate. So are his mouth and all three of his chins. It's everywhere. He reaches down and pulls the lever on the right side of the box. Out slides the wooden tray with a tiny chocolate donkey centered atop it. Winston grabs the chocolate and crams it into his mouth, slurping noisily. "Sooo good," he exclaims, and lifting his arm high above his head, he points a single finger in the air and—never one to pass up on an expansive gesture—twirls it around and around before lowering it in agonizing slow motion until it rests directly atop the red button. He giggles, drooling a rope of chocolate saliva onto his lap—and presses the button. Once. Twice. He looks up then, grinning with stained teeth, and bellows, "There! Now I'm number one in the world!"

Strapped onto her bunk, Gwendy jerked awake with a scream of terror lodged in her throat—and knew exactly what she needed to do.

"Thirty seconds," Kathy Lundgren says.

Gwendy steals a sidelong glance at Winston, who is buckled into his seat and facing the opposite direction. She checks her teeth in the iPad screen—all clean; *no chocolate!*—and releases a deep, steadying breath. "Here goes nothing, folks." She places her finger over the LIVE VIDEO icon and listens to the Operation Commander count down.

"Five . . . four . . . three . . . two . . . one . . . and you're a go!"

Gwendy puts a big smile on her face and taps the icon. "Greetings, earthlings, from my home away from home, Eagle-19 Heavy. My name is Senator Gwendy Peterson from the great state of Maine and I will be serving as your tour guide today. Before I unbuckle and give you a look at the amazing view just outside this porthole, I want to introduce you to our esteemed flight commander, Miss Kathy Lundgren. Say hi to everybody, Kathy! The three handsome gentlemen sitting to my immediate left are . . ."

21

IN JANUARY 2020—AFTER SERVING in a number of high-profile intelligence positions including Deputy Group Chief of Counterterrorism, as well as CIA Station Chief in London, Munich, and New York—sixty-three-year-old Charlotte Morgan became the eighth appointee (and only the third woman) to be named as Deputy Director of the Central Intelligence Agency.

She was also one of Gwendy Peterson's closest and most trusted friends. They'd first met at a budget meeting during the summer of 2003 when Gwendy was serving her second term in the House of Representatives. Charlotte Morgan was temporarily living in D.C., spearheading a six-month training program for overseas operatives. After running into each other at a number of social functions, including a handful of Orioles games, they became fast friends, bonding over their mutual affection for jogging, junk food, and violent crime novels, especially those penned by the dashing John Sandford.

Charlotte returned abroad when the training program ended, but the two women stayed in touch via telephone and email, and visited often during Charlotte's thrice-yearly trips home. When Charlotte got married to her second husband on a private Delaware beach in 2005, Gwendy served as one of four bridesmaids. The following winter, when Charlotte gave birth to a healthy baby girl—on her forty-ninth birthday!—she and her husband chose Gwendy to be the child's godmother.

Years later, when Gwendy's mom passed away on a cold October afternoon, Charlotte hopped on the next available flight from New York and was holding her friend's hand later that same evening. In many ways, Charlotte Morgan became the older sister Gwendy had always wished for.

As Gwendy parked her car by the Lake Fairfax boat ramp in Reston, Virginia, on the morning of December 9, 2023, and spotted her old friend sitting alone on a bench near the water's edge, she prayed that their long history would be enough . . . or at least a start. Charlotte glanced up from the book she was reading, flipped Gwendy a wave, then lifted her hands to her shoulders in a *What's going on?* gesture. Gwendy got out of the car and slowly made her way over to the bench, carrying the canvas bag in her right hand.

"No security?" Charlotte asked, only half-joking.

"I'm driving a rental Kia. That's security enough." *Not to mention the button box*, Gwendy thought.

"You're killing me, dear one," Charlotte said, closing the thick hardcover on her lap. "It's got to be ten degrees out here. Spill it. Why all the secrecy?"

Gwendy took a seat next to her friend, placing the canvas bag by her feet. "Have you ever considered me anything other than completely sane, reasonable, and honest?"

Charlotte's smile faded. She looked closely at Gwendy. "Are you in some kind of trouble?"

"You could say that," Gwendy agreed. "Please answer the question."

"Other than your bullheaded allegiance to the Red Sox, you've proven to be one of the most sane and trustworthy people I know. Top two or three, for sure. You know that."

"Then I need you to listen to me very carefully. Can you do that?"

Charlotte didn't answer right away—she was still too stunned by the turn the meeting had taken. She'd come expecting Gwendy to tell her that she was finally dating someone after the last four years of living like a nun, but this sounded much more serious. She didn't care for the drawn look on Gwendy's face.

"I can do that."

"Be sure, because I'm going to tell you something that will be very difficult to believe. Then I'm going to show you what's inside this bag and give you a demonstration of how it works."

Charlotte leaned forward and gave the drawstring bag a closer look. She opened her mouth to respond, but Gwendy cut her off again. "If you start to interrupt, I'm going to walk back to my car and drive away and pretend this meeting never happened."

"You're scaring me, Gwen. Are you sure we shouldn't call it quits on this conversation right now while we're ahead?"

"Only if you don't want the world to stick around long enough for Jenny to graduate from high school and go to an Ivy League college and have babies of her own one day."

"You're serious?"

"Unfortunately, yes."

The deputy director, never once breaking eye contact, was silent then. It was her job to know when people were telling the truth. "Okay. Tell me."

Gwendy told her.

When she was finished, almost forty minutes later, Gwendy picked up the canvas bag from the grass by her feet, pulled out the button box, and placed it on her lap. It was the first time she'd laid eyes on it in almost twenty-five years. She could hear Richard Farris's voice whisper inside her head:

Don't touch the button box or even take it out of the canvas bag unless absolutely necessary.

Was a thing absolutely necessary when it was absolutely the only way? Of course it was.

"Do you remember the part of my story about Jonestown?"

Charlotte nodded. "You believe you caused it. Or rather that strange box did. May I . . . ?" She reached for it.

Gwendy pulled it away, clutching it to her chest. Because it would be dangerous for Charlotte to touch it, yes, but that wasn't the only reason. There was jealousy, as well. She thought of Gollum in *The Lord of the Rings*: *"It's mine, precious, my birthday present."* Gwendy didn't want to feel that way about the box, but she did.

It was terrible, but there was no denying it.

"I guess I may not," Charlotte said. She was giving Gwendy a measuring look, and Gwendy knew, old friend or not, she was only a few steps from deciding Senator Peterson was barking mad.

"It would be dangerous for you to even touch it," Gwendy said. "I know how that sounds and what you're thinking, because I'd be thinking it, too. Just give me a little more rope, okay?"

"Okay."

"I thought the part of Guyana I was concentrating on when I conducted my experiment back then was deserted. I didn't know about Jonestown. Hardly anyone did before it hit the news worldwide. It's not like there was any Internet to check back then. And remember, I was just a kid. This time I did my research and I'm still not sure no one will be hurt. Or killed." Gwendy swallowed. Her throat was bone-dry. "The red button is the least dangerous by far, but it's still a loaded gun. As I found out when all those people drank the Kool-Aid back in 1978."

"Gwendy, you don't really believe that *you*—"

"Hush. No interruptions. You promised."

Charlotte sat back, but Gwendy could still see the worry in Charl's eyes. And the disbelief. There might be a way to fix that.

"I think you should have a piece of chocolate. That might help to open your mind a little."

Curling her pinky, Gwendy pulled one of the levers on the side of the box. Out came a tiny chocolate animal.

"Oh my God!" Charlotte cried, picking it up. "Is it an aardvark?"

"Not sure, but I believe it's an anteater. No two are ever the same, which is quite a trick in itself. Go ahead, try it. I think you'll like it."

"I'm allergic to chocolate, Gwen. It makes me break out in hives."

"You won't be allergic to this. I promise."

Charlotte lifted it to her nose for a sniff, and that sealed the deal. She popped it into her mouth. Her eyes widened. "Oh my *God*! It's so *good*!"

"Yes. And how do I look to you?"

"How . . . ?" Charlotte really looked. "Clear. It's like I can see every strand of hair on your head, every pore on your cheeks . . . you've never been so clear. And lovely. You always were, but now . . . *wow*." Charlotte gave a small giggly laugh. Not the sort of sound you expected to hear from a CIA topsider, but Gwendy wasn't surprised.

She took Charlotte's hands in both of hers. "What am I thinking? Want to hazard a guess?"

"How could I . . . ." Charlotte began, then: "A pyramid. The *Great* Pyramid. The one in Giza."

Gwendy let go of her friend's hands, satisfied.

"How could I know that?" Charlotte whispered.

"It was the chocolate. But not *just* the chocolate. You've trained your mind to read other people. You could say that telepathy is part of your job. The chocolates just give you a head start. My mother ate some, and they made her feel good, but she never had any mind-reading ability." *They just cured her cancer*, Gwendy thought. "It will fade, but you'll feel good for the rest of the day. Maybe tomorrow, as well."

"Look at the water," Charlotte whispered. "The sun fills it with stars. I never saw that before."

Gwendy reached out and turned Charlotte's face back to hers. "Never mind that now. Do you know what's going on in Egypt as of this week? Probably for the rest of the spring?"

Charlotte did. Of course she did; it would have been part of her daily briefings. "A bad outbreak of coronavirus. It's killing a lot of people and the government ordered a lockdown that will last at least until the middle of May. And they are not fucking around. Show up on the street and you're apt to get arrested."

"Yes," Gwendy said. "And that big old pyramid, the oldest of the world's Seven Wonders, is deserted. No tourists snapping pictures. No workmen. It's as close to perfect for demonstration purposes as I can get."

Gwendy squeezed her eyes closed and thought about the Great Pyramid of Giza, aka the Great Pyramid of Khufu, aka the Pyramid of Cheops. She hated the idea of vandalizing it, but it would be a small price to pay for convincing Charlotte.

She told her old friend what was going to happen and then pressed the red button, really putting her arm into it. Five minutes later she was back in her car, speeding north on I-95, trying to make it in time to a lunch meeting in downtown D.C.

Before leaving, Charlotte asked for another chocolate. Gwendy refused, but invited Charl to pull the lever on the other side of the box. Gwendy wasn't sure a Morgan silver dollar would slide out—they didn't always—but this time one did. Charlotte gasped with delight.

"Take it," Gwendy said. "A little thank-you for listening to me and not calling for the men in the white coats."

Later that night, when her cell phone rang, Gwendy was sitting in bed, watching CNN. It was showing drone footage of a monstrous pile of rubble where the Great Pyramid had once stood. NO EARTHQUAKE, the chyron read. SCIENTISTS MYSTIFIED. After a brief search, she found her phone tangled up in a blanket. She picked up after the third ring, knowing who it was on the other end this time despite the UNKNOWN CALLER tag in the phone's ID window.

Charlotte Morgan didn't bother with a hello or any other pleasantries. All she said was "Holy jumping Jesus."

"Yes," Gwendy said. "That about covers it."

"I'll get you on a space trip, Gwen, if it's what you want. That's a promise. It may take awhile, so hang tough. We'll talk."

"But not about this."

"No. Not about this."

"Okay. Make it as soon as possible. Using it today gave me a very creepy feeling. And some very creepy ideas." Some of them had been violent, and strangely sexual.

"I understand." Charlotte paused. "The Great Pyramid. Holy fuck." Then she was gone, saying good-bye no more than she'd said hello.

Gwendy tossed her phone aside and returned her gaze to the screen. Now the chyron read 6 KILLED IN COLLAPSE. They had been young adventurers from Sweden who had broken out of lockdown to explore the pyramid on their own and had been crushed under tons of limestone blocks. To Gwendy it was relearning an old lesson. No matter how careful you were, no matter how good your intentions, the button box always extracted its due.

In blood.

22

THE VIDEO CONFERENCE IS a big hit, a real smasheroo. No slip-ups, no Brain Freezes, and Gwendy actually manages to have fun. In fact, the entire flight crew has a good time, culminating in a rowdy, impromptu toast—vacuum-sealed pouches of orange juice, apple juice, and lemonade raised high in the air—saluting Senator Peterson for a job well done. Even Gareth Winston, who is grasping a fruit juice pouch in each of his meaty palms, looks almost happy for her. *Or maybe,* Gwendy thinks with a certain mean enjoyment, *he finally managed to move his bowels.*

"Okay, everyone," Kathy Lundgren calls out. "Time to get back to work. We have less than twelve hours until we join our Chinese friends at MF-1."

"May we never see them," David Graves grumbles, and Kathy swats him playfully on the shoulder as he floats by.

Gwendy watches as the others begin to stroke their way back to their flight chairs. "Thank you all again! That was an unexpected and much appreciated surprise!"

Gwendy still feels pretty terrific, but the buzz is starting to fade. If her memory is correct—and that's obviously a big *if* nowadays—the chocolate high used to last much longer. Days instead of hours. But then again, it's been more than twenty-five years since she last ate one, so how much does she really remember? Added to that, she's sixty-four now. Not quite a geezer, but getting there. Or do only men get to be geezers? Maybe she's almost a geezerette.

Either way, she's not complaining. She's thrilled, in fact. Not to mention relieved. The first video conference is behind her. It will only get easier from here on out, now that she knows what to do. And perhaps best of all? Gwendy remembered their names—every last one of the other nine crew members. Plus she remembered their job titles and onboard duties and any other number of details she'd long ago misplaced.

She grabs the iPad from beneath her seat and swipes her way into her secure email account. Scanning the dozens of notices in her mailbox, she stops on an email from Progressive Insurance. It's time-coded from earlier in the day. She opens it.

The email is two pages long and is signed (electronically, of course) by a Progressive representative by the name of Frederick Lynn. She skims its contents. The insurance company is currently working on an estimate of the damage to her house. It has been secured with heavy plastic sheeting and wooden framework where necessary. The power has been turned off and the remaining items in the refrigerator and freezer removed. The Castle Rock Sheriff's Department as well as the Maine State Police will be keeping an eye on it, in case of thieves or ordinary garden-variety souvenir hunters. Also, her neighbors—Ed and Lorraine Henderson—promise to keep a close watch.

The insurance company doesn't expect to hear back from Ms. Peterson until her return from outer space (Mr. Freddy Lynn actually uses those exact words, which brings another smile to Gwendy's face), but they need to ask one important question: Does Ms. Peterson have any pets that may have gotten loose during the fire? They found no food or water dishes, but it's standard procedure to ask. After that, there's a lot of technical policy information she has little interest in reading.

Gwendy thanks God that Brigette has Pippa the sausage dog and hits the REPLY button. She types, "No pets. Thanks for all you're doing." And hits SEND.

I've just sent my first email from outer space, she thinks incredulously.

She refreshes the mailbox screen and scrolls until she finds an email from Norris Ridgewick. It's shorter than the insurance letter, but just barely.

April 17, 2026

Dear Gwendy,

I'm very sorry about the fire. I've spoken with Brian Gardener at the CR Sheriff's Department and he's going to make sure no one gets within shouting distance of your house. I also rode out and talked to your father, so he wouldn't have to hear about the fire on the news. He was pretty down, but I told him the insurance folks would fix it up as good as new. (Although they never do, which we both know.) He asked me to give you all his love.

Now to the real reason I'm writing. I hope you won't be mad, but the last few years I've been doing a little digging of my own about Ryan and his mysterious trip to Derry. A man can only fish so much, you know! You never asked me to get involved, but I figured it was worth a shot. Worst I could do was burn up some gas money and waste a little time. I guess I would've made a pretty crummy detective, because for the longest time I wasn't able to find out much of anything, and I sure didn't get any help from the local constabulary. They basically told me to buzz off. I decided to take one more shot at it last week. No luck. Until, that is, I was getting ready to come on back to the Rock. I stopped to gas up at one of those no-name extra-barrel stations, the kind where a fellow actually pumps your gas and washes your windshield. This guy was named Gerald "Gerry" Keele, an old-timer who was sort of refreshing because he didn't have any of that (excuse the language) "fuck you and the horse you rode in on" Derry attitude. I asked my questions, showed him Ryan's picture, and right away he said yeah. He especially remembered the GWENDY FOR SENATE stickers, because there were three of them plastered across his back bumper.

That makes Gwendy wipe away a tear.

He said Ryan asked directions to Bassey Park because he had to meet a man there, by the big Paul Bunyan statue. Keele laughed and said, "I can give you directions, but you won't find Big Paul because he's long gone." Ryan jotted down the turns and drove off. I thought that was all I was going to get, but then Keele said something else. I was recording on my phone, so I can give it to you exactly. He said, "There's an abandoned warehouse past the gas station, on the corner of Neibolt and Pond. Soon as your boy paid and left, an old Chrysler pulled out from behind that warehouse. Big as a boat it was, and an ugly green color that almost hurt your eyes to look at. I could be wrong, but I almost thought it was following the man you're asking about."

Now I bet I know what you're thinking, Senator Gwendy, because I'm thinking the same: it's a great big damn bust-

out-crying shame that there was no surveillance footage of that accident . . . if it was an accident. I would just about love to know if the car that mowed down your husband and left him dead in the street was an old green Chrysler, big as a boat.

Only that doesn't seem right. Didn't someone call her and say her husband had been hit by some other kind of car? And of a different color? Gwendy thinks so, but she can no longer trust her memory. She isn't even sure there *was* a call. At least she can still read, so she finishes Norris's email.

That's all I have, and I think it's all I'm going to get. That's a strange town, and I could live just as long and die just as happy if I never set foot inside the Derry city limits again. I'll keep digging if you want me to, but I honestly don't think there's more to find out. I hope you're not upset I started in the first place. I meant well. In the meantime, safe travels up there. I respect your courage, but all I can say otherwise is better you than me.

Your friend,
Norris

Gwendy can hear Norris's voice—surprisingly deep for a man of his slender build—as she reads the email for a second time. When she's finished, she just sits there staring at the iPad screen, her eyes gradually losing focus. The good feelings she's been reveling in for the past couple of hours have vanished and been replaced by . . . she doesn't exactly know what. *Shock? Confusion? Fear?* Yes, all of those things. Confusion she's used to since her mind started to go. The others, less so.

"Save my seat," she says to no one in particular. "I'm off

to use the ladies'." She unbuckles her safety harness and swims her way down to the common area on level four. *What in the world were you up to, Ryan?*

The shiny white lavatory door is closed, and once again Gwendy is reminded of the sterile morgue lockers she's seen so often on television. The panel above the latch reads AVAILABLE. Unsure if she really needs to pee or if she's simply going through the motions, Gwendy reaches for the door. Before she can open it, someone grasps her shoulder from behind.

She lets out a squeak and spins around, arms flailing. Gareth Winston is floating a foot or so off the ground, a startled look on his face.

"Jumping Jesus, Winston! Don't ever sneak up on me like that again!"

"Sorry," he says, drifting backward. He doesn't look particularly sorry. "I didn't mean to scare you. I usually make a lot of noise when I come into a room. I'm kinda clumsy that way." He shrugs his ample shoulders. "But I'm as light as a feather up here. It takes some getting used to."

"It certainly does," Gwendy says.

"Anyway, I just wanted to apologize for giving you a hard time before. It's none of my business what's in that case of yours and I shouldn't have said what I said."

Gwendy can't believe her ears. Not that long ago she'd questioned whether the phrase *thank you* existed in Gareth Winston's vocabulary. She would have bet her last dollar that the words *I apologize* did not. She's pleasantly surprised to find that she's mistaken. "Apology accepted."

"When you have as much money as I do, you sometimes fall into bad habits, like always thinking you should get your way. I'm working on it."

"I know quite a few people in Washington, D.C., who could use some help with that. And they don't have a fraction of your bank account."

Winston laughs. "Well, thanks for accepting my apology. I'll let you get on with your . . ." He gestures at the lavatory door. ". . . you know."

Gwendy offers him a genuine smile—she could get used to this new and improved Gareth Winston—and extends her hand. "Thank you for being so gracious."

Winston reaches out and takes it.

Suddenly Winston appears very clear to her, very *bright* and in focus, almost as if he's somehow lit from within, and everything else around him falls away. Thinking about it later, she'll be reminded of a moment from the second time she had the button box in her possession, when she stepped inside the mind of a madman the Castle Rock newspaper called The Tooth Fairy. And, of course, when her old friend Charlotte Morgan knew she was thinking of the Great Pyramid.

Although Gareth Winston is still smiling, he's not smiling inside. He's never smiling inside. But he is in love. The man he's in love with is sitting behind the wheel of a car. Gareth is in the passenger seat, looking at him. It may be impolite to stare, but Gareth can't tear his eyes away from that face. Gareth thinks it's the face of a blond angel. He thinks he would give away everything he owns if the blond angel allowed him just one kiss.

Only in this flash—it lasts maybe two seconds, four at most—Gwendy sees the driver as he really is. His real face is old, haggard, and rotting from the inside out. His eyes are milky with cataracts. His lower lip has lost all its tension and sags away from blackening teeth. She has a terrible premonition that Richard Farris will look this way before too long.

The car is big. And old. The acre of hood is a weirdly vibrant

green that hurts her eyes to look at. The word on the oversized steering wheel—

Winston jerks back, breaking their grip. His eyes are wide in their pockets of fat. "Jesus, woman!" No humble I'm-sorry in that voice now. He sounds pissed off. And scared. "What was *that*?"

"I don't know," Gwendy says. The vision is already fading. If she can't get to her little notebook soon, it will be entirely gone, like a dream ten minutes after waking. "Static electricity, I guess."

Dr. Dale Glen goes floating by, peering at something on his iPad. "Very likely. It's common up here." He says it without looking up from whatever he's reading.

"Whew, it was strong, whatever it was," Winston says, and manages a fake comic-book laugh: *Ha! Ha!* "You'll have to excuse me, Senator. I have some emails I need to answer."

Off he goes, leaving Gwendy by the lavatory door. She has to try twice to unlatch it. Adesh floats by and asks if she's okay. She doesn't say anything—isn't sure she can—but nods, her hair floating above her head like seaweed. She finally opens the door and pulls herself inside. She fumbles for the button that will light the IN USE panel on the outside (there are no locks in the common area, a safety precaution in case someone has a medical emergency) and tries to raise the lid on the toilet. It won't come. A red panel lights up, saying PRESSURIZE.

Right, almost forgot (now she forgets so much). She thumbs the button to the right of the toilet and the red light goes out. There's a low humming as the toilet does whatever it's supposed to do so she can lift the lid without yanking all of the air in the tiny capsule first into the bowl and then into space. It occurs to her that if Kathy is up front in the control area, she will have seen the warning light blink on and then off. And if she's not there, Sam Drinkwater or Dave Graves probably is. She hopes they'll just shrug it off. Probably they will, but it's not good. Forgetting such elementary things from their training sessions is definitely NG.

Gwendy lowers her coverall, sits, and turns the proper dial to its lowest setting. She feels a gentle sucking sensation that means her pee will go down instead of just floating around under her butt in globules. She lowers her face into her hands as she urinates. Something just happened when she took Gareth Winston's hand. Something important. Something about a car. Or two cars, of different colors? Possibly something about Ryan as well, but probably not; probably she's mixing up Norris's communique with what just happened when she took Gareth Winston's hand.

Whatever it was, it's gone.

Goddamn what's happening to me, Gwendy thinks. *Goddamn it to hell.*

She might be able to get it back if she eats one of the chocolates, and it's a tempting idea, but she must not. Even one was dangerous, and it probably doesn't matter.

Does it?

23

THE CREW AND PASSENGERS of Eagle Heavy have seen the MF space station on each of their last six orbits. Because each of these orbits varies slightly, making a fan shape on the computer screens, Many Flags sometimes looks "above" and sometimes "below," but it's always on the starboard side and it's always amazing.

"Looks like the space station in *2001*," Reggie Black comments as they pass on their last non-docking orbit. MF is less than 25 miles away on this one. "Only MF has one ring instead of two."

"And more spokes," Jafari says. The two of them are shoulder to shoulder in front of the porthole, with Gwendy floating above and between them. "I believe that in the movie there were only four spokes."

From the control area Sam Drinkwater says, "MF is very similar to Kubrick's version. You have to remember it's not always art imitating life. Sometimes it's the other way around."

"No idea what that means," Gareth says. He's also looking at the MF station, but since the porthole on the right is taken, he's stuck with his iPad and sounds irritated about it.

"It means that the people who designed the station saw the movie," Sam says. "Maybe as children. To them, this is how space stations are supposed to look."

"Ridiculous," Gareth snaps. "It was built as it was simply

because form always follows function. Not because some space architect saw a movie when he was five."

Sam doesn't argue the point, maybe because Gareth is the paying passenger (in certain confidential preflight files, Gwendy has seen Gareth—and herself—referred to as "the geese," an old airline term for passengers). Or maybe Sam's just bored with the subject. Either way, Gwendy thinks he's right. When looking at her Apple Watch, she often thinks that some gearhead designer was enchanted by Dick Tracy's wrist radio when he or she was a kid.

In any case, the MF station is huge. The actual specs have left her mind, but she does remember that the endlessly curving outer corridor circling its rim is two and a half miles in length. *Even with the Great Pyramid gone*, she thinks, *there are still seven wonders in the world.* Except the new seventh is actually *above* the world. And for the next nineteen days, it's going to be their home. Assuming the next couple of hours go well, that is; docking is the most delicate and dangerous part of the entire mission, even more dangerous than their eventual landing on a floating pad off Malta.

Kathy Lundgren comes on the general comm and tells them to don their pressure suits. For a moment Gwendy is bewildered. She knows what the suit is, of course she does; the question is where did she put it?

She sees Adesh and Jafari pulling their storage cases from beneath their seats and almost slaps her forehead. *Duh. Get it together, Gwendy.* Is her memory worse since the last chocolate wore off? She thinks it probably is. The box always exacts a price.

She gets her suit out and slips into it. For a moment she's distracted by the portside porthole. Did a bird just fly by out there? On the way to the feeder by the picnic table in their—

"Zip up, Senator Gwendy," Dale Glen says, pointing at her open suit.

"Yes. I was just thinking about . . ." Is she going to tell him she thought a bird just flew past, 260 miles above the earth? Or that for just a moment she lost her place in time? "It doesn't matter."

She zips her suit and gets her helmet on and locked, putting her increasingly unreliable mind on hold and letting muscle memory take over. *Click, click, snap,* and done. *Easy as pie,* she tells herself, and connects to her iPad and the screens ahead of her seat. At first there's nothing to see in the forward view, and then that huge and improbable wheel comes over the rim of the earth. It's a majestic, almost heart-stopping sight, revolving slowly and revealing the flags of the sixty-one nations that took part and have the right—theoretically, at least—to use it. *All it needs,* she thinks, *is the soundtrack music from* 2001. *Thus Spake . . . somebody. Can't remember, just that it starts with a Z.*

In the center is a white bubble containing the telescopic equipment Jafari Bankole probably can't wait to get his hands on. Above the bubble is something that looks like a stainless-steel masthead topped with a gray cup lined with glittering gold mesh. It is sending messages to the stars . . . and hoping for a response.

Kathy Lundgren: "Mission Control, are we go for docking?"

Eileen Braddock: "Go for dock, Eagle Heavy, we are green across the board."

David Graves: "Visors down, campers. We've got . . ."

"Seventeen minutes," Kathy finishes. "Crew, roger your visors."

They do.

"Give it to Becky," Eileen says.

"Giving it to Becky, roger," Kathy replies. "No commands, all computer. What do you say, Becky?"

"That I have the bus," the voice of Becky the computer replies.

Dave says, "And what kind of bus is it, Becky?"

"It is a magic bus," Becky says, and actually plays a few bars of the Who song.

"This hardly seems the time for stupid computer tricks," Gareth says. He sounds wound up and pissed off, that amiable tone of voice from earlier outside of the lavatory a distant memory. "Next you'll be asking it to tell knock-knock jokes while our lives are at risk!"

"No one's life is at risk," Kathy says. "This is a walk in the park."

If only, Gwendy thinks.

Now there's a touch of gravity again as Becky fires the aiming rockets in small, feathery bursts.

"Ops, do you want to go around another couple of times?" Eileen asks. "Sunset in twenty minutes, your location."

"Negative, Ground, all good with us, and Becky can see in the dark."

But Kathy and Sam can't, Gwendy thinks, *and computer-directed docking only works if Becky's programming is flawless, and if there's no dreaded holy-shit moment.*

"Roger, Eagle Heavy." This time it's a male voice, Eileen's superior, not a rocket jockey but some political appointee. Gwendy should be able to remember his name—she was the one who appointed him, for Christ's sake—but she can't. She tries some of Dr. Ambrose's tricks, but none of them work.

A sudden brilliant thought strokes across her mind, as scary as a stroke of lightning hitting just feet away: *Where is the button box?* Is it in her tiny capsule of a cabin, or the storage compartment beneath her seat? Oh God, is it sitting home on the high shelf in the garage? What if she forgot to bring it?

She has enough wit to change her comm to private and then select the Bug Man's setting on her iPad. "Adesh, do you know what I did with the steel case I brought on board? The one with—"

"Yes, the one with CLASSIFIED stamped on it." He points down. She looks and sees it's beneath her leg, just as it was on lift-off.

"Thank you," she says. "Forgive the flightiness. I'm a little nervous about the docking."

"Totally understood." He smiles at her through his visor, but there's no smile in his eyes. What she sees there is consideration. Maybe evaluation. She doesn't like it. *They must not know what's wrong with me until the mission is accomplished. After that it won't matter* what *they know.*

There's a thud from above them as Eagle Heavy's docking hatch slides open on its servomotors.

"IDA is in place and green across the board," Becky says. Gwendy has no trouble with that. IDA is the International Docking Adapter, so called because every nation that can send rockets to MF uses the same system. She can remember that, but for the time being her own middle name escapes her.

"Locking hinges in place," Becky says.

The cabin rocks port; rocks starboard; comes steady. Little jerks accompany each movement, as if an inexperienced driver is goosing the gas pedal, releasing it, then goosing it again. A metaphor Gwendy could have done without.

"Ten meters," Becky says.

All at once a huge shadow darkens the cabin, causing the interior lights to come on. Gwendy cranes her neck and sees they are passing under one of the MF station's huge spokes, clearing it by what looks like only feet. She can make out every seal and rivet.

"Jesus, too close!" Gareth cries. "Too fucking cl—"

Then his voice is gone. Someone—probably Dave Graves—has cut him out of the general comm. *Which is a good thing,* Gwendy thinks. *No one needs to listen to him bellow.* Nevertheless, she braces herself for a collision that seems almost inevitable. A gloved hand takes hers. It's Jaff. She turns to him and winks. He looks scared to death, but he manages to wink back.

"Five meters," Becky says.

Seconds later there's a bump—not hard but plenty solid. Gwendy has a moment of vertigo and realizes her body hasn't been fully aware of Eagle Heavy's constant motion until it stopped.

"Soft capture complete," Becky says.

Kathy relays that to the ground, and Gwendy hears applause. Beside *his* porthole, Gareth looks bewildered. He can't hear what's happening.

Gwendy selects OPS 1 on her iPad and says, "Kathy, loop Gareth in. I think he'll be okay now, and he should hear everyone in the down-below is happy."

"Roger that."

Becky tells them to stand by for final docking. There are more thuds, harder this time, as the twelve latches engage, two by two.

"Docking sequence is complete," Becky says.

"Good job, Beckster," Dave says.

"Always glad to help," Becky says. "Shall I handle the hatch opening?"

"I'll do that," Kathy says. "Stand down, Becky."

"Standing down."

Sam Drinkwater says, "The hard line is connected. You're go for hatch opening, Kath."

Kathy turns in her seat. "Everyone pressurized? Let me hear your roger."

They give it. Gwendy thinks the rich guy—name momentarily escapes her—looks grumpy but relieved.

Kathy says, "Mission Control, all valves are closed and I'm opening the hatch."

"Roger, Eagle Heavy. You guys have a great time and don't do anything I wouldn't do."

"That gives us a lot of latitude," Kathy says. "We'll talk to you once we're on board Many Flags. Thanks to everyone in the down-below. This is Eagle, over and out."

24

ONE BY ONE THEY float through the hatch, then up the hard line with its blue foam sides, and finally into Many Flags. Kathy Lundgren is first, Gareth Winston last. Gwendy's between Reggie Black, the physicist, and Adesh, aka Bug Man.

Gwendy feels a slight tug of gravity as she enters. Her mind is currently as clear as a bell, and she remembers that the station's slow spin has returned a fraction of her weight. She and the other newbies look around, bouncing slowly up and down: touch and go, touch and go.

Her first thought is that USA Control would look almost like a hotel lobby if the walls weren't lined with equipment, monitors, and a nightmare spaghetti of cords and wires. And if the walls weren't padded, of course. Her second thought is that it's *big*. After two days in Eagle Heavy, the room looks enormous. The ceiling is at least four feet over her head, and one of the walls isn't a wall at all but a long, gracefully curving window that gives a view of pure black punched through with stars.

"Okay to ditch the outerwear, guys," Sam says. "Stow 'em there."

He points to lockers along one wall. There are at least two dozen. Ten have lighted panels with the names of the Eagle Heavy crew. Gwendy bounce-floats to hers and opens it. There's a hook for her suit and a magnetized shelf for her helmet. She's carrying the steel box with **CLASSIFIED**

MATERIAL stamped on it, and it would stick to the shelf, but she doesn't want to leave it there. Not with Gareth's locker right next to hers. She sees him watching her, and she doubts it's with admiration for her butt in the red Eagle coverall she's wearing.

"Crew to me for a minute," Kathy says. "Gather 'round."

Gwendy closes her locker and joins the others, holding the steel box by its handle. It makes her think of the lunch box she carried to Castle Rock Elementary long, long ago.

"Air smells better, don't you think?" Bern Stapleton asks her.

"God, yes. Sweeter and fresher."

Also, there's instrumental music drifting down from the overhead speakers. Maybe Seals and Crofts, maybe Simon and Garfunkel. *Like in a mall or a supermarket*, Gwendy thinks. She's aware of something else, too. Below the humming of the monitors and equipment, there's a faint *creaking* sound, almost like an old wooden ship in a moderate wind.

That's a little creepy, she thinks. Then: *Check that, it's a* lot *creepy. Like a haunted house in a movie. Or a haunted hotel.* Maybe that feeling is stupid, but maybe it's valid. The MF station is huge, and except for them and half a dozen Chinese doing God knows what, it's deserted.

They circle Kathy, rising and falling, touching and going.

"You know most of this from preflight orientation, but protocol demands I give you a quick refresher upon entry to the station. First, accommodations."

She points at the doors marked SPOKE 1, SPOKE 2, and SPOKE 3.

"Spoke 1 is flight crew: me, Sam, Dave. Spoke 2 is science crew: Reggie, Jafari, Bern, and Adesh. Spoke 3 belongs to our passengers, Gwendy and Gareth, plus Dr. Glen. I think you newbies are going to be delighted by what you find. Someday not far in the future, TetCorp hopes those rooms and many others like them will be occupied by paying guests. Gwendy and Gareth, you have actual suites. Only a bedroom, sitting room, and a small bathroom, but quite luxy."

"Don't tell the taxpayers," Gwendy stage-whispers. Most of them laugh. Gareth Winston does not, perhaps because the current administration has landed him in the forty-five percent tax bracket. Or maybe he's just impatient with the repetition.

"You'll have to bring your own gear up from the Eagle; all the bellmen up here are on strike."

There's more laughter, and once again Gareth doesn't join in. Gwendy wonders when he last had to carry his own luggage. Maybe when he moved into a college dorm. Maybe never.

"I'll cut the rest of the lecture short, if you promise not to tell Mission Control, but I urge you to review the orientation video on your tablet again. It will guide you around the parts of the station available to us . . . which in this extraordinary circumstance is almost all of it. Jaff, you'll want to visit the observatory and power up what needs to be powered up so you can start sending photos back to Earth. I believe your main interest will be Mars."

"Correctamundo," Jafari says.

"Gwendy, you'll want to check out the weather deck. It's small, but it has tons of equipment and its own telescope. Bern, your lab is next to Adesh's bug suite in Spoke 5."

Gareth interrupts. "What happened to cutting this short? I'd like to get settled in."

Kathy registers momentary irritation at this rudeness, but a moment later it's gone. Gareth is important to TetCorp's plans for tourist travel above the earth and therefore must be cosseted. *Up to a point*, Gwendy thinks. *If he has to be busted on his behavior, I think I can be the bad guy.* She certainly busted the man she replaced in the Senate on *his* behavior, and on statewide TV. She just can't remember his name at present. She's never known such feelings of helplessness.

"I suggest we all settle in," Kathy says. "After one more thing."

Gareth gives a long-suffering sigh. But really, what does he have to do? It's not like he has a job up here, and Gwendy certainly doesn't intend to ask for his help on the weather deck.

"You all have the run of the place, except for Spoke 9. That one is currently Chinese territory." She points to an info panel below the big window, where there are eight green lights and one red one. "Should they unlock—which they do sometimes, to use the exercise room and the International Room, where they play video games and use the canteen machines— you will still stay clear. They are not particularly hospitable. But all spokes lead to the outer rim and that's common territory. I always enjoy a run there. In this gravity, which we call lo-no, I can do a mile in just over two minutes."

"*Please?*" Gareth says, and Gwendy knows what he sounds like: a rich type A passenger at the end of a long flight, dismissing the flight crew the minute the plane touches down. Sometimes Gareth can be friendly, even charming, but she thinks that's just thin paint over a man who expects to be obeyed and kowtowed to. "How about it, Kathy?"

"Big Zoom meeting to get to?" Bern asks mildly.

"None of your affair, Plant Man," Gareth says.

"Go," Kathy says, making an amiable shooing gesture. "Get settled. My advice: take today to explore the station before starting whatever job you came here to do."

Most of them head back down into the Eagle, Gareth

Winston in the lead. Gwendy lingers, then makes her slow way to Kathy, who is talking with Dr. Glen. "Got time for a question?" Gwendy asks.

"Of course. How can I help?"

Dale Glen bounces his way over to the window and stands looking out into the infinite blackness, hands clasped behind his back. The others have gone.

"My room," Gwendy says. She can't bring herself to call it a suite. "Does the door lock?"

"None of them do, but your accommodation comes with a security safe, very much like the kind they have in hotel rooms. It *is* sort of a hotel room, actually." She looks meaningfully at the steel box Gwendy's carrying. "You punch in a four-digit combo. Your special cargo should fit quite nicely, Senator."

She's speaking officially because this is official business, Gwendy thinks. "Thank you. That's something of a relief." She glances toward Dr. Glen. He's at a safe distance, but she still lowers her voice. "Mr. Winston—Gareth—has shown . . . um . . . an interest."

"Perhaps he was interested in this, as well." She reaches into the elasticized waist pocket of her jumper. What she brings out, to Gwendy's horror, is her red notebook. The one where she keeps all the things she doesn't want to forget, including the code that opens the CLASSIFIED box.

"He said your cabin door was ajar and he found it floating in the corridor. That must have been the case, because he wouldn't have any reason to be snooping in your cabin, would he?"

"Of course not," Gwendy says, taking the notebook and stowing it in her own pocket. She feels cold all over. "Thank you."

133

Kathy takes Gwendy by the shoulder. "*Do* you think he was snooping? Because I'd have to take that rather seriously, Mr. Moneybags or not."

The hell of it is, Gwendy doesn't know. She doesn't *think* she left the notebook unsecured, she doesn't *think* she left the door of her cabin unlatched, so it could have floated out in the constant circulation of the air purifiers . . . but she can't be sure.

"No," she says. "Probably not. Kathy . . . you have the Pocket Rocket, correct? It's on board?"

"Yes. Although what it's for is apparently above my pay grade."

"And I'm go for a spacewalk on Day 7?"

Kathy doesn't reply at first. She looks uncomfortable. "That's the plan, but plans sometimes change. Several people have been talking to me, including—"

"Including me," Dr. Glen says. He has rejoined them without Gwendy noticing, and now he asks the very question she's been dreading. "Senator, is there anything you want to tell us?"

25

GWENDY GAVE UP TRYING to believe there was nothing wrong with her on a spring day in 2024, about four months after her meeting with Charlotte Morgan. It was a piddling seven-hundred-word essay that did it. The kind of thing she should have been able to bang out in an hour, nothing but fluff and puff, but it brought down her wall of denial as surely as the magic box's red button had brought down the Great Pyramid of Giza.

The *Washington Post* ran an occasional feature called My Five, in which various famous people wrote about five great (or simply overlooked) things in their home states. John Cusack wrote about stuff in his native Illinois. The mystery writer Laura Lippman wrote about Miss Shirley's Cafe in Baltimore and the swimming hole at Kilgore Falls. Gwendy, of course, was asked to write a My Five about Maine. She was actually looking forward to the assignment when she sat down in the small office of her Washington, D.C., townhouse. Going back to her home state was always a pleasure, even if the trip was only mental.

She wrote about Thunder Hole in Bar Harbor, the Maine Discovery Museum in Bangor, the lighthouse on Pemaquid Point, and the Farnsworth Art Museum. She paused then, thinking she wanted to finish with something that was just plain fun. She sat tapping her nose with the eraser of a pencil from her jar—a habit that went back to childhood—until it came to her. Simones', of course.

She tossed the pencil back in its jar and typed: *My fifth choice is in Lewiston, about 20 miles up the road from my hometown of Castle Rock. Turn right off Lisbon Street onto Chestnut, find a parking space (good luck!), and step into Simones'. It's just a little storefront restaurant, but the smell is heaven. The specialty of the house is crankshafts.*

Here she stopped, staring at the screen. Crankshafts? In a restaurant? What was she thinking?

I wasn't thinking. I was on autopilot and had a senior moment, that's all.

Only it wasn't a senior moment, it was a Brain Freeze, and she'd been having a lot of them lately—walking around looking for her car keys while she had them in her hand, deciding to throw a frozen dinner in the microwave for lunch and finding herself looking for the fridge in the living room, more than once getting up from a nap when she didn't remember lying down. And after missing a couple of committee meetings and one roll-call vote (not important, thank God), she was depending more and more on her assistant, Annmarie Briggs, to keep her apprised of her schedule, a thing she had always taken care of herself. *Forget a roll-call?* the old Gwendy would have said. *Never in this life!*

And now this, staring back at her from the screen of her Mac: *The specialty of the house is crankshafts.*

She deleted the sentence and wrote, *You'll never have a better burgomeister.*

Gwendy looked at this and put a hand to her forehead. She felt hot to herself. Hot and strange. A month before, back home in Castle Rock for the weekend, she had gotten into the car with some specific destination in mind and had found herself at the Rumford Rock 'N Bowl instead, with no idea of what she had set out to do. She'd told herself what the hell, a beautiful day for a drive, and laughed it off.

She wasn't laughing now.

What *was* the specialty of the house at Simones'? A frightening spiral of words cascaded through her mind: catgut, dollface, candlewax, mortarboard.

Mortarboard, that's it! She typed it, but it didn't look quite right.

Annmarie poked her head in. "Going to Starbucks, Senator—want anything?"

"No, but I'm stuck here. What are those things you eat?"

Annmarie frowned. "Have to be a bit more specific, boss."

"They come in bread thingies." Gwendy gestured with her hands. "Red and tasty. You eat them with mutchup at picnics and such. I can't think of the word."

The corners of Annmarie's mouth turned up, forming dimples. The expression of someone waiting for the punchline of a joke. "Uh . . . hotdogs?"

"*Hotdogs!*" Gwendy exclaimed, and actually pumped a fist in the air. "Right, right, of cross it is, of cross!"

Annmarie's incipient smile was gone. "Boss? Gwendy? Are you feeling okay?"

"Yes," Gwendy said, but she wasn't. "I meant of cross, not of cross. Bring me a regular black, will you?"

"Sure," Annmarie said, and left . . . but not before giving Gwendy a final puzzled glance over her shoulder.

Alone again, Gwendy stared at the screen. The word Annmarie had given her was gone, sliding through her fingers like a small slippery fish. She no longer wanted to write the goddamn essay. And she hadn't meant to say "of cross" but "of course."

"Of cross, of course, of course, of cross," she murmured. She began to cry. "Dear God, what's wrong with me?"

Only she knew, of cross she did. She even knew when it had started: after pushing the red button to give Charlotte Morgan a demonstration of how dangerous the button box was, and how important it was for the two of them to keep it a dead secret between them until it could be disposed of in the ultimate dumping ground.

But Charlotte couldn't know about this.

No one could.

26

Day 2 on Many Flags.

The crew members have started doing their various jobs, with the exception of Gareth Winston, who has no assigned job. There are many wonders to explore in Many Flags, but so far as Gwendy can tell, the billionaire has spent most of the day in his suite. *Like Achilles, brooding in his tent*, Gwendy thinks. She can relate, because she has spent a certain amount of brooding-time herself since Dr. Glen asked his question. Or rather detonated it in her face.

Unlike Gareth, Gwendy has been plenty occupied. She made a brief trip to the weather deck, checking out the various equipment there, and gaping at the earth below her, watching as darkness moved smoothly over North and South America (blue and violet buttons on the button box). She participated in a Health and Human Services Committee meeting via Zoom. She talked about the importance of space exploration to a class of fifth graders in Boise who had won the videoconference with her in some kind of competition (or maybe it was a lottery). She thinks all those things went okay, but the pure hell of it is she can no longer be sure. She swallowed two Tylenol for a stress headache, but she knows it will take more than Tylenol to get her through what comes next.

They all knew or suspected, it seemed. Everyone on board. Knew what? Suspected what? Why, that Senator Gwendolyn Peterson had slipped a cog or maybe even two. Was a pack of fries short of a Happy Meal. A beer short of a six-pack. That the ever-lovin' *cheese* had started to slip off her ever-lovin' *cracker*. And because they were 260 miles above the earth, with a U.S. senator in charge of some secret mission of A1A importance, Kathy and Dr. Glen had confronted her. They didn't know what was in her steel box, but they *did* know that Gwendy was slated for a spacewalk on Day 7, and when she went out she would be in possession of a small rocket, six feet long and four feet in diameter. No more than a drone, really, only it was powered by a tiny nuclear engine that could keep it driving onward and outward for perhaps as long as two hundred years. After that it would continue forever on pure inertia.

That nuclear power plant, although no bigger than a model train engine, was powerful. If the operator—Gwendy—fucked up the initiation sequence while she was floating around out there, it could either blow a hole in the MF station or possibly destabilize it, sending it either into deep space or plunging into Earth's atmosphere, where it would burn up. Not that Gwendy would know; she'd be incinerated in the first two seconds.

Kathy had been as delicate as she could be. "I wouldn't feel comfortable sending you out there, even with a buddy, if I felt you were suffering some mental debility."

Dr. Glen was blunter, and she had to respect him for that. "Senator, do you suspect you might be suffering from early-onset Alzheimer's Disease? I hate to ask the question, but under the circumstances I feel I have to."

Gwendy had known it might come to this, and had worked out her story with Dr. Ambrose, who had agreed to help her with only the greatest reluctance. They both understood that the best story was one that incorporated as much of the truth as possible. In accordance with that, she told Kathy and Doc Glen that because she had been entrusted with something of gravest importance to the entire world, she'd been under severe stress for *two freaking years*, she hadn't been sleeping well, and that was why she sometimes forgot things. Kathy readily admitted that ninety-five percent of the time Gwendy had handled herself up to or above the accepted standard.

"But we're in space. Things can go wrong. We don't talk about it when we do our PR stuff, but everyone knows it. Even Gareth knows it, which is why he's prepared to perform certain tasks in an emergency situation. Ninety-five percent isn't good enough. It's got to be one hundred."

"I'm fine," Gwendy protested. "Good to go."

"Then you won't mind taking a test, will you?" Doc Glen said. "Just to ease our minds before we send you into space with an important something we don't know about and a powerful nuclear device that we do."

"All right, fine," Gwendy said. Because really, what else *could* she say? Ever since Richard Farris had shown up for the third time, she had felt like a rat in an ever-narrowing corridor, one that had no exit. *It's a suicide mission*, she'd told Farris that night on the back porch, *and you know it*.

The test had been set for 1700 hours, and at this moment it was 1640. Time to get ready.

Which meant it was time to take the button box out of the safe.

27

WHILE SERVING IN THE U.S. House of Representatives, Gwendy had had good connections. As a member of the Senate, she had even better ones, and she never needed one more than after her latest Brain Freeze. *The specialty of the house is crankshafts, for Christ's sake.* She thought of calling Charlotte Morgan, then rejected the idea out of hand. Charlotte was a spook, after all. She might decide that letting Gwendy hold on to the button box was too great a risk. Gwendy knew that letting anyone else hold on to it would be an even greater one.

After some thought she called one of her new friends: Mike DeWine at the NSA. She told him she needed to make an appointment with a psychiatrist who was completely trust-worthy. She asked if Mike knew such a person, knowing he would; the NSA kept a close watch on any developing mental problems in its staff. Secrets must be kept.

"Losing your grip, Senator?" Mike asked amiably.

Gwendy laughed cheerily, as if that wasn't exactly what she was afraid of. "Nope, my marbles are all present and accounted for. I'm involved in a review of the NDS—that's for your ears only, Mike—and I have some very delicate questions."

NDS stood for National Defense System, and that was enough for Mike. No one likes the idea of mentally unstable people in charge of the nuclear arsenal.

"Is there a problem I should know about?"

"Not at present. I'm being proactive."

"Good to know. There's a guy . . . hold on a sec, the name escapes me . . ."

Join the club, Gwendy thought, and couldn't help smiling. Losing one's shit really did have its funny side, she supposed. Or would, if a box that could destroy the world wasn't involved.

"Okay, here it is. Norman Ambrose is our top go-to shrink. He's on Michigan Avenue." Gwendy wrote down the address, plus Ambrose's office number and personal cell. *Thank God for NSA info*, Gwendy thought. "He's probably booked into the twenty-third century, but I think you'll be able to jump the line. Being a United States senator and all."

Gwendy was able to jump it and was sitting in Dr. Ambrose's office the following afternoon. After listening to him reiterate his promise of absolute confidentiality, she took a deep breath and told him she was afraid she was suffering from early-onset Alzheimer's or dementia. She told him that if it was true, no one could know until she completed a certain high-priority task.

"How high?" Ambrose asked.

"The highest, but that's all I can say. It may be a year before I can do the job I need to do. More likely two. It might even be three, but God, I hope not."

"May I assume that if certain people discovered your condition—if it indeed exists—this job would be taken from you?"

Gwendy gave him a bleak smile. "That can't happen. If anyone tried, it would be a disaster."

"Senator—"

"Gwendy. Please. In here I'm Gwendy."

"All right, Gwendy. Is there a history of Alzheimer's or dementia in your family?"

"Not really. My Aunt Felicia went gaga, but she was in her late nineties."

"Uh-huh, good. And you lost your husband fairly recently?"

"Yes."

"I'm very sorry for your loss. Added to that you have all the responsibilities of a new senator to deal with. You may be suffering from simple stress."

"There's no blood test for Alzheimer's, is there?"

"Unfortunately, no. The only way we can confirm the diagnosis—other than by observing the constant deterioration of the patient's mental faculties—is by autopsy after death. There's a written test that is a good marker, however."

"I should take it."

"I think that's a good idea. In the meantime, can I suggest a practical way of dealing with these Brain Freezes, as you call them?"

"God, yes! I'd do enemas three times a day if I thought it would help!"

Dr. Ambrose smiled. "No enemas, just a process of association, and you may have almost come to it on your own." He had a yellow legal pad on his lap. Now he turned back a page and studied the notes he'd made during her story. "When writing about this little restaurant, Simones', you found you were unable to remember a certain word. Do you remember it now?"

"Sure. Hotdogs."

"But you wrote—?"

"Crankshafts," Gwendy said, and felt herself blush.

"You knew it was wrong, so you tried again. Do you recall your second stab at it?"

Gwendy was having a clear day, not even a trace of mental

fog, and she remembered at once. "Burgomeister." Her blush deepened. "I wrote 'You'll never have a better burgomeister.' Stupid, right?"

"I don't think so." Ambrose leaned forward. "What usually goes with hotdogs at a picnic or a barbecue, Gwendy?"

She understood at once. "Hamburgers!"

"I think your mind was trying to form a chain of connections that would lead you back to the word you were looking for. Crankshafts are straight cylinders. So are hotdogs. Burgomeisters are a step closer. I believe if you'd taken your eyes from the screen with your essay on it, and relaxed your mind, you would have found the word."

"Can I train myself to do that?"

"Yes." He said it without hesitation. "This is a trainable skill. Tell me, do you have a pet?"

"No. My father does. A troublesome old dachshund."

"What is the troublesome dachshund's name?"

Gwendy opened her mouth, came up blank, and closed it again.

"Fucked if I can remember. Sorry, that just slipped out. This thing . . . it's infuriating."

Ambrose smiled. "Quite all right. Can you associate your way to it? Look up at the ceiling. Let your mind run in neutral. This is a process we teach to patients in the early stages of Alzheimer's, but also to recovering stroke victims. Don't push. Don't *hunt*. Your mind knows what you want, but it needs to take a detour, and detours take time."

Gwendy looked up at the ceiling. She thought about her father's smile, so warm and welcoming . . . she thought about the maroon sweater he always wore when the weather turned cold . . . watching musicals with him and Mom on TV because they loved them and would sing along . . . Gwendy

PARK

FUN

AMUSEMENT PARK

RIDES

FERRIS

FARRIS!

watching and singing along with them . . . *West Side Story* was her favorite, but her father's was that one with Ben Vereen. That one was—

"His dachshund is Pippa. My dad named her after his favorite musical. *Pippin.*"

Ambrose nodded. "You see how it works?"

Gwendy began to cry, which didn't discommode Ambrose in the slightest. He just handed her a box of Kleenex. She supposed tears in this office were pretty common.

"Will it always work?"

Ambrose grinned, making him look boyish. "Does anything?"

Gwendy laughed shakily. "I suppose not."

"Depending on how your test comes out, Gwendy—we'll do that today, as your situation is clearly difficult—I may prescribe drugs that might slow the progression of your illness. Which, I want to emphasize, is not yet proven. At this point simple stress seems more likely to me."

You may be a great headshrinker, but I don't think you're much of a liar, Gwendy thought. *You've seen all these symptoms before. It's not, as they say, your first rodeo.*

"What drugs?"

"Aricept is my go-to. Exelon sometimes works well in the early stages. But all that is putting the cart before the horse. We need to see how you do on the mini-cog. Come back at five this afternoon, if your schedule permits."

"It does." Gwendy had cleared the day for Ambrose.

"In the meantime, get something to eat and help yourself to a caffeine drink. Coffee, soda, even a Monster Energy."

"Thank you, Dr. Ambrose."

"You're very welcome, Senator."

"Gwendy, remember?"

"Yes. Gwendy. And I don't suppose you can tell me anything about this job that's so important?"

She gave him a level look—her Senator Peterson look. "You wouldn't want to know, Dr. Ambrose. Believe me."

She donned a headscarf and dark glasses and slipped into a nearby Burger King where she ordered a Whopper with cheese and a large order of fries, and slurped a large Coke until the straw crackled in the bottom of the cup. Her first bite of the Whopper made her realize that she was ravenous. She supposed relief spurred appetite. And sharing the burden, of course. Now she had a strategy to cope with the Brain Freezes, and she could hope that Ambrose was right and it was only stress. The test— what Ambrose had called a mini-cog—might confirm that.

She laughed when Ambrose began asking the questions because they reminded her of the test Donald Trump had boasted about passing. *Easy-peasy*, she thought . . . but by the time she completed it she was no longer laughing. Neither was Ambrose.

She did okay on the season (spring) and the date, but could not immediately remember what month it was. She was sure she could have used Ambrose's associative method and come up with it if he'd given her time, but he didn't. She was even worse at counting back from a hundred by sevens. She got to ninety-three, then said eighty-five, which was really just a guess. She was able to repeat back *apple-table-penny* five minutes later but found herself completely incapable of spelling *world* backward. There was plenty of stuff she got right—copying a cartoon drawing, folding a sheet of paper in thirds—but there were distressing and inexplicable (to her, at least) failures. When Ambrose asked her to draw a clock face, for instance, she drew an oblong with a curve like a smile beneath it. She showed it to him and said, "I think this might be wrong."

So *much* was wrong.

And the wait for her trip into space stretched out ahead of her, with no firm date set and so many days to struggle through.

But I have to try!

28

AND NOW THE TIME has come to do that.

Gwendy pulls the lever that dispenses the chocolates. Out comes a butterfly with tiny, perfectly scalloped wings. She pops it into her mouth. Warmth spreads throughout her body and lights up her brain. Then, for the first time in her long and complicated history with the button box, she pulls the lever again. For a moment nothing happens and she's afraid the box is refusing her, but then another chocolate comes out. She doesn't bother to examine it, just swallows it down. The world leaps forward into all her senses. The clarity is painful but at the same time wonderful. She can see every grain in the box's mahogany surface. She can hear every creak as the MF station makes its endless journey through space. She can't hear the Chinese in their spoke, but she senses their presence. Some are eating, some are playing a game. Mahjong, perhaps.

She takes a deep breath and can feel it filling her lungs and enriching her blood. The knock at the door sends waves of vibration across the room. *It's a V shape*, Gwendy thinks. *Like birds heading south for the winter.*

"Gwendy?" Kathy asks. "Are you ready?"

"Just a second!" She puts the button box back in its bag and stows it in the closet wall safe, which is hidden behind her spare pressure suit. She thumbs the CLOSE button and hears the lock engage. She checks for her notebook in the pocket of her jumpsuit, then shuts the closet, bounce-walks to the door, and opens it.

"Ready," she says.

29

THERE'S A SMALL CONFERENCE room in Spoke 1, next to the ops room. Present for Gwendy's mental acuity test are Kathy Lundgren, Dr. Glen, and Sam Drinkwater. Sam doesn't know that Gwendy has a special high-priority mission (unless Kathy has told him, that is), but he's going to be her buddy on her Day 7 spacewalk, so Gwendy supposes he has a right to be here. It would be his responsibility, after all, if she became disoriented and freaked out while they were tethered together.

Doc Glen clears his throat. "Gwendy—Senator—I hope you understand that we have to—"

"To take every precaution," she finishes. She knows she sounds impatient. She *is* impatient. No, more than that. She's angry. Not at them, exactly, but at having to be here and having such a terrible responsibility thrust upon her. "I understand. Let's get to it. I have emails to write and weather info to collate."

The others exchange looks. This isn't the smiling, friendly woman they are used to.

"Er . . . fine," Doc Glen says. He powers up his tablet, then takes an envelope from the breast pocket of his coverall. "It won't take long, an hour max. I'll give you a number of questions to answer and certain tasks to perform. Just relax and do the best you can. To begin with . . ."

He opens the envelope. Inside are eight metal squares. He puts them down in the center of the table on a magnetized rectangle, which he turns to face Gwendy. Words have been printed on the squares in Magic Marker.

go   mother   must   store   the   to   I   for

"Can you arrange these to make a sentence?"

Gwendy moves the words around on the magnetized rectangle with no hesitation. She turns it to face the three crew members—*My judges*, she thinks resentfully—on the other side of the table. "Clever that there's no capital letter," Gwendy says. "Makes it a bit harder. Intentional, I suppose."

They look at how she's arranged the words. "Huh," Sam says. "It's a sentence all right, but not the one I would have made."

"And if there's a handbook that goes with this test," Gwendy says, "it's probably not what the people who made it expected. Which is a bit dumb, if you don't mind me saying. You were expecting 'I must go to the store for mother,' weren't you?"

Sam and Doc nod. Kathy just looks at her with a small smile. Maybe it's admiration, probably it is, but Gwendy doesn't care. They brought her in here like a test animal and expected her to perform—hit the lever and get a piece of kibble. And so she has. Because she has to, and doesn't that just suck?

Gwendy's sentence reads *for mother I must go to the store.*

She says, 'I must go to the store for mother' is the simple way to do it, but simple isn't always best. It's ambiguous. Does it mean 'I have to go there because mother wants pasta and a quart of Ben & Jerry's' or does it mean 'I have to go to the store because mother is there and she needs to be picked up.' Some ambiguity is still there in my sentence, but it's less because 'mother' comes first. My sentence says it's almost certainly an errand." She gives them a hard smile without a shred of good humor in it. "Any questions?"

There are none, and although Doc goes through the rest of his questions and tasks, the test is effectively over with that little lesson in syntax. Gwendy finishes the whole thing in nineteen minutes and stands up, holding the edge of the table to keep her feet from floating off the floor.

"Are you satisfied?"

They look back at her uncomfortably. After a brief silence Kathy says, "You're angry. I get that and I'm sorry, but we're in an environment where there's no room for error. And I think I speak for Sam and Doc when I say you've eased our minds considerably."

"Completely eased mine," Sam says. "I have no hesitation about suiting up with you and going outside."

"I *am* angry," Gwendy says, "but not at you guys. Your jobs are difficult, but so is mine. The difference is that mine is thankless. This damned country is so polarized that forty percent of the electorate in my home state thinks I'm a piece of shit no matter what I do."

She surveys them and yes, she *is* angry at them, at this moment she almost hates them, but it won't do to say so. Still, she has to vent. If she doesn't, she'll explode. Or go back to her room and do something stupid. Something that can't be taken back.

"You haven't lived until you've seen signs saying COMMIE BITCH waving at you from the back of your town hall meetings. On top of that, my husband is dead, half my fucking house burned down, and I had to come in here so you guys could make sure I don't need to be fitted up with Pampers and a drool-cup."

"That's a little heavy," Kathy says mildly.

"Yes, I suppose it is." Gwendy lets out a sigh, thinking, *You want heavy? Try living with what's in my wall safe. That's* really *heavy*. "Can I go now? Got work to do. You guys probably do, too. Sorry about the mouth. It's been building up."

Doc Glen stands up. Floats, actually. He reaches a hand across the table to her. "No need to apologize on my behalf, Gwendy." She's glad he's left her title behind and reverted to her name. "You've got some hard bark on you, and in your job that's a requirement. Get some rest. I can't give you an Ambien, but maybe a glass of warm milk before you turn in will help. Or a melatonin. That I do have."

"Thanks." Gwendy takes his hand. There's no flash, only a sense that he means well. She looks around and forces herself to say it. "Thank you all."

She leaves and returns to her suite in great lolloping leaps, her hands opening and closing. *I could fix this whole problem with the button box*, she's thinking. *And you know what? It would be a pleasure.*

Once inside she opens the closet door, moves the spare pressure suit aside, then makes herself stop. She wants to take the button box out—*it* wants *me to take it out*, she thinks—and in her current state of mind the buttons along the top would look too inviting. She had to eat the chocolates so she could pass their goddamn test, but now she's faced with this *anger*, this *fury*, and it's like a black doorway she dares not go through. What's on the other side is monstrous.

How I hate it, Farris said. *How I* loathe *it*. If she never understood that before, she understands it now. But he said something else, and it resonates in her mind now: *There is simply no one else I trust to do what needs to be done.*

She understands, even in her current state, that if she takes the button box out now, that trust will almost certainly be broken. He gave it to her because she's strong, but there are limits to her strength.

If I have to feel this way, I have to focus it on something other than the box and stay focused until the effect of the chocolates wears off. What?

But with her mind clear, the answer is also clear. She bounces to her desk and powers up her iPad. The emails she sends from her senatorial account are encrypted, and that's a good thing. She writes to Norris Ridgewick.

> *Norris: You said that on your trip to Derry you met with "the local constabulary." The detective in charge of investigating Ryan's death was Ward Mitchell. Did you meet him? And if you did, did you trust him?*

She sends the email to the down-below and walks back and forth through her suite (which doesn't take long), pulling restlessly at her ponytail. She can't seem to sit still, not in her current state. She reaches out for Gareth Winston, like she did for the Chinese in their spoke, and finds him. He is on his computer. Writing an email. She can't see it but she knows that's what it is. There's a word in his mind that she gets clear, although she doesn't know what it means. The word is *sombra*.

Norris may not reply for an hour or more, she thinks, *and Mom used to say a watched pot never boils.*

She decides to walk (maybe even run) the outer rim—anything to burn off this wild and dangerous energy. She puts on shorts and a tee shirt with CASTLE ROCK OLD HOME DAYS on the front, and is just lacing up her sneakers when her laptop chimes with incoming mail. She leaps across the room like Supergirl and settles in front of the screen. The message is brief, to the point, and totally Yankee.

Hey Gwendy,

Met Mitchell, talked to him, wouldn't trust him as far as I could sling a piano. He couldn't wait to get rid of me. Want me to take a trip to Derry and go at him a little harder? Happy to do it. By the way—any idea what got your Ryan haring off to Derry in the first place?

Norris

She wishes she could answer that question, but she can't. Her best guess is that someone told Ryan they had dirt on Magowan, or dirt on her. Either might have gotten him to take a ride north. Did it make any difference? Of course not. No matter what the pretext, Ryan remains dead.

As for sending Norris up to Derry . . . no. Norris isn't the man for that job. She believes the flash she had when she took Gareth's hand was a true insight. She believes that she saw Gareth in one of the two old cars that were in Derry on the day Ryan died. She believes Ryan may have been killed in an effort to derail her senatorial campaign. And she believes that her house was burned after certain men—perhaps driving perfectly maintained old cars—searched it for the button box, came up empty, and reached the logical conclusion: she has it with her in space. Sending Norris to Derry might only succeed in getting him killed.

Without the special chocolates lighting up her brain, she would have doubted this scenario. *No,* she thinks, *I wouldn't have been able to think of it in the first place; I would have been too addled.* With that brain-booster on board, however, she doesn't doubt it. Not one tiny bit. She wonders if Gareth started agitating for a tourist run into space after she didn't drop out of the race against Magowan. No, probably not until after she was elected and got on the Aeronautical and Space Sciences Committee.

"Someone was really thinking ahead," Gwendy mutters to herself. Her hands are clenching and unclenching. Each clench is hard enough to make her short nails dig into the soft meat of her palms. "Someone was really *planning* ahead." Then, for no reason at all, she says, "Sombra sombra sombra." She'll hunt for it on the Net, but she has something else to do first, far more important.

She sits down and sends an email to Deputy CIA Director Charlotte Morgan.

Charlotte—I have reason to believe that my husband may have been murdered in an effort to get me to drop out of the Senate race in 2020. I also think it has to do with the item I am carrying. I suspect that Gareth Winston knows about the item, and he may have the code that opens the safety box containing the item. How that happened is a long story for another time. What I want from you is what's known as a "black bag job," and it has to happen <u>immediately</u>. The detective in the Derry PD who supposedly investigated Ryan's death is named Ward Mitchell. I think he knows more than he's telling. My friend Norris Ridgewick (ex-police, sharp as a knife blade) concurs. I want you to send a team to collar Detective Mitchell, sequester him, and persuade him to talk by any means necessary. I believe someone is trying to stop me before I can dispose of the item under my care, and perhaps (likely!) take possession of it. I believe that someone is Gareth Winston, and if he has the code to the safe box, the only thing standing in his way is an electronic Mesa wall safe. It's the kind hotels use, and a third-rate burglar *could crack it. You know what the stakes are—remember the pyramid? I understand that my chief suspect is a fabulously wealthy man, but he may not be in charge. Whoever is, they're thinking years ahead, and that scares me. Don't even consider that this is paranoia. It's not. Grab Ward Mitchell and shake him he rattles. Let me hear back from you immediately, Charlotte.*

Gwendy

She pauses, then adds a PS: *Does the word "sombra" mean anything to you?*

Gwendy could check that for herself, but now that her two important emails have been sent, she finds herself looking at the closet again, and thinking about the button box. She wonders if she could concentrate on Gareth Winston having a heart attack and make it happen by pressing the red button. *You wonder, Gwendolyn? Is that all?* She voices a humorless bark of laughter. There's no wondering about it; she knows she could. Only there might be collateral damage. What if the station's electrical system shorted out? Or a high-pressure oxy line went blooey?

She comes out of these thoughts to realize she's no longer at her desk. No, she's at the closet. She's opened it, she's pushed aside the spare suit, and she's reaching for the safe's keypad. In fact she's already pushed the first number of its simplistic four-digit combination. Gwendy puts one hand over her mouth. With the other she pushes the CANCEL button and closes the closet door.

She decides she'll go for that run after all.

30

GWENDY BLOWS BY A couple of sweat pants–wearing, AirPods-equipped Chinese women halfway around the rim. They give her a startled look but return her wave. Kathy Lundgren hadn't been exaggerating earlier when she'd boasted about running a two-minute mile. Not by much, anyway. Gwendy hasn't gone for an actual run in over a decade, but it feels as if she's nearly flying. When she gets back to her suite in Spoke 3 her shirt is damp with sweat and she's breathing hard, but she feels more like her old self. She still feels the siren call of the button box when she passes the closet door, but it's not the imperative it was before. More like simple longing. An ache. Sort of like the one she feels for Ryan. It's awful to think of the button box and her dead husband in the same category, but that seems to be the case. Gwendy's glad to feel better again but knows it will come at a cost; she's already starting to lose her crystal clarity of thought. Soon the fog will descend again, and maybe thicker than ever.

The message light is flashing on her laptop. She enters the password that will transform the gibberish of letters and symbols into words (delighted she doesn't have to use the little red notebook to refresh her memory). The message is from Charlotte, and it's entirely satisfying.

Trust you completely. Team on the move to Derry. You
will get a video record of Detective Mitchell's interrogation,

hopefully tomorrow, your Day 3 on the MF. I understand there were some concerns about your mental abilities up there. Although I will be on pins & needles until your mission is completed, that made me laugh. Can't imagine anyone less likely to "lose the plot," as they say.

How does the Sombra Corporation figure into this? Any idea? You can read a certain amount about it on the Net, but it's mostly speculation. We at the Company know more, but not a hell of a lot. They keep a tight lid. Best guess is that their aggregate worth may be greater than that of China and the U.S. <u>combined</u>. Hard to believe but I'm assured it's almost certainly true. If so, they make WinMark LTD, Winston's company, look small in comparison. Not to mention Amazon. So yes, it's possible Gareth Winston might be working with or even for the Sombra Corp if the reward was great enough. No way to tell. All I can say is <u>BE CAREFUL</u>.

C

Gwendy reads this over three times. She has to, because the sense of some lines is getting a bit dim. Her anger is also dimming out. What remains is focused on Detective Mitchell, with his dismissive little smile and empty eyes. *Also the Magowan button on his shirt, don't forget that.* No, she hasn't forgotten it (at least not yet). She wants that video. She wants to see him away from his strangely shitty little city, in a small room with soundproof walls, preferably in a black hood that will be whipped off once he's been wrist- and ankle-chained to the table. Gwendy supposes they don't do it that way anymore; she's sure that the CIA has drug cocktails that will render the likes of Ward Mitchell entirely pliable, but . . .

"But a girl can dream," she says softly.

She showers off her sweat, then goes down to the weather deck. She's scheduled for a video conference with the National Weather Service at 4 p.m. Eastern time. That's hours from now, but she'd had to get out of there. For the time being, at least, being close to the button box isn't safe.

31

Day 3 on Many Flags.

Gwendy is at the desk in the small living room of her suite, going over stacks of appropriation requests. She's thinking that a single look at this untidy pile of paperwork would cause anyone with the idea that the life of a United States senator is glamorous to think again.

What she's really doing, of course, is listening for the chime of her laptop, signaling a message from Charlotte. It's chimed with several incoming messages already, including one from the vice president wishing her well, but nothing from Charlotte. It's probably too early, but that doesn't keep her from hoping.

The other thing she's doing is resisting the call of the button box. It's in the steel CLASSIFIED box, and the steel CLASSIFIED box is in the safe, and the safe is in the closet, but that call still comes through loud and clear. She doesn't want to push the buttons so much as she wants to pull the lever that dispenses the chocolates. She's actually having a pretty good day, memory circuits all firing as they are supposed to, but she misses the weird and wonderful clarity she felt when she was doing the mental acuity test yesterday. A chocolate animal (or two!), and she could fly through this boring paperwork. This is a practical lesson in why drug addicts are addicts.

The knock at her door is a relief. She would welcome a

163

distraction . . . as long as it isn't Winston, that is. She has no urge to see him today. In fact she would be happy not to see him at all until she's completed her task, although she knows that's probably unlikely. For one thing, they all eat together. There's no room service on the MF station.

It's not Gareth. It's Reggie, the physicist. His last name temporarily eludes her, but she doesn't stress about it, just relaxes and uses Dr. Ambrose's chain-of-association trick. Best concert she ever saw? AC/DC, at TD Garden in Boston. Best song? "Back in Black." And whoomp, there it is.

"Reggie Black, as I live and breathe," she says. "What can I do for you?"

He's fiftyish, with fluffs of white hair that float on either side of his bald pate. And he's grinning. "Adesh just showed me something wild. Do you want to see?" He glances past her at the littered desk and his grin fades. "I guess you're busy."

"I can take a break. All you have to do is tempt me."

"Consider yourself tempted. This is crazy cool."

He takes her to the lab Adesh has set up in Spoke 5, where there's lots of space. Based on the signage, Gwendy deduces it was last used by a French team. On the lab's door there's a sign that reads ADESH "BUG MAN" PATEL. KNOCK BEFORE ENTERING.

Reggie knocks. "Okay to come in?"

"Come, come," Adesh says, and opens the door before Reggie can. He sees Gwendy and smiles. "Ah, the esteemed senator! Welcome to Entomology Wonderland!"

They step in. Gwendy sees a row of plexiglass cases with beetles and bugs in some of them, spiders in others. Including Olivia the tarantula: *Ugh*, Gwendy thinks. The far end of the room has been sealed off with floor-to-ceiling plexi, creating a larger cage with smaller cages inside it.

"Show her the trick with Boris," Reggie Black says. And to Gwendy, "It's an authentic mind-blower."

Adesh wags his finger at Reggie in a schoolteacherly way. "It is no trick, Reginald. It is *training* and *adaptation*." To Gwendy: "Besides, I find the flies much more interesting. Ordinary houseflies—*Musca domestica*—but their zero-g behavior is fascinating and illuminating."

"Sure, but the scorpion is cool," Reggie says. "Boris is *money*."

Adesh looks perplexed.

"The best," Gwendy translates. "He means the best. Or maybe the flashiest."

"Oh, it's flashy, all right," Reggie says. "The Bugster's probably got it on video, but it's better live. Assuming you have enough *Musca domesticas*, old buddy."

"Plenty of flies," Adesh agrees. "I am saving the cockroaches."

Ugh, Gwendy thinks again.

Adesh takes a remote control from its magnetized disc and points it into the big cage. The door of one of the small cages—the smallest, not much bigger than a woman's makeup case—slides up and several *Musca domesticas* fly out. But not for long. They stop flying and just hang in the air, as if on strings.

"My God!" Gwendy says. "Are they sick?"

"No, they are in what you might call energy-saving mode," Adesh says. "They used their wings at first, but quickly learned they do not need to. Nor do they need to rest by landing. If houseflies can be said to enjoy anything, they enjoy zero-g."

"Boris, Boris, Boris!" Reggie chants.

Adesh sighs, but Gwendy thinks it's just for show. He's enjoying this, too. She doesn't think it matters if it's men of science or men chopping wood, they all like showing off. Of course, so do women.

Adesh presses another button on his remote control and Boris the scorpion crawls out, claws clicking, his loaded stinger arched over his back. "*Pandinus imperator*," Adesh says. "Emperor scorpion. Its sting is rarely fatal to humans, but for its prey—"

"There he goes!" Reggie cries. "Upsy-daisy, Boris! My *man*!"

Claws still clicking, Boris floats upward and hangs in midair like the flies on the far side of the cage they share.

Adesh raises his voice and calls, "Boris! *Maar*!"

Boris gives his tail a single hard flex, propelling himself across the room like a bullet. Two of the flies escape, but Boris catches the third one in his claws, mashes it, and pops it into his alien maw. Gwendy is repulsed and fascinated in equal measure. The scorpion's forward motion propels it toward the wall, but before it hits, Boris does a forward roll and uses his armored tail to push himself back the other way. He finishes up in almost exactly the same place he started and just hangs there.

"Amazing," Gwendy says. "How do you get him back in his cage?"

"I put him in myself," Adesh says. "I don a glove to do it. I have no urge to be stung, even if it's no worse than the sting of a bee. Boris is trainable, as you see, but he is far from tame. No, no, no."

"And *maar*? What does that mean?"

Adesh goes to the door of the big containment facility, then turns back and gives her a gentle smile in which one gold tooth twinkles. "Kill," he says.

32

WHEN GWENDY GETS BACK to her quarters, the light on her laptop is flashing. Five fresh emails have come in, but the only one she cares about is Charlotte Morgan's. She pushes aside her paperwork and opens it.

Gwen: I didn't think this story could get any stranger, but boy was I wrong. You were on the money about Detective Mitchell knowing more than he was telling. Take a look at the attached video and get back to me with further instructions. It's pretty lengthy—once we got the guy talking, he wouldn't shut up—but most of what you're looking for can be found starting at around the seven-minute mark.

I've also attached a second, much shorter video that came from the iPhone of an eyewitness to Ryan's accident (which as you surmised wasn't an accident at all). The phone belongs (or belonged) to a man named Vernon Beeson, from Providence, Rhode Island. He was on his way to Presque Isle to see his sister. He never arrived. We can't know for sure, but I wouldn't be surprised if he is now floating around in the Derry sewer system. Mitchell claims a patrolman found the phone in a trash can outside Bassey Park. Mitchell also claims not to know what happened to Mr. Beeson. All we could get out of him on that subject was "Maybe the clown took him." Weird, huh?

Very *weird*, Gwendy thinks, and resists the sudden urge to pull the little chocolate-dispensing lever on the side of the button box. She goes back to Charlotte's communique instead.

It's hard to watch, Gwen, even harder to believe, and I wouldn't blame you one bit if you decided to hit the DELETE button without ever opening it. I might even suggest you do exactly that, but I know it's not my place. We found Mr. Beeson's phone locked away in the gun safe in Mitchell's basement, right where he told us it would be.

Last thing I'm going to say and then I'll let you get to it. I've said it before: please be careful, old friend. I know you must feel as though you're all alone up there, but I promise you're not. Sending love and luck your way. Godspeed.

C

The video attachments located at the bottom of the email are labeled MITCHELL and DERRY. Gwendy knows she should open the Ward Mitchell interrogation first—after all, the fate of the world may rest on its contents—but she can't help herself. Taking slow and steady breaths, like she's learned from years of yoga classes, she slides the cursor over to the DERRY file and clicks on it. A window opens in her laptop's upper right-hand corner. She hits the ENLARGE icon and a surprisingly clear wide-angle view of the intersection of Witcham and Carter Streets fills the screen.

On the right side of the video she can see a couple of run-down houses, window shutters hanging crooked or absent altogether, paint peeling in long, curling strips, brown lawns overgrown even at the tail end of November. An old bicycle with a missing rear tire leans against one of the porch railings.

Across the street, kitty-corner from the house with the bike, is an abandoned Phillips 66 gas station, the pumps out front long ago removed. Weeds grow in wild spurts between the cracks of broken pavement. Someone has spray-painted DERRY SUCKS across the faded brick façade. Just beyond the boarded-up office, Gwendy can make out the gated entrance to Bassey Park.

Whoever is filming—Beeson, presumably—has the sound turned on and she can hear the loud undulating whistle of a cold late-season wind blowing across the rooftops. A discarded piece of trash tumbles across the sidewalk—Gwendy's almost certain it's a McDonald's hamburger wrapper—and disappears down the deserted street. It's half past noon on the day after Thanksgiving, but there's not a single living soul or automobile in sight.

And then there is.

An old Volkswagen Bug, traveling north on Witcham, putters through the intersection. The driver, an older man with a wild tuft of scraggly white hair and round John Lennon eyeglasses, is looking around like he's lost. And maybe he is; he's certainly driving slowly enough. Right behind him, riding the VW's rear bumper, is a black truck with jacked-up snow tires and a full-sized American flag flapping from a metal pole jutting out of the rear of its double-wide bed. She can hear the throaty boom of the truck stereo's bass even with the dark-tinted windows closed up tight.

Gwendy has just enough time to take it all in and wonder *why in the world is the person filming this?* when Ryan appears on-screen. It suddenly feels as if all of the air has been sucked from the room. She bites her lower lip and leans closer to the laptop.

He enters from the bottom right corner of the screen, sauntering along the sidewalk with that long, confident stride she remembers so well. He's wearing his favorite winter coat—a long-ago Christmas gift from Gwendy's parents— and a red-and-white New England Patriots ski cap. Every once in a while he sneaks a glance at the row of nearby houses, but it's clear that the main focus of his attention is the cell phone he's carrying in his right hand. He's studying the display like he's following directions.

Reaching the corner of Witcham and Carter, he stops with the tips of his L.L. Beans dangling over the curb. He looks both ways, like an obedient little boy who's promised his mother to always be careful crossing the street, and then down at his phone again.

And then he starts across.

The Cadillac—a garish shade of purple, obscenely wide and long, with a pair of dime-store fuzzy dice dangling from the rearview mirror—slams into him before he reaches the street's center line. Gwendy hears the meaty *thunk* of impact, and then her husband is flying through the air. He hits the pavement and actually bounces, not once but twice, before rolling to an abrupt facedown stop at the opposite side of the intersection. A ragged trail of dark blotches tracks his progress across the roadway.

The Caddy keeps on going without even a flash of its brake lights. It's not until the next day, while showering, that Gwendy realizes she never once heard the sound of the Cadillac's engine. She could hear the sewing machine *putt-putt-putt* of the VW Bug, the angry growl of the black pickup's V-8, the bass thud of heavy metal from the truck's sound system, but when it came to the purple Caddy . . . nothing. Almost as if it *had* no motor.

What remained of Ryan's shattered body lay halfway on the shoulder of Carter Street, his broken legs splayed at grotesque angles atop a narrow strip of dirt and grass separating the curb from the sidewalk. His ski cap, along with one of the boots and wool socks he was wearing, had been torn away by the force of the crash. The boot and sock are nowhere to be found, but Gwendy can see the pale pink skin of Ryan's left foot resting mere inches away from a FOR SALE BY OWNER sign poking out of the frozen ground. The back of Ryan's head—as caved-in and lopsided as a pumpkin left rotting in a field—no longer resembled that of a human being.

Gwendy jerks away from the screen, a loud sob lodging in her throat. For one panic-stricken moment, she fears she might actually choke to death on her grief. She sits back and once again focuses on her breathing. The suffocating sensation gradually loosens its grip. Eyes filled with tears, she turns back to her laptop. And gasps.

There's a car stopped in the road beside Ryan's lifeless body. It's not quite as wide as the Cadillac, and it's sleeker, built lower to the ground, and painted such a dazzling shade of cartoon green that it almost hurts to look at. *It doesn't look real,* Gwendy thinks with morbid fascination. *It looks like a child's toy come to life.*

She immediately recognizes the car as the same vehicle in which she'd seen Gareth Winston sitting beside the blond man when she touched Winston's hand outside of the lavatory on Eagle Heavy. *He was there,* she thinks, squeezing her fists together so hard the color fades from her fingertips. *Maybe not in Derry, and maybe not on the day they killed my husband, but the son of a bitch was inside that car. And was he making some kind of a deal? Of course he was, because that's what guys like Gareth do: they make deals.*

"He's one of them," she says aloud to the empty sitting room.

As Gwendy watches, the doors of the car (*an old green Chrysler, big as a boat*, she suddenly remembers from her old friend Norris Ridgewick's email) swing open and four men step out onto Carter Street.

"What the—" She never finishes the sentence.

The men are unnaturally tall and thin. And dressed identically—wearing long yellow dusters and bandanas over the lower halves of their faces—like a gang of Old West outlaws. They amble to the front of the car and stand shoulder to shoulder, surrounding the body. Looking down, one of the men places a dark-gloved hand on his chest and bends over, howling with a high, barking laughter that Gwendy is somehow able to hear over the whine of the wind. It's an ugly animal sound, and she quickly lowers the volume on her laptop. The others soon join in, gesturing at the fallen body, hooting and guffawing. One of the men abruptly spins in a tight circle and begins hopping from one foot to the other, performing some kind of lunatic jig, slapping at his thighs with furious delight.

Gwendy abruptly stops the video—and hits REWIND. She doesn't go back very far, maybe ten or twelve seconds. She isn't sure if her eyes are playing tricks on her or if what she thinks she just saw is real.

She hits PLAY and watches as the man launches into his bizarre dance, and then it happens again. The man begins to fade in and out—not in and out of focus, but in and out of *existence*. One second he's whole and solid, the next he's blurry and only partially there.

And then it's all four of the men.

While everything else in the video remains crystal clear—if Gwendy leans close enough to the screen, she can almost make out the phone number printed at the bottom of the FOR SALE BY OWNER sign—the four men in the yellow dusters have begun to shimmer. Looking at them now is a little like staring at a heat mirage rising off the highway in the middle of a summer heat wave. *This isn't what they look like,* Gwendy thinks with calm assurance. *This isn't what they look like at all. It's as if they're wearing costumes and masks to make them appear human, but the disguises are only temporary, and I'm sitting here watching as they fade in and out of reality. Even the god-damn car is wearing one. It's lost its edges. Its shape no longer looks quite solid.*

And apparently she's not the only one who notices. For the first time since he started recording, Vernon Beeson, from Providence, Rhode Island, zooms in for a closer look. The houses and gas station and Bassey Park all fall away. As the front end of the Chrysler, with its acre of shiny green hood, rushes forward and fills the screen, Gwendy suddenly wishes she were wearing her flight helmet so she could lower the visor. Looking at the four men and their funny green car doesn't just make her eyes want to water, it makes her *brain* want to water. The camera slowly pans away from the Chrysler and once again finds the men at the side of the road. Even up close, they continue to blur in and out, as if they're being seen from behind a dirty pane of rain-streaked glass. One of the men is standing directly in front of Ryan's body, sparing Gwendy an up-close-and-personal look at the grue-some details. She swears if he moves one step to the left or right, she's going to scream, or throw her laptop across the room, or both. There's a sudden burst of ear-piercing static and then the screen goes dark. And remains that way for what feels like a long time. Just when she's convinced the video is over, it sparks back to life again.

In the interim, cameraman Vernon Beeson has given up on the close-up and is pulling back to the original wide-angle view. As the row of houses reappears on the right side of the screen, the abandoned gas station and Bassey Park creep back into view on the left. The four masked men standing across the intersection gradually regain their focus, albeit from a distance. The static is gone.

Gwendy glances at the time code in the upper corner of the video screen and is astonished to discover that she's only been watching for three minutes and forty-seven seconds. It feels so much longer than that.

The men in the yellow dusters and bandanas have grown quiet. They shuffle closer to each other, standing with their heads pressed together—*palavering*, Gwendy thinks—and then they break up their impromptu huddle. Three of the men return to the car. Even with the volume turned down, the slamming of the car doors is very loud inside the small sitting room. The fourth man waits on the side of the road until the Chrysler speeds away—with not so much as a whisper of its engine—and then he jaywalks across Carter Street and disappears into the cold afternoon shadows of Bassey Park.

Ryan's body remains silent and still on the shoulder of the road.

Nobody else comes, because in Derry, nobody ever does when things like this happen.

A few seconds later, the video ends.

33

GWENDY'S ANGER IS BACK. Her face feels as hot as a furnace and her jaw aches from grinding her teeth. She wipes away tears with a Kleenex, uses it to noisily blow her nose, and then stuffs it in the zero-g wastecan. While her shell-shocked mind is unable to fully comprehend what she's just witnessed, she knows enough to call it what it is: cold-blooded murder. Someone—the blond stranger from her vision, the odd men in their yellow coats, or maybe even Gareth Winston—lured her husband to Derry and ran him down in the middle of the street like a stray dog. *Were they all working for Sombra?* Gwendy guesses they were. *Are.*

Even from across the room and inside the closet, she can hear the steady hum of the button box calling to her. *Just because you hear it*, she reminds herself, *doesn't mean you have to listen to it.* She already knows what it's saying anyway. Ever since they landed on Many Flags, the button box is like a broken fucking record. *Just one more piece of chocolate, Gwendy girl, that's all. Just one more delicious bite-sized animal and you'll think clearer and you'll sleep better and you'll never forget another goddamn thing. Or, better yet, why not press the red button and make all your troubles disappear? Starting with your billionaire friend. You know you want to . . .*

"You're damn right I want to," she snaps, yanking another Kleenex from the box. "And if he'd actually been there in the video, I don't think I could hold back."

Gwendy shoves the voice into the corner of her broken brain—it's getting more and more difficult to do this as her journey nears its end—and clicks on the MITCHELL file. There are a series of loud beeps and then the video begins.

The interrogation room is small and plain. Three gray walls. A tinted viewing window occupies the upper portion of the fourth. It's impossible to tell who is watching from behind the dark glass, but Gwendy guesses that Charlotte Morgan is one of them. Possibly the only one.

There are four men crammed inside the room. One of them, wearing a dark suit and holstered sidearm, leans against the only door. His face is blurred, and for a fleeting instant, Gwendy thinks he's one of *them*—the men in the yellow coats—but then she quickly realizes the man's face has been purposely obscured to protect his identity. A second agent's face has also been hidden. He's sitting behind a narrow desk, studying an open laptop. To his immediate right is the agent in charge, whose unblurred face instantly reminds Gwendy of her father's youngest brother, Uncle Harvey. With his tortoiseshell glasses and bushy mustache, this guy looks like he could be just about anyone's favorite uncle or maybe even a science teacher from the local high school, the one who gets voted school favorite in the yearbook. Both of the agents sitting behind the desk are dressed in slacks and Oxford shirts. No jackets or ties.

The final man in the room is the guest of honor. Ward Mitchell is wearing a loose-fitting orange jumpsuit with the sleeves rolled up. He's seated in a straight-backed metal chair that has been securely bolted to the floor. Gwendy can see he's struggling to keep his head up and his eyes open. There's a darkening bruise rising beneath one of his eyes and both of his lips appear to be swollen. That dismissive little smile of his is nowhere to be seen. Mitchell's arms are propped up in front of him atop the desk. A small surgical tube runs from the bend of his right arm to a portable IV stand. A bag of clear fluid hangs on the uppermost hook, honey-dripping top-secret contents into Mitchell's bloodstream. There's a pressure cuff wrapped around the detective's left bicep, as well as a tangle of wires leading from just inside the collar of his jumpsuit to the back of the agent's laptop.

"Let's start with your name." The agent's voice is firm but pleasant. He even sounds like a science teacher.

Mitchell blinks and looks around the room as if he's just awakened from a deep sleep. He clears his throat. "Ward Thomas Mitchell."

"Age?"

"Forty-four."

You look older, Gwendy thinks, not without satisfaction.

"Address?"

"1920 Tupelo Road. Derry, Maine."

"And you're from Derry originally?"

"Born and raised there."

Well, that explains a lot, the senator thinks.

"Occupation?"

"Derry PD. Almost thirty years. Detective the last twelve."

"Married?"

"Divorced."

"Kids?"

"One. A boy."

"How ol—"

She knows what they're doing, easing him into it with easy questions, but this isn't what she came for. Gwendy presses the arrow button on her laptop and fast-forwards the video. She forgets what she's doing for a moment—a mini Brain

Freeze, here and gone in a matter of seconds—and advances too far. She quickly hits REWIND and watches as the time code begins to reverse. Finally stopping at the 5:33 mark, she presses PLAY. Her hands are shaking.

". . . referenced strange occurrences in Derry. Can you give us an example?"

Mitchell gives a confidential smile. His eyes are drifting around in their sockets. Gwendy thinks she might have seen people this cataclysmically stoned, but not since college. "I've heard voices."

"Like in your head, Detective?"

"No-ooo . . . from inside the drains at my house."

"Really?" The head guy glances at the tinted window and wiggles his eyebrows. "From the drains, huh?"

"Once . . . I'd just turned off the water after taking a shower . . . someone called out to me from inside the drain. And then they started laughing."

"They?"

"It sounded like kids. A whole bunch of kids laughing."

"And this voice, what did it say to you?"

"My name."

The agent in charge scratches his chin. This time he gives the eyebrow waggle to his partner.

"Another time I was loading the dishwasher and I heard that same voice coming from the kitchen sink. It said, 'We're saving you a seat, Warthog.' No one's called me that since I was a snot-nose kid at Derry Elementary."

"Anything else?"

Ward Thomas Mitchell, aka Warthog, laughs. But there's no laughter in his eyes. "There's the clown."

"Want to see a clown, Ward, look in the mirror," one of the others says. He sounds disgusted.

Mitchell pays no attention. "Back when I was a rookie, I started having bad dreams. They got so horrible I was afraid to go to sleep at night. I was being chased in the sewers by someone dressed as a clown."

Gwendy suddenly thinks of her old friend's story about a clown with big silver eyes chasing her in Derry. She's also thinking about her father and his warnings about the town. So out of character for him. She's almost certain that something happened to her father during his short stay in Derry—something horrible—but he's never admitted as much, and she doubts he even remembers now. Or maybe he does and is just too frightened, even after all these years, to talk about it.

"Later that same year, my rookie year, I caught a 911 for a domestic right around Christmas. Neighbor reported loud crashes and screaming coming from the house next door. When I pulled up, a man was sitting on the front porch, covered in blood. He was crying and holding a butcher knife. He'd just finished slicing and dicing his wife and twin girls, and arranging their bodies around the dining room table. He'd placed salads in front of each of them and laid out napkins on their laps. We found a pan of burnt-to-a-crisp lasagna still baking in the oven. The man gave up without a fight, and when we cuffed him and put him in the back of a squad car, he said clear as day—and I'm not the only one who heard him that night—"*The clown made me do it*." And then he never spoke a single word again. Ever. He's still up at Juniper Hill as far as I know."

The lead agent yawns and shuffles his notes.

"Moving ahead, Detective. On Friday, November 29, 2019, Mr. Ryan Brown of Castle Rock was killed in a hit-and-run in your jurisdiction. You were the lead detective on scene and in charge of the case, correct?"

"I wasn't first on scene, but yes, I was the detective in charge."

"And the results of your investigation?"

"We were unable to locate or charge any suspects." Mitchell once more flashes the goofball smile.

"Did you actually search for any suspects?"

"Nope."

"Was there, in fact, anything even resembling an official investigation into Ryan Brown's death?"

"Nope." This time the goofball smile is accompanied by a small chuckle.

"And why not, Detective?"

"Because of the money."

"Are you saying you were bribed not to investigate Ryan Brown's death?"

"Yup."

"By whom?"

"I don't know. Never got a name."

"Are there other members of the Derry Police Department involved in this conspiracy?"

"Yup."

"And who might they be?"

"Officers Ronald Freeman and Kevin Malerman." Mitchell raises a fist. "My *bros*!"

"What can you tell us about the man who bribed you?"

"Tall. Thin. White. Wearing a long yellow coat. Old-fashioned, kinda sharp-looking white dress shoes. He talked funny."

"You mean he spoke with an accent?"

"No, like his tongue was too big for his mouth. Or maybe like his voice box was stuffed with crickets."

All the interrogators stir at that.

"Anything else?"

"Yup," Mitchell says agreeably, "he wasn't human."

"Excuse me?"

"His face . . . it kept changing. Slipping."

Gwendy's throat is suddenly desert-dry.

"His face was slipping? Not following you, Mitchell."

"It was like he was wearing a mask, but not the rubber or cheap plastic kind kids wear on Halloween. It kept slipping, giving me glimpses of what was underneath."

"And what was that?"

"A monster."

"Can you describe what you saw under the mask?"

"Dark bristly hair, scaly skin, red lips, black eyes. And some kind of a snout. Like a wolf or a weasel. Maybe a rat."

"How many times did you meet with this wolf-man?"

"Twice. He initially approached me at the crime scene. And then a second time at my home when he brought me the money."

"How much did the man pay you?"

"One hundred thousand dollars."

One of the others says something. It's off-mic, but Gwendy thinks it might have been "Fuck me."

"Did he explain why he wanted the Ryan Brown investigation to go away?"

"Nope."

"Did he say if he was working for someone else?"

"Nope."

"The man was alone both times?"

"Yup." Mitchell pauses and adds, "I thought he might kill me, you know."

"What kind of vehicle did the man drive?"

"Never saw one. He arrived on foot both times. He had

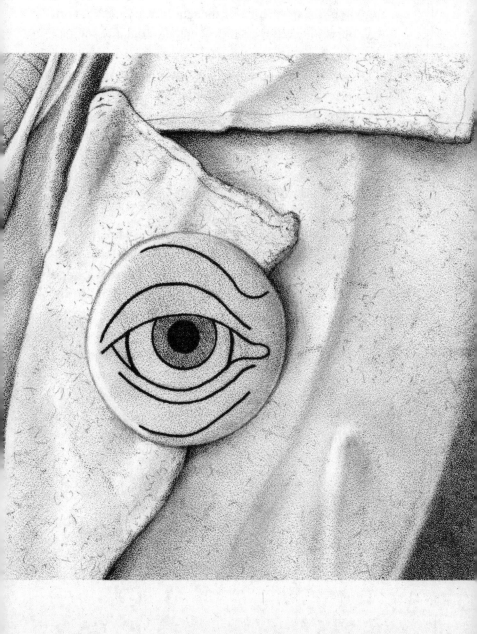

a button on his lapel. At first I thought it was some kind of a badge. But it wasn't. It was a big crimson eye and it was watching me the whole time we talked."

The man by the door says, "A tinfoil hat can help with that." There's some laughter, but the chief interrogator doesn't join in and it dies quickly.

"Had you ever met the victim, Ryan Brown, before his death?"

"Nope."

"Did you play any role in luring Ryan Brown to Derry?"

"Nope."

"How about Gwendy Peterson? You knew who she was?"

"Sure. The bitch always polluting my TV before the election. All those damn commercials. I couldn't watch a single Red Sox game that season without having to listen to her libtard drivel."

Gwendy extends her middle finger to the laptop screen.

"Do you know a man named Gareth Winston?"

"No, but I've heard the name."

"Where?"

Mitchell gives his loopy smile. "Not sure."

"Last question for now and then we can take a short break. Have you ever heard of the Sombra Corporation?"

"Nope."

"You're certain of that?"

"Yup."

And that's all there is.

34

GWENDY FIRES OFF A brief note to Charlotte Morgan, thanking her and commending her for a job well done. There's nothing else Charlotte can do for her at the moment, but that could change in a hurry.

Gwendy's anger has diminished, but it's been replaced by a soul-dragging heaviness that makes her head feel as if it weighs about a million pounds. It was just yesterday that she couldn't sit still—did she really go for a run or did she dream that?—but now she can't seem to make herself get up off the tiny sofa. She considers stretching out and taking a nap, but every time she closes her eyes, she sees Ryan's lifeless body and the trail of bloody smear marks across the road, and all she hears in the dark silence of her mind is that awful high, barking laughter.

Finally, after giving herself a pep talk (at age sixty-four, Gwendy's mental pep talks are still delivered in her mother's voice), she closes her laptop and forces herself to get up and get moving. After depositing a handful of balled-up Kleenex in the zero-g wastebasket and closing the lid, she washes her face with cold water. *Four more days*, she reminds herself again, staring at her reflection in the bathroom mirror. She's not happy with what she sees. Her eyes are swollen from crying, and there's a hint of barely contained hysteria in her gaze. *NG*, she thinks. *Better do something about that before you show up at dinner.* The last thing she needs to do is give Kathy and company a reason to start worrying about her again.

But those men weren't men. They were from . . . somewhere else. Probably the same somewhere else the button box came from. Did Mr. Farris steal it to keep it safe? Gwendy doesn't know—probably never will—but she thinks there's a good chance he did.

It occurs to Gwendy there's one thing she does know: she's about to break bread with a man who had a hand in her husband's death. How heavy that hand was she isn't sure, but that doesn't really matter. Does it? There's a brief moment where she struggles to remember the man's name—she thinks it might be Gary or maybe even Gregory—but then it comes back to her in a flash of certainty that is rare for her during these dark times. His name is Gareth Winston. He's a billionaire, but he'll never have enough money or power. He'll always want more. And he knows the combination to the steel case marked **CLASSIFIED MATERIAL**. She's sure of that, too.

35

THERE ARE FOUR OF them at the table when Gareth Winston bounce-walks his way into the cafeteria. Gwendy is sitting next to Adesh Patel. She looks younger and livelier than the reflection she saw in her bathroom mirror minutes ago. She's just finished telling Kathy Lundgren and Bern Stapleton all about Boris the scorpion's impressive display in the Bug Lab. At the conclusion of her story, she jumps to her feet, exclaiming, "*Maar!*" and lunges across the table toward her former training partner. Bern Stapleton nearly screams and spills half a cup of apple juice, which floats in front of his jumpsuit. He's still trying to catch it with a ball of napkins when Gwendy spots Winston.

Please keep going, she thinks. *Please sit somewhere else.*

But of course he doesn't. Squeezing his considerable bulk onto the chair, Winston settles with a grunt. He immediately reaches for his food tray, detaches it from the magnet holding it to the table, and floats it over to him. He peers through the thin mesh, nods approvingly at what he sees, opens the diagonal zip in the center of the mesh with a thumbnail, and begins to eat pasta in greedy gulps. A few drops of red sauce float in front of him. To Gwendy they look like drops of blood.

"Not bad," he says, finally looking up at the others. "It's not Sorrento's in the Bronx, but it'll do in a pinch."

"I'm so glad you're pleased," Kathy says. "Perhaps TetCorp can hire the head chef from Sorrento's to handle meal preparations for their Mars shuttles."

"Now that's an idea," Winston says, pointing a finger at the flight commander and chewing noisily. He looks over at Adesh. "They even have a vegetarian menu for people like you."

The entomologist leans close to Gwendy and whispers, "People like me, don't you know."

"There's a lovely Italian restaurant in Maine called Giovanni's. You ever heard of it, Mr. Winston?" It's an innocent enough question, but something in Gwendy's tone causes the others at the table to turn and stare at her. Only Winston doesn't seem to notice.

He shakes his head. "Can't say I have. Where is it?"

"It's in a little town called Windham, about forty-five minutes north of Castle Rock. They make a stuffed shrimp *a la Guiseppi* to die for. It's been written up in all the foodie magazines."

"Hmpph." He takes a drink of lemonade and belches into his hand. "I'll have to check it out sometime."

"I've actually been meaning to ask you," Gwendy says. "Have you spent much time in Maine during your travels?"

"Not really. Visited a couple of times. Once to go moose hunting in the Allagash. But the trip was a bust."

"My wife and I went camping at Acadia National Park the summer after we got married," Bern Stapleton says. "Beautiful place. I'm pretty sure we conceived our first child inside that tent."

"TMI," Kathy says. "*Way* too much."

"Adesh," Bern says, "please have the birds-and-bees talk with Commander Lundgren. I think it's time."

Kathy whacks the biologist on the shoulder. Laughing, he gets up from the table and collects his tray. "Off to get some work done. Be good, kids."

"I'm right behind you," Adesh says, standing and clearing his place. "I have a Zoom conference to prepare for."

"Good luck," Kathy calls as the two men walk away.

"I'm surprised you've seen so little of my home state," Gwendy continues, once again staring at the billionaire. "With all that money, I figured you've been everywhere twice."

"Well, excuse me for stating the obvious," he says, "but with all that money, I wouldn't exactly call Maine a desired destination. Paris, Tortola, Turks and Caicos, now those are a different—"

"Have you ever been to Castle Rock?" Gwendy asks, cutting him off. "How about Derry?"

"No and no," he snaps, letting go of his fork. He quickly snatches it out of the air in front of him when it begins to float up toward the ceiling. "I've never been to Castle Rock and I've never been to Derry. Now, can I finish eating my dinner in peace?"

"Of course," Gwendy says, slipping on her Patsy Follett smile. "Just one last thing—I wanted to thank you for returning my notebook. Lucky for me you found it."

"Yeah, well, you ought to be more careful."

She starts away, then stops and turns back. "Maybe you should be, too."

A flush rises in his cheeks. *Gotcha*, Gwendy thinks.

A few minutes later, while scraping their plates into the vacuum receptacle at the other side of the cafeteria, Kathy asks, "What in the hell was that all about?"

"What do you mean?"

"C'mon. You were *poking* at him."

"I was just curious."

"About what?"

"How he'd respond to a poke. Did you see that flush?"

Kathy frowns. "I didn't notice."

Gwendy watches her walk away, thinking: *Test or no test, she still doesn't trust me completely. Well, I've got news for you, lady. The feeling is mutual.*

On the way back to her quarters, Gwendy makes a brief diversion to the weather deck to check on the latest readings. She knows that some staff members back in the down-below—maybe even most of them—don't expect her to perform much more than a lick and a promise when it comes to her climate monitor duties. But that just makes her want to exceed expectations and prove them all wrong; it's how she's always been wired.

Her laptop is back in her room, so she scribbles a couple of notations in a Moleskine ledger and returns it to its place in the top drawer of the desk. When she's finished, she writes a reminder note about tomorrow's video conference with faculty members from the University of Maine and sticks it right in the middle of one of the monitor screens. No way can she forget that. She hopes.

When she gets to her room a short time later, she makes a beeline for the sofa. She's suddenly exhausted and all she wants to do is lie down and rest her brain. *It's strange*, she thinks. She watched a video earlier this afternoon of her husband being murdered—not to mention the four odd creatures in yellow coats and their mile-long ugly green car (*if it even was a car*, she thinks)—but after shoveling a bit of shit in Winston's direction at dinner, she feels a little more in control of things. In fact, she feels surprisingly steadfast. For the first time in days, she's not even thinking about the button box and its magic bag of tricks and treats. Eyes growing heavy, she props a pillow under her head and gets comfortable. Just before she dozes off, she notices her laptop sitting open on the coffee table and thinks: *Wait a minute, didn't I close that before I left? And put it away?*

Probably she didn't. She's gotten so forgetful. Then her eyes slide the rest of the way shut—and she's sleeping the dreamless sleep of the innocent.

RICHARD CHIZMAR

36

Day 4 on Many Flags.

Gwendy brushes her teeth, rinses the night cream off her face, and ties her hair back in a ponytail. Then she dresses in blue shorts and an Eagle Heavy tee. She figures a vigorous walk around the outer rim might help to keep her head clear and increase her appetite for breakfast. She never seems to be hungry anymore, and that worries her. Take last night for example. She enjoyed her time at the dinner table—especially poking Gareth Winston, which was the high point—but she barely touched the food on her tray. She will this morning, appetite or no appetite. Only three more days until her space-walk with the Pocket Rocket, and she can use all the calories she can get.

Gwendy doesn't even consider going for a run. That little act of misguided lunacy—chocolates or no chocolates—could have easily backfired and ended in disaster. She can picture the scene without even trying: *The senator from Maine floating on her back, unresponsive as her misfiring sixty-four-year-old heart sputters. Dale Glen, surrounded by the other crew members, dutifully administering epinephrine and doing CPR. Alas, the sputtering heart quits. After a few more minutes of trying to jump-start it, a grim-faced Dr. Glen calls it. Kathy Lundgren hurries back to Spoke 1 to tearfully notify Eileen Braddock at Mission Control. Before the body of Maine's junior senator has even had time to grow cold in the infirmary* (Gwendy assumes that's where she'd be taken), *Gareth*

Winston slips into her suite and steals away with the button box. End of story. Maybe the end of everything.

Pure crap, of course—her heart checked out fine after half a dozen treadmill stress tests. Plus, paranoid fantasies sometimes accompany Alzheimer's. That was just one of the fun facts about the illness she discovered (and now wishes she hadn't) on the Internet. There's even a name for it: sundowning. And since sundown up here happens roughly every ninety minutes, that leaves plenty of opportunity for weird thoughts.

I am not sundowning!

Maybe not, but still, no running. Best to be safe.

A brisk walk will do me fine, she thinks, sitting down on the edge of the sofa cushion. Bending over, she slips on her sneakers, first the right, then the left. Then she reaches down, picks up the laces—and stops. She has no idea what to do with them.

"Oh, come on," she admonishes herself. "Of course you know how." What was that shoe-tying rhyme she learned in preschool? Something about bunny ears, wasn't it? The bunny ears being the loops you made in the laces? She can't remember, only that it ended *beautiful and bold*. Right now Gwendy doesn't feel beautiful *or* bold. Just scared. She tries—at least a half-dozen times—but doesn't even come close.

Finally, after a brief bout of crying and a thoroughly unsatisfying temper tantrum in which she kicks off both sneakers and sends them floating across the sitting room, Gwendy pulls up a YouTube tutorial on her laptop. The girl in the video is five years old. Her name is Mallory and she's from Atlanta, Georgia. The senator watches the ninety-second video three times from start to finish, murmuring the words to the accompanying song, which she now remembers perfectly: *Bunny ears, bunny ears, playing by a tree. Crisscrossed the tree, trying to* catch me. *Bunny ears, bunny ears, jumped into the hole, popped out the other side beautiful and bold.*

She finally manages to tie her Reeboks. Even then, they're a little loose.

By the time she heads out the door, half an hour later than planned, Gwendy Peterson is daydreaming about the button box again. And singing about bunny ears.

37

SHE'S HALFWAY AROUND THE outer corridor when Adesh Patel catches up with her.

"Good morning, Senator. Mind some company?"

"Not at all," Gwendy says.

But she *does* mind. The last thing she wants on this horrible morning is company. She's cranky and frightened and filled with doubt. *What if I have another Brain Fart? See, that's not even right! What if I have another Brain* Freeze, *and he runs back and blabbermouths to Kathy? What then?*

As if reading her mind, Adesh gently touches her on the shoulder and asks, "Can we stop for a minute? I wanted to tell you something at dinner last night, but we were never alone long enough and I didn't want to say it in front of the others."

Gwendy stops walking and turns to face him. "Is something wrong, Adesh?"

He lowers his eyes and shrugs. "Yes . . . no . . . I mean, I don't really know, I guess."

"Well, spit it out and let's figure it out together."

"I'll try." He takes a deep, wavering breath. "When Doc Glen and Commander Lundgren first came to me asking questions about you, I had no idea what their specific concerns were or what they were thinking. I figured it was because you're . . . well . . ."

"Because I'm *old*? It's okay, it's true. And not a dirty word."

Adesh shakes his head. "No, ma'am. You might be older

than the rest of us, but you're not old. Now my Grandma Aanya, she's old."

"Point taken," Gwendy says. "Say on, O revered Bug Man."

"Well, it was only later, when I found out about the cognitive assessment test they made you take, that I went back to them and spoke my true mind."

"They didn't make me do anything, Adesh. I agreed."

Adesh nods, then shakes his head. "Nevertheless, I was very angry when I heard what they did. And I told them so."

Gwendy is genuinely touched. "You're a good friend. Thank you."

"And when I heard that you passed the test with flying colors, I marched right back in there and said, 'I told you so.' A brilliant woman like you could never fail such a basic assessment."

If only you knew, she thinks sadly.

"Anyway, I needed to get that off my chest. In case people tell you, 'That Bug Man, he spoke out of turn.' It's the correct phrase, isn't it? Out of turn?"

"Yes."

"I just wanted you to know I had to speak my mind."

She floats up a few inches to give his shoulder an affectionate squeeze—and that's when she sees it. Maybe thirty yards behind them, where the inner wall of the corridor curves out of sight, someone is standing in the shadow of the big overhead air purifier, watching them. Before Gwendy can call out or get a better look, the figure disappears. *Winston?* she wonders.

". . . say the word."

She turns back to Adesh. "I'm sorry . . . I missed that. What did you say?"

"I said if there's anything I can do to help you, anything at all, please just say the word."

Gwendy's mind—suddenly very clear, and what a gift that is—flashes to her laptop. Probably she forgot to put it away, just as she forgot her notebook on Eagle Heavy. But if she *did* put it away . . . and then it was not only back on the coffee table but *open* . . .

"As a matter of fact, there might be something." Because of all the people she rode the rocket with, Adesh Patel is the one she trusts the most.

"Tell me," he says.

38

THE ZOOM MEETING WITH the University of Maine faculty and staff goes well. Gwendy experiences one minor hiccup—when speaking with the director of Athletics, she accidentally refers to the Black Bears men's basketball team as the Blueberries—but she catches herself right away and makes a joke of it. Everyone enjoys a laugh and she quickly moves on to other topics.

The rest of her afternoon is spent writing a blog entry for the National Geographic Society (complete with a couple of Dave Graves's photos) and video conferencing with the vice president about climate control issues. She has always found the man well-meaning but stupid . . . which pretty well describes Gwendy herself these days, unfortunately. In between these chores, she catches up on emails and practices tying her shoes (murmuring the bunny song as she does). At some point, she closes her eyes and tries reaching out to Gareth Winston, but nothing comes back to her. Not even the subtlest vibrations confirming his presence on the space station. Another chocolate animal might help, but it also might be a very bad idea.

At one point, Gwendy finds herself looking out the big main window with no idea how she got there. Or when.

NG, she thinks.

At dinner, Winston sits about as far away from Gwendy as is possible. *Wonder why*, she thinks with a satisfied smirk.

For dessert, Sam Drinkwater surprises the crew with a pan of homemade chocolate brownies, still warm from the oven. Gwendy eats two, including a crunchy corner piece, her favorite ever since she was a young girl. They're certainly not the button box's special chocolates—for starters, they taste nothing alike, and for finishers, they possess not even a hint of magic—but the brownies are delicious just the same. A cozy and much-needed reminder of home and simpler times.

After dinner, Gwendy stops by the weather deck. Her work is done for the day, but she's not quite tired enough to call it a night. She also doesn't want to return to her room just yet. Ever since the upsetting incident involving her running shoes, the button box's voice has grown louder and more insistent and more difficult to push away. She's hoping that staring into the enormous telescope for ten or fifteen minutes will be just the ticket for her beleaguered brain. But that's not the only reason she likes coming here.

In some ways the Many Flags weather deck—with its own gigantic window like a hanging glass ornament, and its softly humming monitors—reminds Gwendy of Our Lady of Serene Waters Catholic Church back in Castle Rock. She finds the atmosphere calming for both the body and the soul, and it provides her a sort of celestial cathedral in which to reflect. And the view is—no pun, just truth—downright heavenly.

All of this is a miracle, she thinks, staring out at the dark expanse of . . . everything. *How many other worlds exist in this endless sea of stars and planets and galaxies? How many other life forms might be staring back at me right at this very moment?*

She remembers a warm July night when she was eleven—the summer before the button box first entered her life. A month earlier, just before the end of the school year, Gwendy's fifth-grade science teacher, Mr. Loggins—who more often than not taught his daily lessons with a big green crusty booger visible in one or both nostrils—had taken the class on a field trip to the planetarium. Most of the kids, already snared in summer vacation's web of promise, spent those ninety minutes in the dark throwing jelly beans at their friends, gossiping about who was and who wasn't invited to Katy Sharrett's end-of-year pool party, and making fart sounds by stuffing their hands into their armpits.

Not Gwendy. She had been fascinated. When she got home from school later that afternoon, she'd immediately begged her parents to buy her a telescope. After intense negotiations involving her weekend chore duties, Mr. and Mrs. Peterson agreed to share the cost with their daughter (seventy-five percent mom and dad, twenty-five percent Gwendy). On the first Saturday afternoon of summer break, Gwendy and her father drove out to the Sears store on Route 119 in Lewiston and picked up a Galaxy 313 StarFinder at thirty percent off the ticketed price. Gwendy was ecstatic.

On the July night she's thinking about, the telescope was set up in the corner of the backyard, just a few paces away from the picnic table and grill. Her father, who had come outside earlier, was snoring in a lawn chair, a couple of empty cans of Black Label lying beside him in the freshly cut grass. After a while, her mother appeared and tucked the fuzzy red blanket from the den sofa over him. Then she joined her daughter by the telescope.

"Take a look, Mom," Gwendy said, stepping aside.

Mrs. Peterson peered into the eyepiece. What she saw—a twisting band of shimmering stars as brilliant and bright as rare diamonds—stole her breath.

"It's the constellation Scorpius," Gwendy explained. "Made up of four different star clusters."

"It's beautiful, Gwendy."

"Some nights, when it's clear enough, you can see a huge red star right there in the middle. It's called Antares."

Fireflies danced in the darkness around them. Somewhere down the street a dog began barking.

"It's like looking through a window at heaven," Mrs. Peterson said.

"Do you . . ." All of a sudden Gwendy's tone was unsure. "Do you really think there's . . ."

Mrs. Peterson stepped away from the telescope and looked at her daughter, who was no longer staring up at the night sky. "Do I think what, honey?"

"Do you really think there's a heaven?"

Mrs. Peterson was instantly struck with such an over-powering swell of love for her daughter that it made her heart ache. "Are you thinking about Grandma Helen right now?" Mrs. Peterson's mother had passed away earlier in the spring as a result of complications from early-onset diabetes. She was only sixty-one. The entire family had taken it hard, especially Gwendy. It had been her first intimate experience with death.

Gwendy didn't answer.

"You want to know what I believe?"

She slowly raised her eyes. "Yes."

Mrs. Peterson glanced over at her husband. He had rolled onto his side with his back to them and was no longer snoring. The blanket had fallen onto the grass. When she looked back at her daughter standing there in the dark, Mrs. Peterson was shocked at how small and fragile the eleven-year-old looked.

"First of all, I want you to pay special attention to exactly what I just said. I asked if you wanted to know what I *believed*, right? I didn't ask if you wanted to know what I *thought*. There's a difference between the two. Does that make sense?"

"I think so."

"*Thinking* something is more often than not about logical or intellectual deduction. And that's a good thing. Like the things they teach you about at school. Proper thinking leads to learning and learning leads to knowledge. That's why you know so much about so many interesting things like the scorpion constellation."

"Scorpius."

"Exactly," Mrs. Peterson said, ruffling Gwendy's hair. "But *believing* . . . now that's something different. Something much more . . . personal."

"You mean like Olive Kepnes believing in the Loch Ness monster and aliens? Those are personal choices for her?"

"That's one way to look at it. But I was thinking of God. The Bible tells us that He's real, there are hundreds of stories about Him, but we've never seen Him with our own eyes, right? And no one we know—no one who's even alive right now—has ever seen Him either. Right?"

"Right."

"But many of us still choose to believe that He exists. And that kind of belief, the kind that comes from deep within your heart and soul, the kind that may at times even appear to defy common logic, is *faith*."

"We learned about faith a long time ago in Sunday school."

"Well, there you go. I have faith that there's a God watching over all He's created, and I have faith that there's a wonderful place waiting for all those who choose to live a good life. I don't know what heaven looks like or where it is or even if it's an actual physical place. In fact, I kind of have my doubts about the whole 'angels wearing white robes floating around on clouds playing harps' scenario."

Gwendy giggled, and Mrs. Peterson felt that ache in her heart again. It wasn't a bad ache.

"But yes, I believe heaven exists and Grandma Helen is there right now."

"But *why* do you believe those things?"

"Look around us, Gwendy. Tell me what you see."

She looked to her left and then her right, and then up at the sky. "I see houses and trees and stars and the moon."

"And what do you hear?"

She cocked her head to the side. "A train whistle . . . the Robinsons' German shepherd barking . . . a car with a bad muffler."

"What else? Listen closely this time."

She cocked her head again, to the opposite side this time, and Mrs. Peterson lifted a hand to her face to cover a smile. "I hear the wind blowing through the treetops. And an owl hoot-hooting!"

Mrs. Peterson laughed. "Now tell me quick, what's your favorite memory of Grandma Helen?"

"Her Christmas cookies," Gwendy answered right away. "And her stories! I loved her bedtime stories when I was little!"

"Me too," Mrs. Peterson said. "Now take a look through your telescope again."

She did.

"All of those things you just answered—and so much more; my gosh, *so* much more, dear girl; think of your Grandpa Charlie and your best friend, Olive; think of those amazing star clusters of yours; and before you go to sleep tonight, take a good long look at yourself in the mirror—*those* are the reasons why I believe. Do you think all those miracles could exist without a God? I don't. And do you think—"

Before she could finish, a shooting star raced across the night sky. They stared at it with breathless wonder until it eventually flared out and disappeared. Mrs. Peterson wrapped her arms around her daughter and pulled her close. When she spoke again it was barely a whisper, and Gwendy realized that her mother was either crying or close.

"And do you think God would've bothered to create all those miracles and not have created a heaven to go right along with them?" She shook her head. "Not me."

"Guess I don't, either," Gwendy says now, standing in front of the weather deck's floor-to-ceiling window. And for perhaps the first time in her adult life, she truly believes it. Gwendy has an unobstructed bird's-eye view of Earth below, but she doesn't even give it a glance. Instead, she gazes far off into the mysteries of the up-above and forever-onward, and whispers, "For me, you were the biggest miracle of all, Mom."

39

Day 5 on Many Flags.

Gwendy is almost to the cafeteria—close enough to smell freeze-dried scrambled eggs and sausage in the pleasantly filtered air of Spoke 4—when she realizes she left her red notebook back in the suite. Earlier this morning she put it down on the coffee table next to her laptop so she could type out a quick email and told herself not to forget it. But, like so many other things these days, she *did* forget. *NG*, she scolds herself, and pivots in mid-bounce like a ninja in one of the ridiculous chop-socky movies Ryan used to love so much.

Despite this little speed bump, today has been a good day. Maybe even a great day. For the first time since saying goodbye to Earth's atmosphere—*Who am I kidding?* she thinks; *for the first time in probably five or six years!*—Gwendy Peterson enjoyed an uninterrupted night of sleep. She'd dreamt she was camping out with Olive Kepnes in her backyard in Castle Rock. They'd toasted marshmallows, flipped through a new issue of *Teen Beat* magazine (Shaun Cassidy oh God such a hunk!), and giggled about cute boys until the sun came up.

When she'd awakened, fifteen minutes before her alarm was set to go off, she felt like a brand-new woman—brimming with energy and determination and, most importantly, clarity. *Don't forget hope*, she'd told her reflection in the steamed-up mirror after a long, relaxing shower. *Two more days and all of this madness will be over.*

Gwendy is humming the theme song to *The Sopranos* and practically skipping down the main corridor in Spoke 1 when she runs into Dr. Glen heading in the opposite direction. When Dale looks up and sees the senator, he flashes a grin. "Someone got up on the right side of the bed this morning."

"Absolutely, Doc. I'm a free woman. No Zoom meetings, no conference calls, no weather girl duties. Not a single thing on the schedule today. I just might crawl back into bed after breakfast and stay there for the rest of the day! So I ask you, who's got it better than me?"

He raises his eyebrows as he glides past her on the tips of his toes. "I guess that would be no one, at least not up here."

"See you at breakfast in a few," she says, cheerfully waving a hand over her shoulder. "Just need to grab something from my room."

"Want me to wait?"

"Nope, go on ahead. I'll be right behind you."

Gwendy is still smiling when she opens the door to her suite. She takes a couple of steps inside—and freezes.

Gareth Winston is down on one knee in front of her sitting room closet. The door is open and Gwendy's extra pressure suit has been pushed out of the way. She can see some kind of gadget— shiny black metal, not much larger than an iPhone— attached to the keypad on the safe. Several dark wires run from the base of the gadget to what looks like a small calculator with a digital readout screen. Winston is holding the calculator thingamajig in his hands. When Gwendy bursts into the room, he drops it and scrambles to his feet, leaving the gadget to float.

"What are you doing here?" She's pretty sure she already knows the answer. Her brain may be broken, but she's not stupid. "Do you have any idea how much trouble you're in? Tampering with classified material is a federal offense."

"I don't believe I'm in any kind of trouble at all, Senator." Winston's eyes look nervous, but his voice never wavers.

"I guess we'll see what Commander Lundgren has to say about that." She turns to leave.

Rattlesnake quick (*and twice as mean*, she has just enough time to think), Winston lunges across the sitting room and grabs her arm. If Gwendy hadn't just seen it with her own eyes, she never would've believed the man was capable of moving that quickly. *Of course*, she thinks, *that's zero-g for you.* His fingers dig into her flesh as he drags her toward the center of the room and shoves her down onto the sofa. "Even if you somehow managed to get away, it would be too late by the time you got back with the others."

"What do you mean, *too late?*"

"You see that little black box over there?" He gestures to the gadget affixed to the safe's keypad. "That marvel of technology is called a LockMaster 3000. It's available to the public for not much more than the cost of a decent laptop. It usually takes no more than ten minutes to reset a four-digit combination and provide a new entry code. These Many Flags safes are a little trickier, probably because Tet is expecting some high-powered people to eventually be using the quarters up here, but in the end it'll do the job. May take twenty minutes or even half an hour, but oh yes, it'll get there."

"I'd be back here a lot quicker than half an hour—and with plenty of help, too."

He scratches his chin thoughtfully. "That's assuming I let you go anywhere. It's a fair assumption on your part, I suppose—as a U.S. senator, you're used to going wherever you want, whenever you want—but this time the assumption would be wrong. I don't want to go all Snidely Whiplash on you, dear, but why would I set you free to roam before I get my hands on the button box? And once I do . . . goodness! Who knows what might happen?"

When she hears the words *button box* come out of Gareth Winston's mouth, for a dizzying moment Gwendy thinks she may pass out. *That would be a very bad idea*, she thinks. *That would be the end of everything.*

"What do you know about the button box?"

"Some, but not enough. I'm counting on you to fill me in on the rest."

"Never," she says.

He smiles. "Spoken like a true movie heroine, but I think you will."

"Let's cut to the chase, Winston, okay? We sit and wait for your little gadget to do its thing, you take possession of the box, and then what?"

"Then you have an unfortunate accident. If the box can't provide it, I have something that can."

She bares her teeth in a humorless grin. "They'll all know, Winston. My God, you have to see that. And you'll go to prison—federal prison, not some state dump—for the rest of your life."

"I don't think so," he says, shaking his head so rapidly the flesh on his cheeks jiggles back and forth like Jell-O. "Several on board suspect you're . . . how shall I say this? Mentally challenged."

"The cognitive test—"

"Sam Drinkwater and Dave Graves think you cheated somehow—that nobody could score as high as you did."

"I'm losing my mind, but I'm still smart enough to cheat?"

Gareth snickers. "I believe you just described most of your colleagues in the House and Senate, not to mention the president himself: just smart enough to cheat. But let's not talk politics. Let's get back to you instead. A fatal accident would be mourned, of course—you'd be a national hero, maybe get your face on a postage stamp, not to mention a million tee-shirts—but no one would be that surprised. Not really. Cognitive issues so blatant you were forced to take a test? I wouldn't even be surprised if some of the bigwigs at TetCorp lose their jobs as a result of it. The media will say your unsound mind should have shown up sooner, that somebody missed it. Doctor Glen will undoubtedly come in for his share of the blame."

"I've sent emails," Gwendy says, gesturing to her laptop on the coffee table. "Friends in high places back in the States know all about you, Winnie. They know you stole the combination to the security case, for one thing."

The lizard smile disappears from Winston's face. It's a possibility he hasn't considered. "Suspicion is one thing, but providing proof is quite another. And that would be nearly impossible without any witnesses."

He pulls a small object from his pocket and holds it up for her to see. It looks like a tube of lipstick, and it's the same weirdly vibrant green as the Chrysler from the Derry video. A cartoon green. It hurts Gwendy's eyes to look at it.

"A good friend of mine gave this to me. No idea what it's made of but I can tell you this: it's virtually undetectable by modern security systems. And it's lethal. All you have to do is point, then twist the little metal loop in the base. One spray and it turns your insides into jelly. There's plenty of juice inside this canister to take care of the entire crew if necessary."

"How would you get back? You gonna fly the ship home yourself?" And then before she can stop herself: "Your little blond friend teach you how to do that, too?"

Before Gwendy can react, Winston has her pinned against

the back of the sofa, his meaty forearm pressing down on her throat. There's a thunderstorm in Winston's eyes, and for a terrifying moment Gwendy is certain he's going to kill her right now. "How do you know about Bobby?"

"I . . . saw it in a dream," she manages to get out. "You were sitting inside a car with him. A green car."

For the first time, Winston looks unsure. And scared—that, too. "Then you know enough not to fuck around with these people." He removes his arm from her throat. "I don't think Bobby's his real name and I don't think he's human. He and his friends mean business, and so do I." He pauses. "He's beautiful, though. Like an angel. Except sometimes it looks like there's something inside him, his real self, and that's not so beautiful." He lowers his voice. "His real self has *fur*."

Sudden tears spill from Gwendy's eyes, and she silently scolds herself for showing weakness. She lifts a trembling hand to her neck and rubs the already sore muscles. It feels like something inside of her is broken.

"If you were to kill me and the rest of the crew, you'd be stranded here. You'd *die* here, Winston."

The ugly grin resurfaces on Winston's overfed face. "Let's just say I could hitch a ride back with my Chinese friends."

"They would never allow . . ." She stops as the reality of his words hit home. "They . . . you . . . you son of a bitch, you bribed them."

"I wouldn't necessarily call it a bribe." He chuckles into his fist. "Bribes are for pikers, dear. This was an investment in their future."

"Why are you doing this? Is it money?" *Keep him talking, keep him talking.*

"Don't be foolish. I have more money than I could spend in a thousand lifetimes."

"Then why?" Almost pleading now. "Why do you want it so badly?"

"That's quite a story." He glances over at the closet where the LockMaster 3000 is busy doing its thing. "But since we have time, why not?" He props his feet up on the coffee table and crosses his arms behind his head, like he's back home in his MetLife Stadium skybox watching the Giants and the Eagles square off on a Sunday afternoon. "In October of 2024 I was in St. Louis for my father's funeral . . ."

40

THE NAME OF THE *funeral home is Broadview & Sons, and once he signs off on the bill, Gareth Winston beats feet out of there. Winston hates funeral homes. Almost as much as he hated his father.*

It was the oldest story in the book—nothing the devoted son accomplished was ever enough to please the overly critical father with the razor-sharp tongue, so at some point, the son simply stopped trying.

Lawrence Winston III, also known as dear old Dad, made his piddling fortune selling commercial real estate and collecting rent checks on almost five hundred two- and three-bedroom apartments in a string of downtown high-rises. In the late '80s, a reporter from the St. Louis Post-Dispatch referred to the senior Winston as "a part-time slumlord and full-time scumbag." When Gareth banked his first billion at age thirty-three, the first thing he did was FedEx his father a photocopy of that newspaper article and a handwritten note on company stationery:

> **I still can't hit a curve ball or a 2 iron. I still don't have an Ivy League diploma. I'm overweight. And I'm still not married to a beautiful Catholic virgin from across the river. But I'm filthy-ass rich and you're not. Have a miserable fucking life.**
> **Gareth**

And then he never spoke to the man again.
Not even when his father called to make amends from his deathbed.

The hard truth of the matter is if it weren't for his mother—whom Winston still adores and makes a point of calling every Sunday night no matter where he is in the world, a tradition that first began after Winston left home for college—he wouldn't have even come home for the funeral, much less footed the bill. But she begged him over the telephone, and if there is one person in this world Winston can't refuse, it's his mother. Corny but true.

After the obligatory reception, there's a car waiting to take Winston back to his hotel suite, but he decides to walk instead. He needs the fresh air, plus he'd skipped breakfast this morning and is starving. Walking at a rapid pace, he cuts across McKinley Avenue, picks up South Euclid, and then takes a left onto Parkview. From there, he stops to buy three hot dogs and a bottle of Diet Pepsi from a street vendor and settles his considerable bulk on an empty bench overlooking the northeastern corner of Forest Park. From where he's sitting he can spot the pale oval of the skating rink—still six weeks out from opening weekend—as well as the seventh fairway of the Highlands Golf Course, which he wouldn't be caught dead playing. It's strictly for small-timers.

He's wiping a dribble of mustard off his shirt when a fluorescent green Chrysler swings up to the curb beside him. It looks to be roughly two miles long. Winston gives the car a once-over but is unable to determine what year it rolled off the assembly line. All he knows is that it looks very old and in cherry condition, and he's never seen another car like it. I wonder if it's for sale, he thinks idly.

The driver's-side window glides down. A man with short blond hair and striking emerald eyes, the bottom half of his face hidden behind a red bandana, leans his head out of the car and says, "Hop in. Let's go for a ride."

Winston grins. He's always liked a cheeky bastard, having been one himself all his life. "Nice ride, mister, but that's not gonna happen." He starts to ask the stranger why he's wearing a mask—few people wear masks anymore, not since the arrival of the vaccines a couple years ago—but he never gets that far.

"I don't have much time, Mr. Winston. Get in."

Winston's eyes narrow. "How do you know my name?" The answer to that is obvious: he's seen it in the papers or on one of the business channels, where Gareth Winston is a fixture. "Who are you?"

"A friend. And I know lots of things about you, Mr. Winston."

Because of the red bandana, Winston is unable to see the stranger's mouth, but he's nonetheless certain that the man is smiling. "I don't know who the hell you think you're talking to, but—"

"When you were twelve, you broke into your neighbors' house while they were away on vacation. Frank and Betsy Rhineman. Nice people. It's a shame their son died so young."

"How do you know the—"

"You stripped out of the swim trunks you were wearing and slipped on a pair of Mrs. Rhineman's panties—pale yellow with a black lace border, not too frilly—ate an ice cream sandwich you found in their freezer, and shot some billiards in the game room. Then, before you changed back into your trunks and scooted home for dinner, you returned upstairs and masturbated on the bedspread in the Rhinemans' guest bedroom."

"You're lying!" Winston bellows, startling a young mother walking by pushing a baby stroller. She quickly crosses the street to put some distance between them. "Stop it right now!" The billionaire's face has gone beet-red and his eyes are bulging.

"You still have the yellow panties to this day. They're tucked away in a safety-deposit box at your bank in Newark. Along with a few other equally distasteful treasures."

"Fake fucking news! None of what you're saying is true!"

"Would you like to hear some more?"

Winston is quiet for a moment, his broad chest rising and falling in great heaves. Then he asks in a quiet voice, "What do you want?"

"To make you an offer. The most generous offer you've ever been presented with. Get in the car, Mr. Winston. Let's chat."

"Sounds too good to be true, and what sounds that way never is." But he's already getting up from the park bench, leaving behind his lunch trash and walking toward the car.

"Could be," the stranger says, and removes the bandana from his face.

Winston takes a good look at the stranger and does a double take, then a triple take. And suddenly there's no longer any question in his mind about getting inside the car. He isn't gay—has never found the male form even remotely attractive, especially his own—but the blond man is so breathtakingly beautiful Winston wants to hold the man's face in his hands and kiss him. He wants to feel those lips and taste that breath. He looks like an angel, Winston thinks, opening the passenger door and sliding into the seat. As soon as he closes the door, a loud buzzing rises in the basement of his brain, like thousands of flies crawling over a rotting corpse. He turns to the man as the car pulls away from the curb. "Where are we going?"

"Just up the street and around the corner. For a little privacy."

A chill dances along Winston's spine at the mention of the word privacy. He feels an instant tightening in his groin. The man cruises two blocks east and pulls into the parking lot of an abandoned warehouse. He drives around back and stops in front of an empty loading dock. Winston can see shards of broken glass, several rusty needles, and a scattering of used condoms lying on the asphalt outside of the car. But he doesn't care. Just like he doesn't care about the insistent buzzing deep in his brain. All that matters now is the blond angel sitting next to him.

The man switches off the engine and turns to him. "Allow me to properly introduce myself." He extends his right hand. "You can call me Bobby."

Winston reaches over and takes his hand. The man's skin feels smooth and pleasant, like warm butter. The tightening in the crotch of Winston's slacks deepens to a dull throbbing.

"What I have to say to you, what I have to offer you, won't take long," the stranger says. "But I need you to listen very carefully."

Winston, adrift in a haze, slowly nods his head.

"My associates and I are well aware of your great wealth, Mr. Winston. But, as you know, there are other standards by which to measure one's legacy." He leans across the seat, close enough for Winston to feel the man's breath wash over him. Winston's already wide eyes widen some more. "Power. Control. Territory.

"There are other worlds than these. Many. You can rule one of them. Not just a company, not just a continent, but an entire world. And you can do it for an eternity."

The buzzing sound inside of Winston's head has diminished. Now he hears something else: the sound of distant waves crashing on a rocky shore. He likes the idea of ruling a world; who wouldn't? It's bullshit, of course, but it would be very nice. Excellent, in fact. He could see himself in a castle by the sea . . . listening to those crashing waves . . . a thousand people bowing down as he stands above them . . . hell, ten thousand! As the Beach Boys' song says, wouldn't it be nice.

"All we need from you is a particular item. It is in possession of a woman named Gwendolyn Peterson—"

"The senator?"

"The very same. We can try to take it ourselves—in fact, we have tried—but the Tower is strong."

"What tower?" Winston asks in a voice that sounds nothing like his own.

"The only one that matters." The blond man reaches over and places a hand on Winston's knee. Winston shudders in pleasure. He might be gay after all—at least in this man's presence. "Gwendolyn Peterson has what we need to destroy the Tower. You must find it and

bring it to us. Because of your enormous wealth and political connections, you are uniquely fitted for this task."

"You're insane." The roar of the ocean swells inside Winston's
head.

"Close your eyes," Bobby commands.

Winston is helpless not to obey. It's like being hypnotized. He feels
the kiss of a cool breeze upon his face and smells a tinge of salt in the air
as soon as his eyes are shut. And then he can taste it on his tongue—
the ocean! The sound of crashing waves grows louder, only now it's not
just inside his head; it's everywhere. A bird cries out somewhere above
him—a gull of some kind—and a chorus of birds answers it.

"Now open them."

Gareth Winston opens his eyes and he's no longer sitting in the
green Chrysler behind an abandoned St. Louis warehouse. Instead,
he's sitting beside the blond man in a meadow of windswept grass.
He stands up and looks down at a churning sea of emerald water.
Hundreds of feet below, white-tipped waves crash upon an endless
shoreline of jagged rock and sand. The sky above them is streaked
with purple and yellow, and there are birds—hundreds of them!—
floating on the wind. The sun rising over the watery horizon is a deep
crimson.

This is real, he thinks. My God, this is real.

"What have you done to me?"

"Turn around, Mr. Winston."

He does. Slowly. Like moving in a dream, but this is no dream.

The man points off to the west at a distant city that stretches as
far as Winston's eyes can see. The early-morning sunlight glints off
the windows of scores of tall buildings. A complex spiderweb of road-
ways and bridges weaves its way through the shimmering metropolis.
It's too far away for Winston to determine the type of vehicles that are
currently traveling those roads, but there are many of them. In the sky
above the city, there's nary a hint of smog or pollution.

"How big is it?" Winston asks in dazed awe.

"Bigger than New York City, Chicago, and Los Angeles combined. And still growing. Surrounded by nearly fifty thousand acres of virgin woodland."

Winston whistles appreciatively.

"There are another two dozen cities just like it scattered throughout the world I'm offering you."

Winston points a finger at a long, dark scar of barren land a few miles directly in front of them. Tiny black figures, like busy ants in a child's ant farm, scurry back and forth in staggered lines. "What's that over there?"

"That," the man says, a satisfied smile creeping across his face, "is your diamond mine."

"Really?"

"Really." For the first time since he stood up from the park bench, there's a glimmer of the old Gareth Winston. His eyes look greedy—and hungry.

"And over there," his new friend continues, pointing to a sprawling castle sitting atop a hilltop overlooking the ocean, "is your home. One of many, I might add. For this residence alone, you employ—a rather kind way of wording it considering you tender none of them a salary—more than two hundred men and women from a nearby village. In exchange for their loyalty and labor, you might allow them to grow their own food tax-free."

"Of course," Winston mutters. In spite of his amazement, his businessman's brain is ticking over. "And possibly medical care. People who think loyalty can't be bought are idiots. There'd have to be some sort of retirement benefits . . . at least for those close to me . . ."

Bobby laughs. The teeth that are momentarily exposed are not those of an angel; yellow and crooked, they are the teeth of a rat. "See? You've already begun to plan. Given your extraordinary mind, you should be quite the successful ruler. And as the years, the decades . . .

the centuries! . . . roll by, you will become not a man but a god to those you rule over."

"And there are women?" Winston asks, looking and sounding more and more like his old self with each passing minute. "Not that I've ever had much luck with that."

"Luck plays no role here. Not when you're the king. Not when you're young and handsome and strong."

Winston laughs. "Not so young and strong anymore. And never very handsome, I'm afraid."

"I respectfully disagree, Mr. Winston." He gestures behind them. "Take a look."

When Winston turns and sees the tall, ornate mirror—with its glittering gold trim and polished, hand-carved oak legs—positioned in the long grass, his mouth drops open. When he sees his reflection in the mirror, he gasps.

He appears as young and slim as the morning he drove away to college.

"Here, in your world, you'll look this way forever. And as for being handsome, although you never truly believed it thanks to your father's constant disparagements, you were, at one time—and remain so here, as you can see for yourself—a young man of considerable physical appeal. Your father stole from you the most important gift a young man can possess: self-confidence." The blond man grins. This time his teeth are very straight and white. "But your father is no longer with us, now is he?"

"No, he is not." Winston looks around. "This is real?"

"Yes."

"Could I come here again?"

"To visit, yes. To live and rule . . . not until you bring us what we want. The button box."

Winston finds himself remembering a class he had in college, and a particular line from that class. He didn't understand it then, but now he does. "If it's real, and if I can, I will. I promise."

The man—Bobby—turns Winston away from the mirror. Bobby wants his undivided attention. "Gwendolyn Peterson has been tasked with getting rid of this rather special box once and for all, and there is only one place in her world—or any of the others—where this can happen."

"Where?" Winston asks.

The blond man stops walking. "How would you feel about taking a trip to outer space, Mr. Winston?"

41

"DON'T TELL ME YOU actually believed that cock-and-bull story about ruling your own private world," Gwendy says. "You're one of the most successful businessmen in history. I can't believe you'd take a few moments of . . . I don't know . . . hypnosis as reality."

Winston gives her an odd, knowing smile. "Do *you* believe it?"

Gwendy actually does. She can believe in other worlds because she cannot believe the button box came from hers. Before she can open her mouth to tell a lie that might not sound very convincing, there's a *beeeep* sound.

"Ah!" Gareth says. "I believe the safe has a new code and can now be opened. So why don't we—"

Before he can finish, both of their phones give off the distinctive double tone that means an incoming text from the station rather than a message from the down-below. They both take out their phones, Gwendy from the center pocket of her coverall, Winston from the back pocket of his chinos. Gwendy thinks, and not without sour amusement, *We're like Pavlov's dogs when it comes to these things. The fate of the earth may be at stake, but when the bell rings we salivate. Or in this case, read the text.*

The identical messages are from Sam Drinkwater: **Joining us for breakfast?**

"Text him back," Winston says. "Say we're in a serious

conversation . . . no, *negotiation* . . . about the future of the space program, and they should eat without us."

Gwendy is on the verge of telling Mr. Billionaire Businessman Gareth Winston to stuff it . . . but doesn't.

This has to end, here and now.

That thought sounds like Mr. Farris. Whether it is or isn't doesn't matter. Either way it's true.

She moves closer to Winston (*ugh*) so he can read the text she's preparing to send. It's exactly what he told her to say, with one addition: **Important we not be disturbed until 1100 hours**.

"Excellent. I'm going to open the safe. I can't wait to see what Bobby was so excited about. You, my dear, should sit right where you are like a good little Gwendy." He shows her the green lipstick tube. "Unless, that is, you want to find out what it feels like to die with your guts melting inside you."

He starts to rise, but she takes his arm and pulls him back down. In zero-g, it's easy. "Help me get my head around this. One hypnotic trance and you just fall into line? I don't believe it. You're not that stupid. In fact, you're not stupid at all."

Winston probably knows she's just trying to buy time, but he preens at the compliment anyway. Gwendy gives him her best wide-eyed tell-me-more look. It usually works in Senate committees (at least with men), and it works now.

"I have been back to Genesis many times," he says. "That's what I call my world. Nice, eh?"

"Very," Gwendy says, doing the wide-eyed thing for all she's worth.

"It's real enough. Bobby—he says I'd never be able to pronounce his real name—has given me certain instructions for going there. I could go there now, if I liked. My visits are necessarily short, but once I give him—and his controllers—this box of yours, I'll go there for good." He gives her a goony smile that makes her doubt his sanity. "It's going to be *great*."

"A hallucination," Gwendy persists. "Had to've been. This Bobby sold you a grander version of the Brooklyn Bridge." She shakes her head. "I still can't believe you fell for it."

He smiles indulgently and reaches inside his shirt. He brings out a pendant on a silver chain. In the gold setting is a huge diamond. "From my mine," he says. "I have others at my home in the Bahamas, some even bigger. This one is forty carat. I had one of similar size appraised, first to make sure it was real and second to determine its worth. The Swiss jeweler who looked at it almost had a heart attack on the spot. He offered me a hundred and ninety thousand dollars, which means it's probably worth twice or three times as much."

He drops the pendant back inside his shirt. "Genesis is real enough, and when I'm there I'm young and virile. The women . . ." He wets his fat lips.

"No more panty stealing, I take it," Gwendy says.

He gives her a glowering look, then actually laughs. "I suppose I deserve that. Don't know why I told you. No—no more panty stealing." He looks away from Gwendy, and she thinks that while he's distracted she might be able to grab something and whack him on the head. Except everything is fastened down, and the idea of clonking someone hard enough to knock them out in zero-g conditions is ridiculous.

When he looks back at her, he's wearing a rueful smile that's almost likable . . . or would be if he were not threatening her life and planning to steal the button box she's been charged with guarding and ultimately disposing of.

"When Bobby took me that first time, I remembered something a teacher said in an Ancient History class I took in college. I didn't want to take the damn thing, cut most of the classes and hired some grind to do my final paper, but that one thing stuck in my head. It was from an old Greek—I think he was a Greek—named Plutarch. Or maybe he was a Roman."

"Greek," Gwendy says. "Although he *became* a Roman."

Winston looks annoyed at the interruption. "Whatever. This Plutarch wrote something about a conqueror named Alexander. I can't remember the exact wording, but—"

Gwendy interrupts again. She likes interrupting him, and why not? He has not only interrupted her task, he's threatening to permanently interrupt her life. " 'When Alexander saw the breadth of his domain, he wept for there were no more worlds to conquer.' "

Instead of looking pissed off, Winston smiles so widely that the bottom half of his face almost disappears, and Gwendy thinks again that he's insane. *The prospect of having his own world, one where he can rule forever, has driven him over the edge. Maybe it would anybody.*

"That's it! Exactly! And I was like Alexander, Senator Peterson! I had no more worlds to conquer! I had reached my limit! And what did I have to look forward to? Growing older? Watching helplessly as I grew fatter, as my face began to wrinkle, as my body began to deteriorate? And my mind!" The smile becomes a nasty grin. "You'd know about that, wouldn't you?"

Gwendy doesn't take the bait. "For the sake of argument, let's say that world exists, Gareth. Even if it does, you won't get it. Not if you give them the button box."

Winston's grin fades. What replaces it is a look of narrow distrust. "What do you mean?"

"What I say. Give it to them and the world ends. If this Tower is as powerful as you say it is, *all* worlds end. Including yours, diamonds and all."

He gives a scornful laugh. "Why would these people—Bobby's people—do that? They'd die along with everyone and everything else."

"I think . . . because Bobby's people, those who pull his strings like he pulled yours, are the lords of chaos." And then, in a voice she doesn't recognize as her own, Gwendy cries, "Let the Tower fall! Rule, Discordia!"

Winston recoils as if that voice were a hand that had struck him. "Are you insane?"

It was Farris's voice, Gwendy thinks. *I don't know how or why—he must be dead by now—but it was.* Then she remembers the last time she saw him, on her porch in Castle Rock. *I'll help if I can*, he said that night.

"Think about what you're doing, Winston. For God's sake, *think*."

"I have. And I know when someone is trying to fuck with my head. Let's get a look at this fabled button box. Sit where you are, Senator. You won't get a second warning."

Of course not, Gwendy thinks. *The only reason I'm still alive is because he needs to make sure he has it. Once he does, he'll point that tube at me and—*

"Ah," Winston says. He's peering at the safe, which puts him between Gwendy and the door. "The reset combo is 1111. I believe even someone who's losing her mind could remember that one."

He removes the LockMaster and pushes the combo—*beep-beep-beep-beep*. She hopes the gadget didn't work, that the safe will remain shut, but the door swings open when Winston pulls the handle. Out comes the steel case with **CLASSIFIED MATERIAL** stamped on it. "I don't need to consult your little notebook again for the code to this one," Winston says. "One look was enough. Unlike yours, my memory is in perfect working order. People are amazed at my recall."

"Don't sprain your shoulder patting yourself on the back," Gwendy says coldly.

Winston laughs. Now that he has the case Gwendy swore to protect with her life, he seems quite cheerful. Perhaps he's thinking of his diamond mine. Or having a ménage à trois with two beautiful young women. Or a ticker tape parade in one of his fine new cities with thousands of people shouting his name. Gwendy could tell him about the black button—the Cancer Button that supposedly ends everything—but would he listen? No. He is Alexander, with a new world to conquer.

"1512253 . . . and presto!" He opens the steel box. He looks inside. His eager smile dissolves. "What . . . the *fuck* . . . is *this*?"

He takes out a white feather. When he lets it go, it floats in front of his face. Winston bats it away. He turns the security case so she can see inside. With the feather now out of it, the case is completely empty.

"Surprise, Mr. Winston," Gwendy says, and the slack-jawed shock on his face makes her laugh. But then shock is replaced by a look of fury Gwendy hasn't seen before. Suddenly she can see the Gareth Winston who lives inside, and he's no laughing matter.

I'm looking at a human wolf, she thinks.

Then he grins, which is even worse.

He lets go of the CLASSIFIED case, leaving it to float near the longtime talisman she calls her magic feather. He glides across to her. She shrinks back involuntarily and raises her hands to protect her throat.

"Oh, I'm not going to choke you," he says, still smiling.

"I might kill you"—he raises the green cylinder—"but it won't be a hands-on affair. And it will be *very* unpleasant."

Gwendy thinks, *The black button is the Cancer Button and that green thing is the Tube of Death. I've wandered into a fucking comic book.*

He shows her the ring on the bottom of the tube. "If I twist this all the way while it's pointed at you, the disintegration of your organs will be instantaneous. I know, because I've tried it."

"On one of your subjects," Gwendy says. Her voice sounds far away. "In Genesis."

"You *are* a bright one, at least when you're in your right mind. Too bright for your own good. The point is, my dear, that if I twist the ring slowly . . . a teeny-tiny bit at a time . . . you'll die in excruciating agony. You may actually feel your heart come loose from its moorings and drop into your stomach *while it's still beating.* Wouldn't *that* be something to experience!"

Yes, it's a comic book, all right, she thinks. *Too bad I can't just shut it and toss it in the UV waste disposal. Too bad it's actually happening.*

"You see," he says, as if speaking to a child, "I've come too far to turn back now, Senator. I have burned my bridges. Which is all right because, unlike you, I have an escape hatch. One that will take me to another world. A world I've already come to love. Let me tell you what's going to happen if you don't get with the program, you smartass bitch. You die—miserably, screaming through your disintegrating vocal cords—and then the rest of our Eagle Heavy compatriots die. Once the killing's done I will call in my Chinese allies and we will search this place until I find what I came for. When I do, I will exit my current abode in a kind of space taxi provided by a corporation you may have heard of—"

"Sombra."

"Yes! Good for you! I'll turn over the box to those who want it so badly, and exit this reality for a much more pleasant one. Do you understand?"

"I believe the smartass bitch is following you," Gwendy says.

"None of that has to happen, Gwendy. You can live. The rest of the crew can live, which will please me. You might not believe it, but I've come to like them. I will take the button box and go."

Given a choice between believing that and believing in the tooth fairy, I'd opt for the fairy, Gwendy thinks, but she nods as if she believes him. He's pointing the tube at her and fiddling with the ring on the bottom in a way that makes her very nervous. Only *nervous* is too mild a word for it. She's scared to death.

"Now we come to the Final Jeopardy question," Winston says. He's still grinning, but Gwendy can see beads of perspiration on his forehead. He's scared, too. That gives her at least some comfort. "Where is it?"

She opens her mouth, closes it, then opens it again.

"You're not going to believe this, Gareth, and I know you won't like it, but it's true. I can't remember."

42

HE STARES AT HER, eyes slitted. "You're right. I don't believe it. You aced the cognitive test they gave you. Dr. Glen was very impressed."

"I had the chocolates then."

"If you don't start making sense, dear, you are going to be very sorry."

Note to self, Gwendy thinks. *Having a panty thief call you dear is extremely repulsive.*

"The button box dispenses chocolates. They're brain boosts." They do much more, some of it not good, but this is no time for lengthy explanations. "I took a couple before the test. As you see, I can't do that now because the box isn't h—"

"I don't believe you. It's hogwash."

"Says the man who believes he's going to rule an entire planet, complete with pulp novel slave women and a handy nearby diamond mi—"

He slaps her. In zero-g it's not hard, like a slap underwater, but it shocks her. She has been hit before, but not since childhood. The one who hit her lived to regret it . . . but not for long. Her eyes flash wide, and he sees something in them that makes him dance-float backward, leveling the tube at her.

She thinks, *I'm not a proponent of the death penalty, but if I get a chance, dear, I'm going to kill you. If you'd been involved in Ryan's death, I'd try to kill you twice. Luckily for you, that happened before you got involved in this business. At least if I can believe your story.*

And she does. According to Winston, he met Bobby four years later, and what reason would he have to lie? All their cards are pretty much on the table now.

"You don't want to make fun of me, Senator. That's one thing you absolutely don't want to do."

"I'm not. *I can't remember where I put it.*"

"In that case I have no use for you, do I? I'll have to find it on my own, with the help of my Chinese associates. After I negate the rest of the crew, that is." He raises the tube, and she sees in his eyes that he means to do it.

"Give me a minute to think. Please."

"I'll give you thirty seconds." He lifts his watch to his face. "Starting right now."

Gwendy knows Winston thinks she's faking; Gwendy knows she isn't. She needs to use Dr. Ambrose's trick, find a chain of association and follow it to the location of the button box. Only her time is fleeting and she can't find a starting link. Her mind is whirling.

Yes, Richard Farris says, *this isn't good. You are in dire straits.*

That lights her up, and when Winston aims the tube, she raises a hand. "Wait! Wait! I can get it!"

Dire Straits. Not Ryan's favorite band, but one of them . . . and he loved that song about how sometimes you're the wind-shield and sometimes you're—

"The bug! Sometimes you're the windshield and some-times you're the bug!"

"What in Christ's name are you talking about, woman?"

"About the Bug Man. The only person in the crew I trust one hundred percent. The only one who believes in me com-pletely. Adesh. I gave him the button box. I told him to put it in his lab."

"Really?"

"Yes."

"Do you know *where* in the lab?"

Gwendy doesn't have a clue. "Yes. I'll show you."

"I should kill you and find it myself," he says. He raises the green tube . . . then lowers it again. And smiles. "But you've been troublesome, dear. *So* troublesome. I think I want you to watch me take possession of your precious box. I might even let you live. Who knows?"

You know, Gwendy thinks. *And I know.*

"Let's go, while they're still all at breakfast." He gestures with the tube. "After you, Senator."

43

SPOKE 5.

They float-walk down the corridor past signs in French:
LAVEZ-VOUS LES MAINS and RAMASSE TA POUBELLE
and even NE PASSE FUMER, which Gwendy would have
thought a no-brainer. But with the French and their Gauloises,
who could tell?

There's that steady low creaking. Gwendy has gotten used
to it, but Winston, it seems, has not.

"I hate that sound. It's like the whole place is coming
apart."

"No," Gwendy says, "you'll be the one tearing it apart.
Tearing *everything* apart."

It doesn't even touch him. *Classic narcissist,* she thinks.
Maybe it's true to some degree of all mega-successful businessmen and women. God, she hopes not.

"Why did you give it to the brownie? And what did you
tell him?"

The brownie, Gwendy thinks. *Jesus. And he probably thinks
of Jafari as the blackie.*

"Because I trusted him, I told you that. As for what I told
him . . ." She shook her head. "Can't remember."

This is a lie. Now she remembers everything. How hard
it was to actually hand it over, for one thing. She remembers
Adesh's look of curiosity, and most of all she remembers telling him he must not touch the buttons. *You may feel an urge*

to do just that, but you must resist it. Can you? Adesh had said yes—yes, he was quite sure he could—and because Gwendy had to trust someone, she gave him the box. Then had to resist her own almost insurmountable urge to snatch it back, cradling it to her breasts and shouting, *Mine! Mine!* She even remembers thinking about Gollum again, and how he called the One Ring his precious.

But she had given it over.

"Well, here we are," Winston says. He examines the sign on the door: ADESH "BUG MAN" PATEL. KNOCK BEFORE ENTERING. "Maybe we'll skip the knocking part."

Gwendy wishes, not for the first time, that the doors of the rooms, suites, and labs on the MF station had locks. But they don't.

"You first, dear. I'm not expecting a surprise, but always safe, never sorry."

She depresses the latch and steps inside. Soft sitar music is playing from a boombox, which is strapped to the center worktable to keep it from floating away. Some small gadget is tucked under the strap.

The second thing she sees is the last thing she expected. She told Adesh to put the button box in one of the drawers, there are at least fifty of them, but it's right out in the open, lying on the floor of the large cage where Adesh does his insect flight experiments. She can clearly see the tiny levers on the sides, and the colored buttons lining the top. The door to the cage is standing open.

"What's with the flies?" Winston asks. There are six or seven of them hanging motionless above the button box. "Are they dead?"

"Resting," Gwendy says. "According to Adesh, they've adapted quite well to zero-g conditions." She's looking at the boombox and the thing on top of it. Now she understands. How Adesh could have foreseen this situation is beyond her, but yes, she understands and knows what she must do.

If she can.

"Go in there, Senator. Get the box and give it to me."

She says, very slowly and clearly: "The fuck I will. I protected it as long as I could and as well as I could and I'm not handing it over to you or anyone. Get it yourself."

"Very well. But I think you'll come with me." He grabs her by her shoulder, fingernails digging into her flesh. "*Dear.*"

She pretends to struggle, backing up just far enough so her butt is against the worktable with its microscope, monitors, and centrifuge. She puts a hand behind her, hoping she looks like she's trying to hold on to the table but actually grabbing for the gadget on top of the boombox. *Please God, don't let him see and don't let me drop it*, she thinks. Not that it will drop; it will float.

She almost does lose her grip, but then the controller is in her hand and pressed against the small of her back. Winston snarls and points the green tube at her. "Enough! Get in there!"

"All right. I'll go. Just stop hurting me."

"I'll do more than hurt you. *Get in there.* You're not running for the door, if that was in your mind."

If he looked down he'd see she's hiding something, a flat eight-inch rectangle that looks like a TV remote. It's pretty obvious. But Gareth Winston's attention is mostly focused on the thing he's come so far to obtain. His prize. *His precious.*

They float into the large cage, Gwendy first. She manages to get the controller into the center pocket of her coverall while pretending to rub her hurt shoulder. Winston has slipped behind her, shoving her along.

"Over there. Against the wall."

235

He gives her a hard push. Gwendy floats backward.

Please let this work. Oh God, please.

He bends down and picks up the button box. A soft sigh escapes him. To Gwendy it sounds almost sexual.

"I feel it," he says. "It's powerful, isn't it?"

"Very powerful," Gwendy agrees. The controller Adesh has left for her is just another button box, only with four buttons instead of eight. She doesn't know which of them opens Boris's cage, so she lays her index finger across all four and pushes them.

Winston doesn't notice. He's running his own finger over the buttons: light green and dark green for Asia and Africa, blue and violet for North and South America, orange for Europe, and yellow for Australia. Plus the two at the ends: red for wishes that turn dark no matter how well-meant, and the black one. The Cancer Button.

Meanwhile, the buttons on the controller have opened four cages. The doors rise soundlessly. Black ants float up from one, red ants from another, cockroaches from a third. From the fourth comes Boris. *Pandinus imperator.* He rises, tail cocked.

"What do they do, these buttons?" Winston asks. He has forgotten Gwendy completely in his absorption. "What happens when you press them?"

"Bad things," Gwendy says.

"And the levers on the sides? What do *they* d—"

"Turn around," Gwendy says. And then, with great pleasure: "Look at me, you fat psychotic piece of shit."

His mouth drops open in surprise. His eyes widen in their pockets of puffy flesh. He turns. Gwendy suddenly realizes that Boris may not respond to her voice, so different from Adesh Patel's, but it's too late to worry about that now.

She screams, "*MAAR!*"

She need not have worried. Boris lashes his poison-laden tail and speeds across the room, ignoring the flies in favor of a much bigger target. Winston cries out and raises a block-ing hand, but in zero-g he's far too slow. Gwendy is savagely delighted to see Boris's stinger bury itself dead center between Winston's eyes.

He shrieks in pain and horror as he flails at the scorpion with both hands. There's a hole the size of a pencil point where the stinger went in. It's dribbling blood and the flesh around it is already beginning to swell.

"Get it off me! Jesus fucking Christ GET IT OFF ME!"

Winston is batting at it with both hands. Boris disengages and avoids him easily, flicking his armored tail and zipping away. The button box floats in front of Winston, forgotten. His weapon—*the Green Tube of Death*, Gwendy thinks—is also floating, but the rapid batting of Winston's hands, which continues even when Boris has cruised out of slapping range, sends it in Gwendy's direction, lazily turning end over end.

She reaches for it.

Winston also reaches for it, but the eddy set up by Winston's hands is in Gwendy's favor. She snatches the tube. Winston tries to grab her ponytail and she sends it flying away from him with a shake of her head. She risks a glance down at the tube, wanting to make sure the ring end is pointed at herself. *If it was the wrong way around and I blew my own guts to soup, I probably wouldn't even have time to appreciate the irony*, she thinks, at the same time ducking in slow motion to avoid Winston's equally slo-mo roundhouse punch.

"Say goodbye to the smartass bitch, Winston." Gwendy points the tube and twists the ring in the base.

There's no sound. There's no comic-book death ray. Gwendy has a moment to think it was all a bluff, and then the front of Gareth Winston's white shirt blooms with red flowers. His eyes melt and roll down his cheeks in thick blue tears. Gray stuff begins to pour out of the empty sockets and from his nostrils. Gwendy realizes she's looking at his liquified brains and begins to scream.

Adesh has also left his phone, powered up, on the central worktable, and set his smart watch to monitor it. The crew is sitting around the mess room table, shooting the shit and drinking post-breakfast coffee, when his watch lights up. Adesh pushes the stem and they all hear Gwendy's screams.

The screams have stopped by the time they get to the Spoke 5 entomology lab. Gwendy is backed up against a wall as far from the big enclosure as she can get, with her fisted hands pressed to her mouth and the button box in her lap. There's a babble of exclamations.

Kathy: "What in the hell—"

Adesh, shaking his fists in the air: "You got him! He said you would!"

Jafari: "Got who?"

Dr. Glen: "Oh my dear God in heaven."

Doc has followed Gwendy's frozen gaze to the big cage, where the late Gareth Winston's clothes are floating in a pool of blood and decomposing organs. His throat has been blasted open. What remains of his face looks like a wrinkled and deflated rubber mask. It's crawling with red and black ants.

Even at this moment, Adesh is the scientific observer rather than the horrified witness. "The ants, they swam down to him! Adaptive behavior! Remarkable!"

Reggie Black leans over and loses his breakfast. Which floats around him in wet chunks. Sam Drinkwater and Dave Graves do the same. Sam manages to catch most of his ejecta, but soon it's oozing through his cupped hands.

"Get out of here!" Kathy snaps. "Everyone out! We're sealing this room! If he's got some kind of Andromeda Strain–type disease—"

"He doesn't," Gwendy says. "His only disease was greed. And he died of it."

AN HOUR LATER THE nine remaining Eagle Heavy crew members are sitting in the conference room. At Gwendy's strong suggestion, which has been seconded from the down-below by CIA Chief Charlotte Morgan, the Chinese have been locked off. They will still be able to access the outer rim, but they won't be able to enter any spokes but their own. Neither Charlotte nor Gwendy thinks the Chinese will be a problem, but Gwendy is a believer in the late Gareth Winston's mantra: always safe, never sorry. *Of course*, she thinks, *he never expected Boris.*

The button box sits in the middle of the table beside an open (but highly protected) downlink to Charlotte's office in D.C. Kathy reaches for the box, and Gwendy has to restrain herself from pushing the commander's hand away.

After one touch, Kathy pulls her hand back on her own, and fast. Her eyes are wide. "What *is* that thing?" And without waiting for a reply: "I want a complete report, Gwendy. You may be a United States senator, but up here I'm in charge, and I'm ordering you to tell me everything." She sweeps a hand around the table. "*All* of us."

Gwendy has no problem with that, and not just because they deserve to know. She will also need their cooperation to complete her final task. Charlotte is silent, but Gwendy knows she's listening.

"I will, but I need to know something first." She turns to Adesh. "You set a trap for him, didn't you?"

Adesh nods.

"How did you know to do that? Did you see a man? About your height, wears a black derby hat?" The idea that Farris—sick or well—can be here is ridiculous. At the same time it seems perfectly reasonable to Gwendy. In her experience, Farris can appear anywhere, and disappear just as quickly. It makes her think of an old song by Heart, the one about the magic man.

"I saw no one," Adesh says, "but I heard a voice. In my head. You see . . . I'm sorry, this is embarrassing."

"No need to be embarrassed," Gwendy says, and takes his hand. "I believe you just played a very large part in saving the Earth and everyone on it."

Sam Drinkwater makes a scoffing sound. Kathy, who has touched the button box and felt its power, makes no sound at all. Her attention is riveted on Gwendy and Adesh "Bug Man" Patel.

"You said not to push the buttons, not to even touch them, and I kept that promise. You must believe me, Gwendy."

Gwendy nods. Of course she does.

"But . . . you said nothing about the tiny levers on the sides."

Now Gwendy gets it. She smiles.

Adesh unbuttons his pocket and brings out a Morgan silver dollar. He floats it across to her, heads and tails spinning lazily above the table. She doesn't have to look at the date to know it's 1891.

"The first lever I pulled produced that. I was always going to give it to you, Gwendy—I hope you believe that, too."

"Yes," she says, and floats it back with a flick of her finger. "But I want you to keep it. As a souvenir. Then you pulled the other one, yes? And got a chocolate."

"It was a thing of beauty," Adesh says, almost reverently. "A little chocolate scorpion, just like Boris."

"*Pandinus imperator.*"

He smiles and nods. "Who could say anything is wrong with your memory? It was too perfect to eat, but . . ."

"You ate it anyway."

"Yes. Something told me to. The desire was too strong to resist. And that is when I heard the voice. It sounded very old . . . very tired and rather far away . . . but completely sure of itself. It said you would see . . . and know what to do . . . when the time came."

Gwendy's eyes fill with tears. It was Farris, all right, her private deus ex machina. Old and tired, perhaps even dead, but still *somewhere*. And if anyone deserved a deus ex machina, it was she. And didn't her personal god from the machine have to be the man who'd gotten her into this in the first place?

"Maybe we could go back to the beginning?" Bern Stapleton suggests. "I for one would like to hear how one of the richest men on Earth ended up a puddle of goo with ants crawling on what remains of his face."

"A very good idea," Kathy says. "Let's hear it, Senator. From the beginning."

While I still can, Gwendy thinks, because Adesh is mistaken—there's *plenty* wrong with her memory. It has begun to fog over again. She knows where she is, she knows these people are the crew she came up here with . . . but she can't remember any of their names except for Adesh Patel and Kathy London. *Is* it London? No matter. She leans across the table, pulls the lever on the right side of the button box, and pops a chocolate koala bear into her mouth. The fog rolls away. But of course it will be back, and soon the chocolates will disappear into deep space.

"The beginning was when I was twelve," she says. "That's when I saw the button box for the first time and took possession of it . . ."

She talks for forty-five minutes, pausing for sips of water. No one interrupts, including Charlotte Morgan, who is hearing the whole story for the first time.

45

WHEN SHE'S FINISHED, THERE'S thirty seconds of silence while the eight of them digest what she's told them. Then Reggie Black clears his throat and says, "Let me be sure I understand you. You claim to be responsible for Jonestown, where nine hundred people died. This woman in Canada was responsible for the coronavirus, which killed four million and counting—"

"Her name was Patricia Vachon," Gwendy says. Nothing wrong with her memory now. "And it wasn't her fault. In the end, she just couldn't resist the pull of the box. Which is exactly what makes it so dangerous."

Reggie makes a seesawing gesture with his hand—maybe *si*, maybe *no*. "And you also destroyed the Great Pyramid in an earthquake, killing six more."

Charlotte speaks up for the first time. The speaker is so good she could almost have been in the room with them. "Not an earthquake, sir. No cause has been attributed."

"I didn't want anyone to die," Gwendy says. She can't keep the tremble out of her voice. She is thinking about her old friend Olive Kepnes, who died on the Suicide Stairs between Castle Rock and Castle View. "Not ever. I thought the part of Guyana I was concentrating on was deserted. The Pyramid was supposed to be locked down, totally empty, because of a fresh COVID outbreak." She leans forward, scanning them with her eyes. "But those young people were there, on a lark.

This is what makes the button box so dangerous, don't you see? Even the red button is dangerous. It does what you're thinking of . . . but it does more, and my experience has been that the more is never good. I don't think the button box could be destroyed even in a nuclear furnace, and it works on the possessors' minds. Which is why Farris kept passing it on to new owners."

"But always coming back to you," Jafari said.

"Tell me," Reggie says, smiling. "Was the box also responsible for 9/11?"

Gwendy suddenly feels very tired. "I don't know. Probably not. People don't need a button box to do horrible things. There's plenty of evil fuckery in the human spirit."

Sam Drinkwater says flatly: "I'm sorry, but I can't believe this. It's a fairy tale."

From the speaker, Charlotte says, "Is that Ops Drinkwater?"

"Yes, ma'am."

"All right, Mr. Drinkwater, listen up. I have seen the interrogation with Detective Mitchell. Everything Gwendy has told you about the death of her husband is true. The cell phone footage is very disturbing, but our techs tell us none of it has been rigged or spiced up with special effects. As for the Great Pyramid, I was there when Gwendy named it and pushed that red button hours before it fell to pieces for reasons the science guys still can't figure out. I'm lifetime CIA, I don't believe anything unless I can prove it, and I believe this. I don't think the man who bribed the detective was human . . . or not precisely human. And I believe that box you're looking at is more dangerous than all the nuclear weapons on Earth put together."

"But—"

"No buts," Charlotte says briskly. "Unless you think a hardheaded businessman like Gareth Winston died for a fantasy." She pauses. "Which reminds me, we have to come up with a cover story to explain his death. Whatever it is, it's going to shock the markets."

"Need to think about it carefully," Kathy says. "Maybe . . . Gwendy? Are you all right?"

"Fine," Gwendy says. "Little bit of a headache." Actually, an idea.

Doc Glen says gloomily, "We'll have to shovel him up, you know. And that gadget he had is enough to convince me that something beyond our understanding is at work here. That gadget goes with him."

"Absolutely," Kathy says.

Reggie Black—who, Gwendy believes, would have sided with Doubting Thomas in the Bible—shakes his head. "I'm willing to accept that it's all very strange. I'm not willing to accept that pushing that black button could destroy the whole world." Gwendy almost expects him to add, *Let's try it and see, shall we?* But he doesn't. Which is good. If he even made a move toward the button box, Gwendy would have leaped across the table to stop him.

"It doesn't matter," Adesh says. "Surely you all see that?"

They turn puzzled looks on him, Gwendy included.

"We send the box away in the device we call the Pocket Rocket. Whether it's a thing of supernatural evil or just a box that gives out chocolates and silver dollars . . ." He shrugs and smiles. It's a very sweet smile. "Either way, it's gone. The Pocket Rocket won't even be orbiting the earth with the rest of the space junk we have been charting." The smile becomes dreamy. "It will be off to the stars, never to come back."

This logic is irrefutable.

Kathy Lundgren turns to Gwendy. "We'll do it tomorrow. You and me. My ninth spacewalk, your first. The one that's televised back home to your constituents will be your second, but no one has to know that, do they?"

"No," Gwendy says.

Kathy nods. "We'll watch the Pocket Rocket heading out toward the moon, and Mars, and the great beyond. With its cargo on board."

"It sounds fine. What about Winston?"

"For the time being, until we can decide how he died, Mr. Winston is okay. Just suffering a touch of zero-g space sickness and holed up in his cabin. Not feeling well enough to communicate with the down-below. Or do you disagree?"

"No," Gwendy says. "That's fine for now."

She's still sorry about what happened in Jonestown, even though she guesses much of it was the fault of the Reverend Jim Jones. She's sorry about the destruction of the Great Pyramid, and sorrier about the lives lost when it disassembled. But she's not sorry about Gareth Winston.

"Which one of the levers dispenses the chocolates?" Reggie Black asks.

"That one." Gwendy points.

"May I?"

Gwendy doesn't want him to touch the box, but she nods.

Reggie pulls the lever. The slot opens and the shelf comes out. It's empty.

Gwendy turns to Adesh. "You try."

The tiny shelf has gone back in. Adesh hooks his pinky around the lever and pulls gently. Out comes the shelf, this time bearing a small chocolate weasel. He looks at it, but gives it to Bern. The biologist examines it, then puts it in his mouth, fingers ready to take it out if it's nasty. Instead, his eyes half-close in an expression of ecstasy.

"Oh my God! Delicious!"

Reggie Black looks put out. "Why didn't it work for me?"

"Maybe," Gwendy says, "the box doesn't like physicists."

46

That night.

Gwendy is walking the outer rim of the Many Flags space station. It makes its usual creaks and groans, haunted house sounds that the other man, the bad man, didn't like, but Gwendy doesn't mind them. She can't remember the bad man's name, although she's sure she could come up with it using Dr. Ambrose's chain of association. *I'd just start with cigar,* she thinks.

The man walking beside her doesn't seem to mind the creaking sounds, either. His face is serene and he's very beautiful. Except his beauty is a mask. Sometimes his features waver like water in a pond blown by a strong breeze and she can see his real face and head. He's some sort of weasel, like the chocolate treat the biologist got. Gwendy can't remember his name, either. That's all right. She can remember the name of the man-who-isn't-a-man, though: it's Bobby. That's what the bad man called him. She thinks: *Cigar.* She thinks, *Who smoked cigars?* Winston Churchill did. And there it is.

"The bad man's name was Garin Winston," she says.

"Close enough," Bobby says. "It doesn't matter, he's dead."

"Melted," Gwendy says. "Like the Wicked Witch in *The Wizard of Ooze.*"

"Close enough," Bobby says again. "What matters is this: there are other worlds than these."

"I know," Gwendy says. "Someone told me, but I don't remember who. Maybe Mr. Farris."

"That meddler," Bobby says.

They walk. The space station creaks. They see no one, because this is sleep time on MF. Except for the Chinese, holed up in their spoke, they are alone in the haunted house.

"There are twelve worlds," Bobby says. "Six beams, twelve worlds, one at each end of each beam. And in the center is the Tower. We call it Black Thirteen."

"Who is we?"

"The taheen."

This means nothing to Gwendy.

"The beams hold the worlds and the Tower powers the beams," Bobby says in a lecturely tone. "Only one thing can destroy it, now that the Crimson King is dead."

"The button box," Gwendy says, but Bobby smiles and shakes his head. He makes a come-on gesture with hands that sometimes blur into paws with sharp claws at the ends. The gesture says *you can do better.* Gwendy starts to protest that she really can't, she's suffering from early-onset Alzheimer's (probably caused by the box, but who knows for sure), then realizes she can. "The black button *on* the button box. The Cancer Button."

"Yes!" Bobby says, and pats her shoulder. Gwendy shrinks away. She doesn't want him to touch her. It makes her feel the way the station's creaks and groans made the late Garin Winship feel. "You must not send the box away, Gwendy. What you need to do is push the black button. Destroy the Tower, destroy the beams, destroy the worlds."

"Rule Discordia?"

"That's right, rule Discordia. End the universe. Bring the darkness."

"Like in Jonestown? Only everyone and everything?"

"Yes."

"But *why*?"

"Because chaos is the only answer."

He looks down. Gwendy follows his gaze and sees she's holding the button box.

"Push it, Gwendy. Push it now. You must, because—"

47

GWENDY WAKES AND IS horrified to discover she really is holding the button box, and her thumb is actually resting on the black button. She's standing in front of the open safe in her closet, the spare pressure suit crumpled at her feet.

"Chaos is the only answer," she whispers. "Existence is a dead equation."

The urge to push the button, if only to end her own misery and confusion, is strong. She would like Farris to step in as he did for Adesh and rescue her, but there is no voice in her head and no sense of him. She groans, and somehow that sound breaks the spell.

She puts the button box back in the safe, starts to swing the door shut, then decides she's not done with it quite yet. She doesn't want to touch it for fear that horrible compulsion might come back, but she has to. She pulls one of the levers and a chocolate comes out. She pops it into her mouth and the world instantly clarifies.

She pulls the lever again, afraid the little platform will slide out empty this time, but another chocolate appears. It's a dachshund that looks exactly like her father's longtime companion, Pippa. She goes to put it in her pocket—it's for later—but then realizes she *has* no pockets. She's in her sleep shorts and a University of Maine tee. But that's not all. She's got a sneaker on one foot, a sock on the other, and she's wearing a pair of the insulated work gloves each member of the crew has been issued. There's probably a reason for the gloves—on Eagle Heavy and the MF station there's a reason for every bit of clothing and equipment—but she can't remember what it is. Sudden temperature drop, maybe? Her deteriorating condition keeps manifesting itself in different ways, and she sees now that she has written LEFT and RIGHT on the gloves.

But how long before I forget what those words mean? How long before I can't read at all?

These thoughts make her feel like crying, but she can't waste any time on tears. She doesn't know how long the chocolate will keep her in the clear, and the spare is for tomorrow, right before she and Kathy Lundgren suit up for their spacewalk at 0800 hours.

Kathy.

With her mind right, she realizes what she should have known much earlier.

Gwendy goes to her phone, selects Kathy's name from the MF directory, and makes the call. As the officer in charge of the mission, First Ops, Kathy always keeps her phone on. She'll hear the beep and respond. She *must* respond, because what Gwendy has realized is that she can't do this on her own. If she tries, Kathy will stop her. Unless, that is, she has reasons not to.

The phone only rings once, and when Kathy answers, her voice is clear and crisp. Maybe not sleeping at all, no matter how late the hour. "Gwendy. Is there a problem?"

"A solution, I think. I need to talk to you."

"All right." No hesitation. "Come to my quarters."

48

KATHY LUNDGREN'S QUARTERS ARE smaller and more austere than Gwendy's, but she has cocoa packets squirreled away and makes them each a cup. The sweetness reminds Gwendy of her early childhood—cocoa with her dad on early summer mornings with a mist still on the lawn.

After one sip, she puts her cup on the little table beside Kathy's narrow bed (no sitting room here) and tells Eagle Heavy's First Ops what she's been trying to hide. "You were right. Doc was right. Even Winston knew. I do have early-onset Alzheimer's, and it's now progressing very rapidly."

"But the test we gave you proved—"

"It proved nothing. I aced it because of the chocolates, but the effects don't last. A few minutes ago I woke up wearing gloves and one sneaker. The sneaker wasn't tied, because I can't remember how to tie my shoes anymore."

Kathy looks at her in silent horror, which Gwendy understands, and sympathy, which she hates.

"For awhile I still could, because I found a jingle on the Net that I learned when I was in primary school—"

"Something about bunny ears?"

As anxious and afraid as she is, that makes Gwendy laugh. "You too, huh? Only now I can't remember the jingle. Unless I've eaten a chocolate, that is."

"You ate one before coming here, I assume."

Gwendy nods. "But they're dangerous, like everything

to do with the button box. And the box is getting stronger while I get weaker. When I woke up, just before I called you, I had it in my hands and I was getting ready to push the black button. My thumb was actually on it."

"Thank God you're getting rid of it!"

"*We're* getting rid of it. And that's not all." Gwendy takes a deep breath. "I want to go with it."

Kathy has been bringing her cup to her mouth. Now she sets it down hard. "Are you *crazy*?"

"Well, yes. That's sort of what Alzheimer's *is*, Kath. But at this moment I've never been saner. Or more present." She leans forward, pinning Kathy's eyes with her own. "When the button box goes, the chocolates go. If I'm still here, my decline will be very rapid. By the time we get back to Earth, I might not even know my own name."

Kathy opens her mouth to protest, but Gwendy overrides her.

"Even if I do, the time will come when I don't. I'll be wearing diapers. Sitting in my own piss and shit until someone comes to change me. Staring out the window of some expensive rest home in D.C. or Virginia, not knowing what I'm staring *at*. Having just enough brainpower left to know that I'm lost and can never find my way back to myself." *Rule Discordia*, she thinks.

She's crying now, but her voice remains steady.

"I could tell you that I'd find a discreet way of committing suicide when we get back to the down-below, but I don't think I could be discreet, and I don't think I'd know how to do it. I might *forget* to do it. And Kathy, I'm only sixty-four, and physically healthy. I could go on like that for ten years before pneumonia or a mutated form of COVID took me. Maybe fifteen or twenty."

"Gwendy, I understand, but—"

"Please don't condemn me to that, Kathy. Listen. When I was a little girl, my folks bought me a telescope. I spent hours looking at the planets and stars through it, often with my father, but once with my mom. We looked at Scorpius and talked about God. I want to go with the box, Kathy. I want to point the Pocket Rocket toward Scorpius and know that someday millions of years from now, I might actually get there." She smiles. "If there's life after death—my mother believed that—I might be there in spirit. To greet my perfectly preserved body."

"I do understand," Kathy says, "and I would if I could. But you have to think of me a little bit, okay? Think about what would happen to me afterward. Losing my commission and my job—which I love—wouldn't be all. I'd probably go to jail."

"No," Gwendy says. "Not if everyone else goes along with what I have in mind. Sam, Jaff, Reggie, Adesh, Bern, Dave, and Doc. And they will, because it will stop an investigation that would shut down TetCorp's plans for space exploration and tourist travel for a year. Maybe two or even five. Tet's in a race with SpaceX and Blue Origin now. That guy Branson, too. Do you think our guys want to get years behind?"

Kathy is frowning. "I don't know what you're . . ." She stops. "Winston. You're talking about Winston."

"Yes. Because any story you cobble together to explain his death will be suspicious."

"Explosive decompression—"

"Even if Dave Graves could rig the onboard computers to show there had been such a decompression—and I have my doubts—a story like that would shut down the MF," Gwendy says. "All those tourist plans—Tet's *and* SpaceX's—would be frozen. That's in addition to the investigation into you and the whole crew." Gwendy pauses, then plays her trump card. She has saved it for last, as she always did in contentious committee meetings. "Plus there's me. I'd be questioned, and with my ability to think rapidly bleeding away, who knows what I might say?"

"Jesus Christ," Kathy mutters, and runs her hands through her short hair.

"But there's a solution." This is also the way she played it in committee hearings, learned from Patsy Follett. *First hit 'em with the sledgehammer*, Patsy used to say, *then offer them the painkillers.*

"What solution?" Kathy is looking at her mistrustfully.

"Our spacewalk tomorrow is unauthorized, right? No one knows about it but Charlotte Morgan and our Eagle Heavy crew mates."

"Right . . ."

Gwendy sips her cocoa. So good, with its memories of Castle Rock on summer mornings with her father. She puts it down and leans forward, arms on her thighs, hands clasped between her knees.

"We're not going to take that spacewalk."

"We're not?"

"No. *Gareth* and I will take it, unbeknownst to you or anyone else in the crew. We decided to do it on our own, and because we're inexperienced, we didn't use tethers or a buddy cable. Something went wrong and we just floated away into the void."

"Why would you do a crazy thing like that?"

"Why did the *Mary Celeste* show up deserted, but seaworthy and under full sail? What happened to the crew of the *Carroll A. Deering*?" There's nothing wrong with

Gwendy's recall for the time being; she hasn't thought about the *Carroll Deering* since a book report she did in the eighth grade. "No one knows. And if you eight can keep a secret, no one will ever know why Winston and I decided to go for a little stroll in space."

"Hmm," Kathy says. "To be cold-blooded about it—"

"I want you to be."

"It would solve two problems. We wouldn't have to explain the gooey death of Gareth Winston, and we wouldn't have to worry about you saying certain things as your . . . umm . . . *condition* worsens."

"Charlotte Morgan will help you," Gwendy says. "She'll make sure she's in charge of debriefing the crew, and she'll apply a coat of whitewash, for obvious reasons. Also, she'll want to get her hands on that disintegrator thingie."

"I suppose she would. I need to think about this."

Gwendy takes her hands and squeezes them lightly. "No," she says. "You don't."

49

BACK IN HER QUARTERS, Gwendy sits down at her desk, opens the RECORD app on her phone, and begins talking immediately. There's no time to waste—the chocolate may start wearing off anytime—but it doesn't take long to say what she has to say. When she's finished, she scribbles a quick note. She rubber-bands it to her phone and puts the phone in a manila envelope. She begins to close it, then thinks again and adds something else. She seals it and writes ADESH on the front in big capital letters.

Then she goes back to bed. She falls asleep with two hopes: no more dreams of the monster that calls itself Bobby, and that when she wakes up, her mind will wake up with her.

50

THE CREW MEETING IN the conference room takes place at 0600. Kathy lays the situation out with a crisp conciseness Gwendy couldn't possibly have matched now that the effects of her late-night chocolate treat are almost gone. They are bright men and they understand. They also understand the solution Gwendy has proposed will save a great deal of trouble, expense, and possible Senate hearings where they will be mercilessly grilled on nationwide TV.

There is only one substantive question and it comes from Reggie Black. "What happens to Winston? Or what remains of him?"

"Vaporized with the rest of the trash before we leave the station," Sam Drinkwater says, and makes a sucking sound. "Poof. Gone."

No one has anything to say to that.

When the meeting ends, the crew stands in a kind of receiving line. Each of them hugs Gwendy. Adesh is last. "I'm sorry," he says as he hugs her. "You've been so brave. You don't deserve this and I am so, so sorry."

She hugs him back. "I have an envelope for you. My phone is inside, with a message for my father. Would you take it to him?"

"It will be an honor."

He wipes his eyes, but his tears—emblems of his grief and regard—float in front of his face.

"And I'm going where no woman has gone before, so don't cry for me, Margentina." She frowns. "Is that right? Margentina?"

"Absolutely," Adesh says. "Absolutely right."

51

0730.

There are airlocks on the MF, one in the outer rim beyond each of the even-numbered spokes, but Gwendy and Kathy will egress from Eagle Heavy, where the air tastes stale and the three crew station levels feel abandoned. Before suiting up, Gwendy pops the chocolate she saved into her mouth.

"Don't suppose you have another one of those, do you?" Kathy asks.

Gwendy considers, shrugs, and then loosens the drawstring top of the aluminum-quilted bag on the bench beside her. She brings out the button box. It feels dull now, powerless, as if resigned to its fate, but Gwendy doesn't trust that. She pulls the lever that delivers the chocolates. The cunning little platform slides out, but there's nothing on it.

"Sorry, Kath. The button box giveth and sometimes it don't giveth."

"Roger that. Would have liked to try one, though. Are you good, Gwendy?"

Gwendy nods. She's very good. With the chocolate on board, she's clear as a bell. The woman who had to print RIGHT and LEFT on her gloves is gone, but she'll be back.

Or maybe not.

"What's funny?" Kathy asks. "You're smiling."

"Nothing." But because something more seems required, she adds, "Just excited about my first spacewalk."

Kathy makes no reply, but Gwendy can read her thought: *First and last.*

"Are you sure the computers in Mission Control won't register us opening the airlock down here?"

"Positive. These computers are all off until the return. To conserve power."

They float their way into the airlock, helmets under their arms, and sit on the two benches. The space is tight—all spaces are tight on Heavy—and their knees touch. Gwendy starts to put her helmet on, but Kathy shakes her head. "Not yet. Sixty inhales and exhales first. Prebreathing, remember?"

Gwendy nods. "To purge the nitrogen."

"Right. Gwendy . . . are you sure?"

"Yes." She answers with no hesitation. Everything is in place, the story they will tell later set and agreed to by all hands. Gwendy and Winston weren't at breakfast, but no one thought that was unusual because they are passengers, super-cargo, and have the luxury of sleeping in. No one will start to worry until at least 1000 hours, and by then Kathy will be back on board the MF. There will be a search. It will be at least 1400 before Sam Drinkwater calls the down-below to tell them the VIPs are missing and may have drifted away while attempting a spacewalk. Terrible accident, God knows why they would have done something so foolish, blah-blah-blah.

Gwendy gets a little woozy from the fast respiration. Kathy tells her that's normal and will pass by the time they egress Eagle Heavy. After two minutes of breathing, Kathy tells Gwendy it's time to put on her bucket. "And remember, helmet-to-helmet comm *only*. No one hears but just us girls. Let me hear your roger."

"Roger that," Gwendy says, and dons her bucket. Kathy moves to help her secure it, but Gwendy waves her off, does it herself, and looks for the green light on the little control panel at mouth level. When she sees it, she dons her gloves, secures them, and waits for a second green light. She makes a thumb-and-finger circle to Kathy, who returns the gesture.

Kathy closes the door to Eagle Heavy and the two of them sit waiting for the airlock to depressurize.

"Reading me, Gwendy?"

"Loud and clear."

"Set your suit temp to maximum hot, then adjust it down."

"How long will the heat last?"

"In theory, as long as your breathable air, just shy of six hours. The heat may actually last longer, but . . ." Her shrug says the rest: *But you won't feel it.*

There's a belt around Gwendy's waist with two ordinary high-altitude carabiners attached. She knots the drawstring bag with the button box around one of them. Kathy attaches the buddy cable to the other. They are now tethered together like scuba divers: the instructor and the pupil.

"Ready to EVA?" Kathy asks.

Gwendy makes another thumb-and-forefinger circle. She thinks, *Oh yes, very ready. Been waiting for this ever since I first looked through my telescope, over fifty years ago. I just didn't know it.*

"Don't wait too long to lower your outer visor. Night pass ends in just about seven minutes."

"Roger."

Kathy turns the red lever in the center of the airlock's outer door, then pulls it.

0748.

The airlock opens on the stars.

52

THEY FLOAT INTO SPACE, tethered. Gwendy can hear her own breathing and, through the helmet-to-helmet comm, Kathy's. Beside them is Eagle Heavy, and she can see where someone from the ground crew has printed GOOD LUCK YOU GUYS on the fuselage in Sharpie. Below them is Earth, blue and cloud-streaked, with a golden nimbus growing on one gorgeous shoulder. *Here comes the sun*, Gwendy thinks.

Kathy leads them slowly downward, using indented handholds on Heavy's flank. Near the bottom, these handholds are smudged from the blast of the last rocket bursts, as Kathy lined them up for docking.

On the way down they pass hatches labeled A through E. The last one, Hatch F, is just above the rocket boosters. It's the only one with a keypad; the others can be opened with a simple socket wrench. Kathy has to duck under a solar panel to get at it. She raises the little plexi shield over the pad and punches the combination Gwendy has given her. It's the same one that opened the CLASSIFIED case.

The thing Kathy floats out makes Gwendy smile. The Pocket Rocket is four feet long, or maybe a bit less. To Gwendy it looks almost exactly like the craft that brought Kal-El, aka Superbaby, to Earth. Her father gave away most of his old comic books (or lost them), but Gwendy found a box of *Superman*s in the attic and read them eagerly, again and again.

Kathy floats the Pocket Rocket up between them. There's

a hatch on top, held by simple latches that look about as high-tech as the ones on the Scooby-Doo lunch box Gwendy carried to elementary school. Kathy flips them, reaches inside, and brings out a controller that looks like the one Gwendy used to release Boris in Adesh's lab. Except this one is smaller, and there are only two buttons.

Another button box, Gwendy thinks. *Those damn things are my destiny.*

Kathy points to the drawstring bag floating around Gwendy's waist, then points at the open hatch on top of the Pocket Rocket. Her meaning is clear, *put it inside*, but all at once Gwendy doesn't want to.

Mine, it's mine. This one really is my destiny.

Kathy raises her outer visor and Gwendy can see she's frightened. Even though Kathy has never seen the button box in action, she's scared to death. That expression is enough for Gwendy to free the bag from the carabiner holding it. She can feel the corners of the button box inside.

No, the thing called Bobby whispers in her head. *Don't do this. The Tower must not stand. Rule Discordia!*

Then she thinks of Richard Farris's weary face when he said, *How I loathe it.*

"Rule my ass," she says. She doesn't just place the button box in the Pocket Rocket's belly; she rams it in.

"Say again?" Kathy asks.

"I wasn't talking to you," Gwendy says, and flips the latches closed.

Meanwhile, the controller is floating away. Gwendy reaches for it, but at that moment the sun comes over the curve of the earth's horizon, blinding her. She forgot something after all—to lower her outer visor. She slams it down, panicked. If the controller is lost . . .

But Kathy has snatched it just before it can drift out of reach. She hands it to Gwendy.

"Last chance, hon. You don't have to go with it."

"No," Gwendy agrees, "but I'm going to. I *choose* to. Give me a hug, Kathy. Probably ridiculous, but I need it."

The two of them hug clumsily in their bulky suits while the newly risen sun turns their visors into curved oblongs of amber fire. Then Kathy lets go, unclips the buddy cable from her waist, and reattaches her end to a D ring on the Pocket Rocket's rounded nose. Gwendy supposes that handy ring allowed some crane operator to lift the Pocket Rocket up to the F hatch.

Kathy says, "The engine is nuclear powered—"

"I know—"

Kathy ignores her. "And no bigger than a cigarette pack. Marvel of technology. Push the top button to power it up. You'll start moving immediately, but very slowly—like a car in low gear. You understand?"

"Yes."

"Tap the lower button and you'll speed up. Each time you tap it, you'll speed up more. Following me?"

"Yes." And she is, but she's looking at the stars. Oh, they are gorgeous, and how can anyone look at that spill of light and believe life is anything but a hall of mysteries?

"There's no guidance system. No joystick. Once you start you just *go*, and you can't come back. *You can't come back, Gwendy.* Do you understand?"

"Yes."

"All right, then." Kathy reaches behind herself and grasps one of the handholds. Soon she will follow them back up, kicking her feet like a diver seeking the surface. Back to warmth and light and the companionship of her crew mates. "If you meet any ETs, tell them Kathy Lundgren says hello."

"Roger that," Gwendy says, and gives a salute. *Six hours*, she thinks. *I have six hours to live.*

"God bless you, Gwendy."

"And you."

There's nothing left to say, so Gwendy pushes the top button on her last button box. A dull red ring glows in the Pocket Rocket's base, a paltry light that's no match for the sun's splendor. Is it giving off harmful radiation? Possibly, but does it matter?

The slack runs out of the buddy cable, it pulls taut, and then Gwendy is moving away from Eagle Heavy and beneath the outer ring of the Many Flags station. She knows no one is watching, but she gives it a wave anyway. Then it's behind her. She taps the speed control button twice, lightly, and begins to move faster, flying horizontally behind the Pocket Rocket with her legs splayed. It's a little like surfing, but it's really like nothing she has ever experienced. *Like no one has ever experienced*, she thinks, and laughs.

"Gwendy?" Kathy's voice is growing faint. Soon it will be gone. Already the MF is receding, glowing in the sunlight like a jewel in the navel of the earth. "Are you okay?"

"Brilliant," Gwendy says, and she is.

She is.

53

FIVE HOURS LATER.

Now there's just the red ring of the Pocket Rocket's nuclear drive ahead of her as it tugs her steadily onward into the black. It reminds Gwendy of the dashboard cigarette lighter in her father's old Chevrolet. There's a temperature gauge among the dozen or so digital readouts inside her helmet and it registers the outside temperature as −435 Fahrenheit, but her suit is a toasty-warm seventy-two degrees. Her remaining oxygen is down to seventeen percent. It won't be long now. Of course there's no speed gauge among the readouts, so Gwendy has no idea how fast she's going. There's little or no sensation of movement at all. When she peers over her shoulder (not easy in the suit, but possible), Earth looks exactly the same—big, blue, and beautiful—but the MF station is lost to view.

Gwendy looks ahead again, at the Milky Way. She wishes the brightest of its stars was Scorpius, but she's pretty sure it's Sirius, also known as the Dog Star because it's part of the Canis Major constellation. That makes her think of her father's sausage dog, Pippin. Only that's not right, is it?

"Pippa," she whispers. "Pippa the dachshund."

She's losing it again. The fog is closing in.

Gwendy fixes her eyes on Sirius, which is roughly at ten o'clock in her field of vision. *Second star on the right and straight on till morning*, she thinks. *What's that from?* Hansel and Gretel, *isn't it?* But that's not right. She trawls her dimming mind for the correct story or fairy tale, and finally comes up with it: *Peter Pan.*

Fifteen percent oxygen now, and it will be a race between the end of her breathable air and the end of her ability to think. Only she doesn't want to go out that way, not knowing where she is . . . or if she does know that (outer space is kind of hard to mistake for the bus station in Castle Rock, after all), why she's out here. She'd like to go out knowing all this happened for a *reason*. That in the end, she completed the task set before her. That she saved the world.

"*All* the worlds," she whispers. "Because there are more worlds than ours."

She doesn't *have* to go out puzzled and confused, nor does she have to go out cold and shivering if her heat quits before her breathable air. (She seems to remember Carol—if that's her name—saying the heat would last longer, but her suit's temp has begun to drop a degree at a time.) She has another option.

She has only one disappointment. In 1984, ten years after Richard Farris gave her the button box, he came to take it back. He sat in her small kitchen with her. They had coffee cake and milk, like old friends (which they sort of were), and Mr. Farris had told her future. He said she was going to be accepted at the Iowa Writers' Workshop, and she was. He told her she was going to win an award (*Wear your prettiest dress when you pick it up*), and she did. Not the Nobel, but the Los Angeles Times Book Prize was not to be sneezed at. He told her she had many things to tell the world, and that the world would listen, and that had been true prophecy.

But the mysterious derby-wearing Mr. Farris had certainly never told her she would end a mostly warm and loving life in the deep cold of outer space. He'd told her she'd live a *long* life. Sixty-four wasn't young, but she didn't consider it old, either (although in 1984 she probably would have considered it ancient). He told her she would die surrounded by friends, not alone in the universe and being tugged ever deeper into the void behind a tiny rocket that would continue running on power for seventy years or more and then continue in an endless inertial glide.

You will die in a pretty nightgown with blue flowers on the hem, Farris had told her. *There will be sun shining in your window and before you pass you will look out and see a squadron of birds flying south. A final image of the world's beauty. There will be a little pain. Not much.*

No friends here—the last ones she made were far behind her.

A spacesuit instead of a pretty nightgown.

And certainly no birds.

Even the sun was gone for the time being, temporarily eclipsed by the earth, and was she crying? Dammit, she was. The tears didn't even float because she was under constant acceleration. But the tears were fogging up her visor. The star she'd been watching—Rigel? Deneb?—was blurring.

"Mr. Farris, you lied," she said. "Maybe you didn't see the truth. Or maybe you did and didn't want me to have to live with it."

No lie, Gwendy.

His voice, as clear as it had been as they sat in her kitchen forty-two years ago, eating coffee cake and drinking milk.

You know what to do, and there's still enough of that last chocolate in your brain to give you time to do it.

Gwendy uses the valve on the left side of her helmet to begin bleeding the remaining air from her suit. It disappears behind her in a frozen cloud. Her visor clears and she can see that star again: not Rigel, not Scorpius, but Sirius. Second star on the right.

A kind of rapture steals into her as she breathes the last of her thinning air.

I am in bed now, and I am old—much older than sixty-four. Yet the people who surround me are young and beautiful. Even Patsy Follett is young again. Brigette Desjardin is here . . . Sheila Brigham . . . Norris Ridgewick . . . Olive Kepnes is here, and . . .

"Mom? You hardly look twenty years old!"

"I was, you know," Alicia Peterson says, laughing. "Hard as that might be for you to believe. I love you, hon."

And now she sees—

"Ryan? Is it really you?"

He takes her hand. "It is."

"You're back!"

"I never left." He leans down to kiss her. "Someone wants to say goodbye."

He stands aside to let Mr. Farris come forward. His sickness is gone. He looks like the man Gwendy first saw sitting on a bench near the Castle View playground when she was twelve. He's holding his hat in his hand. "Gwendy," he says, and touches her cheek. "Well done, Gwendy. Very well done."

She's not in space, not anymore. She's an old woman lying in her childhood bed. She's wearing a pretty nightgown with blue flowers on the hem. She has done her duty and now she can rest. She can let go.

"Look out the window!" Mr. Farris says, and points.

She looks out. She sees a squadron of birds. Then they are gone and she sees a single shining star. It's Scorpius, and heaven lies beyond it. All of heaven.

"Second star to the right," Gwendy says with her final breath. "And straight on . . . straight on til . . ."

Her eyes close. The Pocket Rocket with the button box in its belly drives onward into the cosmos, as it will for the next ten thousand years, towing its spacesuited figure behind.

"Straight on til morning."

EPILOGUE

ONE NIGHT SOME TIME after all these things, Gwendy Peterson's father sits at his window in the nursing home where he lives—frailer, more unsteady, but, as he often says, *not too bad for an old fella*. He's looking out at the stars and thinking that somewhere out there in their endless multitude, his daughter continues her pilgrimage. Her phone, brought to him by a nice Indian man named Adesh Patel, is in his lap.

Patsy Follett, Gwendy's mentor, might not have had as many witty sayings as Oscar Wilde, but she'd had her share. One of them was *A scandal lasts six months. A scandal that's also a mystery lasts six years.* It's only been three years since Senator Peterson and the billionaire businessman disappeared into space, but the march of current events has driven it from the forefront of people's minds. Not from Mr. Peterson's, however. It's hell to outlive your only child, and the fierceness of his loss is mitigated by only two things: the knowledge that he can't have much longer himself, and that he has her voice to comfort him. Her last recorded message. The world doesn't need to know she died a hero; it's enough for Mr. Peterson that he knows.

A week after Adesh Patel's surprise appearance, Gwendy's dad had another visitor. A woman this time. The day manager of the Castle View Nursing Home—a haughty little fellow with a pencil-thin mustache who insisted the residents address him as Mr. Winchester—sauntered into the sun-room where Alan was playing hearts with Ralph Mirarchi, Mick Meredith, and Homer Baliko. He introduced the tall blond lady towering over his shoulder as Deputy Director Charlotte Morgan of the Central Intelligence Agency. He quickly shooed the other men out of the room, and after offering their guest a ridiculous half-bow, left them alone.

The woman flashed Mr. Peterson a bemused look—a look that said *I'm sorry you're stuck here with such a first-class tool*—and sat down across from him. "Please call me Charlotte, Mr. Peterson. I'm an old and dear friend of your daughter's."

"In that case, you better call me Alan." He rubbed the gray whiskers on his chin, wishing he'd shaved this morning. *This lady is a looker.* "And I don't figure you came all this way to talk about spies and foreign policy."

"No, sir, not today." She smiled and reached over to touch his hand. "But I do have something important to tell you. Something highly confidential that you must promise to never repeat to anyone else."

He raised his right hand in the air. "So help me God."

"That's good enough for me." She took a quick glance over her shoulder to make sure they were still alone in the sun-room. Mr. Peterson, suddenly feeling as if he were playing a bit role in a James Bond spy film, did the same. When he looked back at his daughter's old friend, he was surprised to see that there were tears shimmering in her eyes.

"I could lose my job and end up in Leavenworth for what I'm about to tell you, but I don't care. I loved Gwendy. She was family."

"Whatever it is, it'll go to my grave with me." *And probably sooner than later*, he thought.

"Your daughter didn't sneak out for an illicit spacewalk. Anyone who truly knew her knows that part of the story is bullshit." She took a deep breath—the kind that says *you're past the point of no return now*—and continued. "Gareth Winston was a bad man, Mr. Peterson. And he'd gotten a very bad idea into his head—a *dangerous* one. Gwendy found out and put a stop to it before it was too late. She sacrificed her life so that others—*millions* of others—could live. I suppose that sounds awfully dramatic, but I swear to you it's true."

Alan nodded. "That sounds like our Gwendy."

"I can't even begin to imagine the courage it took for her to do what she did. But she completed the task willingly, and I believe with only one regret: that she would never return home to see you again. She talked about you and your wife all the time. She adored you, Mr. Peterson."

"The feeling was mutual," he said in a choked and tired voice.

With the memory of her visit fading, he stares down at the iPhone resting in his lap. And as he has done on so many other occasions, he presses the PLAY button and closes his eyes.

Hi Dad. I don't have much time, but I wanted to tell you I'm sorry. Please don't be too sad, and whatever you do, don't waste a precious minute on being angry or bitter. And no matter what you hear or see on the news, just remember this: I had a job to do, an important one, and I did it the best way I knew how. A long time ago, back when I was a little girl in pigtails running around the playground at Castle View Park, you told me something I've never forgotten: when faced with the choice of doing the right thing or nothing at all, you do what's right. Every single time. I am so proud to be your daughter. There isn't a better father anywhere in the world. Please smile when you think of me. Please remember the good times. How lucky we were—you and me and Mom! The Three Musketeers, she used to call us! Okay, I better get going. You know how I hate to be late. Goodbye for now, Pa. I love you with all of my heart, and I will see you again. Mom and I both will. I left you a surprise inside the enve-lope. It's yours now. Take good care of it. It's very special. You might even say it's . . .

"Magic," he whispers in the silence of his dark room.

Alan Peterson pulls out the small white feather from the pocket of his robe. It's never far from him these days. He stares at it, remembering, and then places the feather upon the windowsill beside him. It's immediately bathed in moonlight. His eyes are once again drawn to the night sky outside the window. There are so many stars tonight. Even with the oak tree blocking much of his view, he can spot the Milky Way and Taurus the Bull. High above its tallest branches, Orion the Hunter peers down at him. The words suddenly slip into his head unbidden. Mr. Peterson has no idea where they came from or what they mean, but he likes the sound of them so much he says them out loud: *There are other worlds than these.* Sitting there, staring up at the infinite darkness, he thinks they are easy words to believe.

ACKNOWLEDGMENT

It's usually plural, as in *acknowledgments*, but we decided not to do the whole Academy Awards shtick, since there's no music to play us offstage. Lots of people helped, including our families, who give us the time and space to do this crazy job, and all those helpers know who they are. But Robin Furth, who aided Steve on the last three volumes of the *Dark Tower* books, deserves special mention. All that stuff about prepping for takeoff, the takeoff itself, the docking with our (decidedly fictional) space station? That's all Robin. She sent us fact sheets, she sent us videos, and when we got things wrong she corrected us (gently, lovingly). If it feels real, that's because most of it really is. *Gwendy's Final Task*—and her final adventure—isn't dedicated to Robin, but it could have been; her help was enormous.

Oh, and before we let you close the book (assuming you haven't already), we want to thank *you*, Constant Reader. We're so happy you invested your time, money, and imagination in our little story.

—Stephen King & Richard Chizmar

ABOUT THE AUTHORS

STEPHEN KING IS THE author of more than sixty books, all of them worldwide bestsellers. His recent work includes *Billy Summers*, the novella collection *If It Bleeds*, *The Institute*, *Elevation*, *The Outsider* (now an HBO television series), *Sleeping Beauties* (cowritten with his son Owen King), *End of Watch*, the short story collection *The Bazaar of Bad Dreams*, *Finders Keepers*, *Mr. Mercedes* (an Edgar Award winner for Best Novel and now a television series streaming on Peacock), and *Under the Dome*. His novel *11/22/63*—a Hulu original television series event—was named a top ten book of 2011 by *The New York Times Book Review* and won the Los Angeles Times Book Prize for Mystery/Thriller as well as the Best Hardcover Book Award from the International Thriller Writers. His epic works the *Dark Tower* series, *It*, *Pet Sematary*, and *Doctor Sleep* are the basis for major motion pictures, with *It* now the highest-grossing horror film of all time. He is the recipient of the 2020 Audio Publishers Association Lifetime Achievement Award, the 2018 PEN America Literary Service Award, the 2014 National Medal of Arts, and the 2003 National Book Foundation Medal for Distinguished Contribution to American Letters. He lives in Bangor, Maine, with his wife, novelist Tabitha King.

RICHARD CHIZMAR IS THE coauthor (with Stephen King) of the *New York Times* bestselling novella *Gwendy's Button Box*.

Recent books include *Chasing the Boogeyman* from Gallery Books, *Gwendy's Magic Feather*, *The Long Way Home*, his fourth short story collection, and *Widow's Point,* a chilling tale about a haunted lighthouse written with his son Billy Chizmar, which was recently made into a feature film. Chizmar's work has been translated into nearly twenty languages throughout the world, and he has appeared at numerous conferences as a writing instructor, guest speaker, panelist, and guest of honor. Follow him on Twitter (@RichardChizmar) and Instagram (richard _chizmar) or visit his website at: RichardChizmar.com.

RICHARD CHIZMAR

ABOUT THE ARTIST

KEITH MINNION MADE HIS first professional story sale to *Asimov's SF Adventure Magazine* in 1979. His third story collection, published in 2020, is *Read Me & Other Ghost Stories*. Also published in 2020 is his second novel, *Dog Star*. Keith is a former book designer and illustrator and only gets pulled out of retirement—kicking and screaming—for worthy book projects like this one. He is a former schoolteacher, DOD project manager, GPO printing contract specialist, and officer in the U.S. Navy. He currently lives in the Shenandoah Valley of Virginia, pursuing oil painting and woodworking, and is well into his third novel, tentatively titled *The Demon of Bushwick*.